CHATEAU BEYOND TIME

CHATEAU BEYOND TIME

Michael Tobias

COUNCIL
OAK BOOKS

SAN FRANCISCO & TULSA

First printing, first edition, 2008

Printed in Canada

Cover image: Roelant Savary, *Landschaft mit Vögein* (GG1082) Kunsthistorisches Museum, Wein

Cover and interior design by Carl Brune

All images photography by Michael Tobias

LIBRARY OF CONGRESS CATALOGING-IN-PUBLICATION DATA

Tobias, Michael.
Chateau beyond time / Michael Tobias. -- 1st ed.
    p. cm.
ISBN 978-1-57178-213-7
1. Eden--Fiction. 2. Paradise--Fiction. I. Title.

PS3570.O28C48 2008
813'.54--dc22

2008001537

DEDICATION

This novel is dedicated to Jane Gray Morrison, who lives there.

CHARACTERS

Martin Olivier

Margaret Olivier

James Olivier

Edward Olivier

Anthony Olivier

Max Hardiman

Lance Sèvre

Jean-Baptiste Simon

Jacques Simon

Henri Simon

Dr. Gosha Krezlach

Hubert Mans

Paul Le Bon

Julia Deblock

Hans Maybeck

Father Leopold Bruno

Father Bladelin

Edouard Revere

Fabritius Cadiz

Raoul Fougeret

Gouge de Bar

Berndt

Jacob Hythlodae

Luis Adornes

Jimmy Serko

Maggie

Housekeeper

Security guard

French policemen

Half-dozen poachers

Miscellaneous others

CHAPTER 1

Jean-Baptiste Simon was sleeping soundly for the first time in months when the phone jarred him awake at 3:30 in the morning.

"Jean, it's Hubert. Sorry about the time."

"What is it?"

"I'm not sure. Only a hunch."

"Uh-huh?"

"Twenty minutes ago, some sort of animal escaped from a cargo crate at the port, was chased by at least a dozen men, then dove into the water and vanished."

"What was it?"

"Not sure."

"What genus?"

"Don't know."

"Family?"

"Nobody's sure."

"Hubert?"

"Jean, here's the thing." He hesitated to convey the next bit of information. "The security guard I spoke with says it had a unique antler or horn."

For Simon, that set the parameters, at least. Obvious ones.

"OK. That could be several hundred species that come to mind. A dozen South African ungulates alone or a steer, for example. Not a pretty picture, but also not our problem."

"Jean, he says it had one horn."

"Hubert, you're starting to annoy me."

"One horn—center of the forehead."

CHAPTER 2

Simon sighed wearily. He'd been there before.

One horn. Rhinoceros. The word *rhinoceros* derived from the Greek and meant *nose horn*. There were five species of the family Rhinocerotidae left on earth, but only two of them, the huge Indian species and the Javan, were endowed with a single horn. The others—from Nepal, Sumatra, and Africa—had two. A mental map rose up in his mind's eye, with its deserts, jungles, and savannahs. Lowland swamps, merciless ecosystems, unforgiving poachers.

At least the white rhino had a slight chance. But as for the black African rhino, they were lost souls, spooked by anything, understandably, and would charge with the slightest provocation. The patchwork of farms, industrial estates, cities, and highways had all but banished them from the planet.

As for the Javan and Sumatran rhinos, they had little if any future whatsoever. Fewer than three hundred of the small Sumatran and a mere couple of dozen of the Javan remained.

A one-horned rhino showing up on the docks of Antwerp had to be from either India or Indonesia. Simon hoped it was from India, at least, where numbers had rebounded somewhat from a few hundred in the mid-1900s back up to nearly 2,500 today—possibly enough to ensure their fragile survival. But if this particular refugee was Javan, a single rhino equated with possibly ten percent of the entire living population. That much could be said with some confidence. It would be a tragedy few people would ever know about.

Port authorities at Antwerp had apprehended numerous smugglers from India and Indonesia in the past, not to mention a fair share of tourists with items fashioned from rhino horn in their carry-ons. Such travelers often masked their malfeasances in a parade of screaming children and in the chaos of nicely wrapped Christmas presents before customs officials—a "playing dumb" game. And it often worked. Young wildlife sentinels meagerly scattered about airports were insufficiently trained, as a rule, to detect a rare snakeskin from Mozambique or ivory jewelry from the Democratic Republic of the Congo. If more veteran-level inspectors happened to be on duty, the items might be properly identified and confiscated. Sometimes the individuals were fined, sometimes not. The system was vastly imperfect.

But the odds of getting away with outright poaching were dreamy for hardened criminals. If the horn were scraped and powdered, as was the prescribed preparation for so much Asian medicinal hocus pocus, particularly in China, it could sell for more than 50,000 USD per kilo on the black market.

Airports were easy compared to shipping yards. Simon knew that there would have been no way for a dozen men to stop a frightened, charging rhino on a dock in the middle of the night, especially one that had just endured nightmarish capture and transport from Asia. Ketamine doses, the most common component in tranquilizer drugs for wildlife, were always imprecise because the weight of any wild animal could never be exactly gauged. Xylazine, a muscle relaxant, was likely to have no impact on a rhino. Moreover, there were only a few square inches of area on a rhino that would not deflect the .22-caliber air-pumped bullet with its cocktail of chemicals.

Even assuming the poachers had gotten it halfway right, with the right compression of air, length of syringe, rubber piston inside the barrel, and so forth, the unknowns of a terrified, stressed rhinoceros were incalculable. The defiant animal would have been doped up during weeks of hell. Few ever survived such journeys, which of course drove up the price even more. Scarcity was profitable.

Simon now envisioned the rhino charging against impossible odds, like Hemingway's "faithful bull"—bewildered, surrounded, groggy, adamant—as if weeks concealed in a stifling container with little food and the minimum of fluid were not bad enough.

First there would be the shock of the water in its eyes and throat and lungs—cold water, even in summer months, because of the depths. Antwerp's docks embodied seventy-five kilometers' worth of berths suitable for deep-draft ships. And the sea locks—a maze of concrete, steel, embankments, enormous cranes, hundreds of square miles of machinery rooted to sharp-edged platforms, and crosscurrents—worked nicely in company with super-tankers but would act on a lone rhino, all too few tons of it, with unrelenting ferocity. Currents rippling all across Europe rendered a perfect configuration for a port advantaged by a delta leading to three major rivers, the Meuse, the Rhine, and the Scheldt, not to mention the Albert and ABC Canals. One could swim from Antwerp to the Black Sea, but only theoretically. You'd have to be suicidal to attempt it.

It was this unique water world which made Antwerp's port the fourth largest in the world, where nearly 150 million tons of goods were shipped to and from nearly three dozen countries each year. Such quantities were a nightmare for wildlife inspectors. But from the perspective of a rhino, caught in this otherworldly labyrinth of hazards, this monster of human machinations was worse than a nightmare. It was certain death, for there was the problem of barges—64,000 of them each year, or nearly one every eight minutes—plying the 1,500 kilometers of Belgian waterways. A barge would make pâté out of a flailing rhino at the moment of impact.

All this passed through Simon's mind in a glance. "It will never be found. It's dead," he sighed heavily. "What about the container? The shipping company? Other animals? A rhino is not an easy thing to conceal. Someone is there, hiding. Someone who had a hand in this."

"Yes, it must be," Hubert replied nervously.

Simon was feeling the pressure. There was no time to be lost. Somewhere in that maze of a harbor were conspirators who had worked the system. IW (the Interpol Wildlife Division, the acronym varying from country to country) could not seal off the port. It was too big, too complex—31,336 acres of land; container terminals in all directions, including the huge Zandvliet and Berendrecht locks; and, to complicate matters, the Deurganck dock on the Left Bank, as it was known.

Then Simon's partner finally owned up to what was really on his mind.

"I don't think it was a rhino."

He knew what such a suggestion was bound to trigger in his boss at 3:33 in the morning.

With his head blazing over the critical time frame, the need to gather witnesses, and the pain of a hangover, Simon was in no mood for an unidentified one-horned creature, the biological equivalent of a UFO. It happened sometimes. An explorer in Africa who insisted he'd seen a brontosaurus. And the American couple some years back who were certain a great auk—probably the most celebrated of (allegedly) extinct avians—had scuttled off the side of a freeway somewhere east of Paris where they'd been leisurely tasting wine. The odd thing about that was the fact that the man taught zoology at an American university, and he insisted he certainly knew a great auk when he saw one (the literature of ornithology was rife with well-rendered illustrations dating back to the 17th century when the bird was still surviving on remote North Atlantic island groups).

"Ridiculous," Simon finally replied, turning on his nightlight, grabbing pen and notepad, getting out of bed. "It was either a rhino, or it had two horns, in which case it could still be a rhino or five hundred other sorts of creatures."

"Maybe," Hubert said with an air of strangeness.

CHAPTER 3

Simon was in no mood for Hubert's odd departure, lack of sobriety. Yes, the two partners of several years had been out drinking with impartiality, boozing convivially until about midnight with fellow wildlife crime busters attached to IW. Then Simon had taken a taxi back to his eclectically furnished two-bedroom bachelor pad in the old city, managing to slip out of his running shoes and rayon t-shirt before passing out. His mind had been fixed on the image of a needed getaway with his widowed daughter, Sylvie, and her newborn, on a remote spit of warm sand somewhere in western Cyprus, near the sleepy village where the first new European mammalian species in a century had been discovered, a large primeval mouse.

Simon's condo lacked the slightest charm. It was all business. His ex-wife (who disliked mice and other aspects of Simon's obsessive-compulsive traits) had taken the antiques, although Simon retained what he deemed the essentials: memorabilia of his parents and grandparents, seashells, wildlife books, some avant-garde furniture made of plastic, aluminum, and cardboard à la early Frank Gehry. And a closet full of impressive firearms.

He'd not had time to do more than that, not given his career trajectory.

Two years before, the 48-year-old Simon had been seconded from his police unit in Dijon to Deputy Director of the IW Secretariat, responsible for a broad, taxonomic sweep of CITES identifications (Convention on International Trade in Endangered Species of Wild Fauna and Flora, based in Switzerland), which included the coordination of undercover operations and well-timed stings, mostly in unlikely apartments, at loading docks and harbors, railroad stations, and airports throughout Europe.

His promotion had come just in time, for Simon had grown restless in Dijon, with only the occasional foray into the neighborhood outback, usually to negotiate quietly with small-time farmers who were in violation of the new European Union Animal Welfare legislation, particularly when it came to treatment of pigs, geese, and chickens. In Westphalia, farmers had to look each of their pigs in the eye for at least twenty seconds a day, a gesture that was thought to convey at least a modicum of humaneness. The pig farmers were up in arms. They said twenty seconds per pig, times millions of pigs, meant a loss rather than profit at the end of the day.

Farmers, particularly the poorer ones on properties less than five hectares were difficult to deal with for reasons that were ultimately personal for Simon. In the past, his parents had kept more than a hundred Charolais, the bulging white native cattle breed now popular in many other countries. Their meat ended up on plates at high-end restaurants throughout Burgundy in eastern France, where Jean-Baptiste had grown up, but also where the fifteenth case of Mad Cow Disease had recently shown up, probably from the waste-tainted wheat flour fed to the animal or that was the current supposition. Hard economic times, as well as arthritis and quiet depression, had forced Simon's father to scale way back. He traded the Charolais for a few dozen hormone-free Jersey milking cows, milked once a day, not twice, on a single plot of thirty hectares surrounded by American oak, elm, maple, and plane trees.

Simon's father, Jacques, was nothing like *his* father, Henri, Jean-Baptiste's grandfather—a man who evidently resisted the idea of ever killing an animal, period. He would have had his share of heated debates with nearly every other resident of his village, because *everyone* killed. It was a way of life in France, a tradition that presumed honor, nobility, and survival.

So Henri Simon had entered the monastery at Cluny and embraced the spiritual life. Though Jean Baptise was still a boy when his grandpa, Henri, died, he had imbibed enough information over the years to know that his father's father had eventually moved away from religion to embrace the life of a struggling painter. This enigmatic Burgundian was enamored of cows, not on a dinner plate but on canvas. He drew in the manner of traditional pastoralists, at a time when such scenes had fallen out of vogue. Simon had inherited his grandfather's genes, preferring to forego meat and fish. He never talked about it, but his mother had noticed rather early on that her only son ate nothing but salads, fruit, and cereal. She had no outright quarrel with such behavior, aberrant though she believed it to be for a proper Frenchman.

The end result was that Simon had his own ethical views, but also understood and had great compassion for farmers, whom he knew to be among the hardest working, most witty, and practical people he'd ever known. Good people sadly caught, too often, in a changing world of factory farming and chemicals.

Global warming was adding to the farmers' woes. Two summers before, eleven elderly denizens of his parent's village had died from heat prostration. A year before that, the rains seemed endless. The rivers and canals flooded, and farmers lost hundreds of millions of dollars collectively. Some committed suicide rather than putting bullets through their animals' heads, cows and horses and donkeys who were starving or half drowned.

However much Simon respected the history of farming and the farmers he knew firsthand, whose own children he went to school with, he had also developed a zero tolerance for cruelty, something he had never discussed with his parents. His discrete consumer and dietary habits continued into his adult life.

And, it was the cruelty business meted out by humans against animals, sometimes deliberately, often by hunters sneaking into forests out of season, as well as the international cartels profiteering in the tens of billions of dollars globally by capturing and/or killing threatened and endangered species (so-called T & Es) that had informed his professional life, a life that was beginning to wear him down. He was tired. Tired of arguing ethics, tired of contradictions, frustrated by dogma and the sheer plight of animals worldwide, a situation that was only getting worse by the day.

Although he could manage on five hours of sleep per night, the last few months of so-called Operation Blue Wing, now successfully put to rest, had seen him going frequently on a regime of nothing but espresso with brandy, an excess of aspirin, and too many antidepressants. Such sleep deprivation had taken a serious toll, and a call at 3:30 A.M. from his partner and (officially) second-in-command had a distinctly unwelcome effect. His head was screaming in pain. He had lived with migraines for years, originating in some vertebra in his neck, he'd been told, but this one was a howler.

A rhinoceros running free in downtown Antwerp.

Just what I need . . .

He got dressed, holstered his sidearm, grabbed his notebook and small microtrack tape recorder, and headed downstairs.

CHAPTER 4

S ix Months Before . . .

Edward Olivier pressed hard with his left hand against his upper right chest where a bullet had lodged ten minutes before. He grabbed hold of the chain around his neck, clinging to the silver oval with its Benedictine hallmark.

The forest was as dense as any equatorial jungle, despite it being winter in France, drizzling, and the middle of the night. The drizzle had turned to sleet, as it nearly always did. A thick vine ensnared the stumbling seventy-eight-year-old ornithologist, and he felt his chain ripped from his body. He tried to bend down, groping with his hands through the underbrush to retrieve it, using a small penlight he held in his teeth. A pain shot through his chest as involuntary spasms jerked him back upward in a frozen angle, breathing hard. He bit down on the flashlight, cracking a tooth. The tool fell away and darkness subsumed his fading thoughts when . . .

He heard the distant sound of another blast. Almost immediately, a bullet ripped through his shoulder.

"I'm sorry," he whispered, looking all around at the discernible bright eyes peering out from the ancient forest. He felt blood running down his arm.

A charge of large ungulates and a flurry of others headed deeper back toward the uplands, through a breach in the old wall, followed by the distinctive cries of an unprecedented array of birdlife all around, rare in the dark. He recognized some, the puffins, snipe, and carrion crow. A Levant sparrowhawk shot past him, terrified.

Then silence. *They're gone*, Edward surmised. *I've got to get back inside the periphery . . . .* His head was fighting for clarity. He knew the route from this portion of grounds, a complex map long memorized, knew every trap, every grid, every hole in the ground.

When suddenly a third burst of firepower issued, as if from all sides, he fell stunned and muted into the mud. It had been raining hard for many days and nights. A huge easterly, sixty to seventy miles per hour, had come in from the Atlantic, blowing trees down. The front brought heavy snows to some parts of the region. Here, snow fell less frequently than might be expected for its elevation. More usually, the hills were perpetually fraught with mistral-warm drizzle, sheet lightning, heavy rains, and impenetrable clouds that were ever-present for as long as he could remember, since just after World War II. Frost was frequent, however. It might be sunny everywhere else in France, but these mountains, this strange geologic twist of landforms, engendered a microclimate that was perdurable, defied cell phones, even satellite reconnaissance. It had always proved to be a comfort, but not on this night.

Somehow, his worst fear had materialized, something that had not happened in family memory. Intruders had gotten in.

There was an echo, and another, and another. He knew that the bullet, which hit him like a missile, had issued from somewhere within the mile-wide sinuous valley surrounded by largely inaccessible hills of limestone dating to the beginning of time.

"Lance!" he tried to call, but only a faint murmur issued from his lips. It was too late.

They had been scoping him out. Even through dense mist. Some new kind of night vision binoculars. No doubt about it, he reckoned.

He raised his other hand, feebly thinking to scratch a sign in the mud, but it proved pointless, then to touch the unfortunate gash on his head. Not even time enough to close his eyes, or utter words to dispel the demons. He'd seen them on the inside, over the wall—demons in the guise of men.

"I'm so sorry."

CHAPTER 5

P resent Day . . .
  Hubert arrived at Simon's apartment with his patrol car's red and gold lights lazily flashing. It was just short of four in the morning, with scarcely a vehicle on the road. A boy on his bicycle delivering newspapers with news of an Iranian showdown, a baker making his rounds, far off the first grating sound of an approaching garbage truck.

Simon was waiting on the sidewalk in the darkness. A drunk slept outside the adjoining coffeehouse that would not be open for three hours.

He quietly slipped into the Renault, and Hubert sped away without speaking, through streets still saturated with the night's rain.

Simon took out his notepad and pen. "Has anyone been questioned yet?"

"No," Hubert replied. "I've asked Inspector Le Bon to cordon off the immediate area of the chase and hold all those who were involved or saw anything in the harbor master's office until we get there. IW has issued an all-points alert. Every barge will know to keep an eye out for a wild animal in the water."

Simon held no hope for the beast. Barges were like supertankers, zero torque, poor visibility. What mattered most to him was the time. It was probably already too late to ensnare the conspirators on site.

On the other hand, evidence in these matters was always a sort of game: part logic, part serendipity. Clues might be as subtle as a single hair, with its DNA echoes, a missing line item or unsigned bill of lading, even the print of a gloved hand on the sea-moist side of a demolished crate.

Within twenty minutes, they had arrived at the Port Authority, passing the BLEU (Belgo-Luxemburg Economic Union) offices and heading into the industrial expanse with its endless containers stacked fifteen, twenty high. Fertilizer, fruit, steel, sugar, truckloads of new Mercedes, grain bound for Angola, warehouses full of registered agrochemicals, stretching for tens of miles. Four hundred million cigarettes headed for China, seventy tons of Canadian zinc ore waiting to be transferred to Munich.

The sign: ALFAPORT ANTWERPEN.

The harbor master's headquarters, directly above the Scheldt, oversaw this hegemony of European consumption. It was, after all, along with Rotterdam, the historic capital of import/export.

Entering the large open secretarial workstation, Simon counted fourteen individuals in addition to the harbor master. None looked too pleased. Longshoremen, caught up in the fanfare of something that had happened just ninety minutes before. These were heavy brutes, not the sort to screw with.

Simon wearily acknowledged his uniformed IW fellows, most of whom had been drinking with him hours before. All shared the same look of sleep-deprived annoyance, and not a little curiosity. Something strange had happened. It was in the cold moist air.

The harbor master himself had seen nothing, but everyone present had taken part in the chase, and the key witness had nearly been killed in the fracas, or so the present flight of rumors suggested.

"You are a dockworker?" Simon asked the first man before him matter-of-factly. He could see by his hands and his clothes that he was.

The man nodded.

"Is that a 'yes'?" Simon added, his Dijon patois hitting up against an antagonistic Flemish. The linguistic enmity between Belgian and French was nothing new. Two of the IW team were Englishmen, one attached to Scotland Yard, the other an Interpol wildlife crime geneticist from London University. English was the common parlance of all who spent their lives around shipping lanes, the same universal language wielded in commercial airline cockpits and control towers.

"I am Jean-Baptiste Simon, Deputy Director, IW," Simon attested with a tone of efficiency. "What did you see?"

The worker spoke reluctantly. "I heard the commotion coming from inside one of the crates. They were supposed to be cars, from Paris. The crate had already been severely damaged. The animal got out and charged. I was maybe ten feet away."

"What was it?"

"I don't know."

"But you must know, if you were ten feet away."

"At first I thought it was a rhino. But as it ran past me, I saw that it was a different sort of rhino."

"A buffalo?"

"No."

"There are countless varieties," Simon reminded him. "Cape buffaloes, various jungle buffaloes, bison."

"It had one horn, and it was white. But I am sure it was no white rhino."

"How can you be sure?"

"I saw the one Steve Irwin got up close to on Animal Planet. This was different." The man was adamant about it.

"Different how?"

"The horn was spiral."

"A kind of antelope, perhaps?" Simon ventured. "Some are huge and have spiral horns. Maybe the second horn had been poached or broken off. It happens."

"No. Fast, manner of an antelope, yes. But horselike, enormous. Fierce. I don't know. It was pretty dark."

One man insisted it was an Arabian oryx. He'd seen them at the zoo. Another joked that it kind of resembled the unicorn he'd seen in some exhibit of tapestries years before at an underground museum in Anvers. But about three times the size and "very hairy."

Another confirmed the size, but couldn't remember anything about it being hairy. It did "snort hugely," the man attested. It struck Simon suddenly that this witness was German. No penchant for overstatement. Not at four in the morning.

"It was almost prehistoric," he concluded.

Each witness had a similarly confused account. *Red . . . black . . . ferocious . . . A huge mutant goat . . . The horn of a narwhal, like a whale . . . A deep, bellowing cry. A high-pitched whine, like some infant needing mother's milk.*

Now Simon caught the currents of a freaky fact: fourteen adults, a few possibly involved in what appeared to be a crime, though possibly not. But the majority told, each one separately, of a different beast that shared some characteristics. The lack of consensus among such practical men made Simon wonder if something really bizarre had emerged from the crate and disappeared into the waters of oblivion.

Simon knew the mystical tales of the unicorn, beginning with an alleged skeletal find at Einhornhöhle in the Harz Mountains of Central Europe in the early 1660s. Legends persisted about the horn—its medical properties purported to prolong life indefinitely, an antidote to numerous toxins, and velvet that could be rendered into the most potent human aphrodisiacs ever known. One animal was worth a king's ransom.

Fifteen thousand years ago, survivors of the Ice Age across the continent still had occasional encounters with the woolly rhinoceros, or *Coelodonta antiquitatis*, as it used to be called by taxonomists. And it is possible that some had heard of its horselike relative, known as the Elasmotherium, a single-horned ancient rhino, native to the Eastern Steppes leading into modern Russia. That animal was enormous, living strictly on the leaves of trees, and traditionally was referred to as the "giant unicorn." It went extinct by 10,000 B.C., whereas numerous breeds of bull, with their varied horns, carried on the legend. Some were blue-black. None could be mistaken for horses, but some—bred with African long-horned cattle—might be white. An Italian painter of the late 16th century, Aldrovandi, had sketched both one- and two-horned creatures he called Pirassouppi and Camphurch. The latter had rear webbed feet like a duck and the body of a bewildered wild dog, though without the gorgeous painted splashes of contemporary African wild dogs, more like the rough rust-colored South Indian wild dog. The former, the Pirassouppi, strode with the confidence of a Lipizzaner.

Simon didn't know what to think.

By this time, the regional chief inspector, Paul Le Bon, a decorated career policeman who had attended United Nations conferences on global crime syndicates and worked hand-in-hand with Interpol, had surrounded the main docks with a bevy of policemen, the officers conducting a crate-by-crate search.

Hubert and Simon were escorted to the container in question. It had been smashed, dowels, metal hinges, nails flattened. The heavily damaged steel cover was an inch thick. The remains were numbered in large stenciled code. It conformed, said the harbor master, to the log on the computer system that accounted for over a quarter of a million crates every twenty-four hours.

"It was loaded four days ago outside Paris," the master relayed. "No doubt about it. Along with 124 other luxury vehicles. Mercedes. Jags."

There was no damage to any other crate. The animal had kicked itself out.

Not possible, Simon reasoned, playing the scenario over in his mind.

A young rhino's horn would not have stood a chance against such steel. Nor would an adult have had enough space to deliver a punch sufficient to break out.

It was then that Simon noticed something on one of the ruptured steel flanks. Something, or someone, had made it easy for the animal. With his finger, Simon marked the points where fracture lines had been amplified with a torching tool or pneumatic drill of some sort.

"Where were these vehicles going?" Simon asked Le Bon, who had taken a full accounting from the harbor master.

"The Emirates."

CHAPTER 6

Martin Olivier was just leaving for lunch from his office on Bond Street when his secretary, Alicia, told him he had a phone call.

"Take a message," Martin said distractedly. He was meeting his wife, Margaret, at a private gallery where she had served as curator of an exhibition on Flemish iconography of the Renaissance, still on the walls. The show had received glowing reviews all over the world. After the Fra Angelico retrospective at the Metropolitan Museum in New York in late 2005, this was considered by many to have been the most complex, expensive, and daunting exhibition ever mounted, particularly for a private institution. With its more than one hundred pieces—paintings, musical instruments, maps and globes, letters and rare books, the exhibition would travel nowhere else—insurance premiums were too high.

"Whoever it is says it's urgent," Alicia declared.

"Who is it?" Martin replied.

"He says he's your uncle. The phone shows a three-three country code."

Martin cut short his flight toward the lobby. He had not heard from James Olivier, his father Edward's only sibling, in many years.

"Transfer the call to my office, and do me a favor, call Margaret and tell her I'm running a few minutes late. And be sure to tell Max just to wait." Max was Martin Olivier's personal chauffer. London had become impossible without one, at least for people like Martin Olivier.

Martin had a queer sensation in the pit of his stomach. He'd not been in touch with his father for almost a year. There had been no single estranging event but a systematic alienation over time that was never above the surface. The backstory was complicated. They had very different personalities, father and son, that either clashed in mutually internalized silences, or proffered courtesies that would have worried families of a more intimate character. In any case, the time since they had last had a good talk, taken supper together, had slipped away. Martin always assumed that his father disapproved of his having gone into real estate, although his father had never articulated the exact reasons for his apparent discontent with his son.

Anthony, Martin's own son, had turned eighteen without so much as a card from his globetrotting grandfather. That was not like Edward Olivier, who always managed to dispatch a uniquely Edward sort of reliquary from wherever he happened to be traveling. He delighted in generous if unpredictable gifts symbolic of his connection to the natural world: African carved stones, the odd feather from some waterfowl in Newfoundland, a Brazilian fossil. Once Martin had received a round of cheese from a monastery in France, manufactured by the monks and cured in the finest cow's urine. It certainly smelled of it. How the parcel made it through the postal system Martin never quite figured out.

And then there was the extravagant four-volume reference work with hand-colored chromolithographs from the 1800s which catalogued the European birds "not found in Great Britain." It was valued on abe.com at nearly £ 2,500, the color reproductions in perfect condition.

Edward's presents frequently consisted of expensive wildlife books. Anthony received them now as Martin had when he was growing up. As a young man, Martin had tried to break his father's peculiar habit by arguing for a Mustang convertible when he was eighteen instead of Buffon's *Histoire Naturelle*, a fifteen-volume set published in the mid-1700s, as complete an encyclopedia of mosquito bites or the intricacies of a salamander's alimentation as one was likely to find.

"Did you know," Anthony once remarked to Martin sometime after the boy's eleventh or twelfth birthday, "that bats will not eat flies until they have first removed their wings, which they consider indigestible?"

"You're joking," Martin replied bemusedly, a complete déjà vu. Edward had shared the same anecdote with Martin at about that age.

The last book Martin remembered receiving from his father on a birthday was a handsome copy of *Alice's Adventures in Wonderland*. He remembered its topsy-turvy world with fondness as a welcome foil to the pressured formalism of growing up in an atypical English household where one's parents were precocious, oftentimes away, and harbored high expectations for their son.

"James. What a surprise," Martin said coolly. He couldn't help his response to his uncle's voice, which instantly took him back to a lonely childhood, one with an absent father and uncle. Their participation in his young life could be measured by the eccentric gifts and little else.

Martin detected a fumbling, labored weight in the voice, hesitant and strange. "My dear boy."

James's use of this endearing phrase alarmed Martin. "What is it? You sound dreadful."

"I have some rather troubling news."

Martin said nothing, then, "OK?"

"Your father's dead."

Martin slowly sat down on his fine 18th century teakwood and silken chair of Japanese origin, which he'd acquired at auction, and for just an instant, he stared at the portable phone, holding it at arm's length.

"Martin, are you there?"

"Yes, I'm listening. What happened?"

"I mustn't go into the details. Not over the phone."

Martin could hear a whimpering, a sort of panic on the part of James.

"Alright, I'm coming. Where are you?" Martin removed his Mont Blanc pen and specially inscribed notepad from his vest pocket to write down the particulars.

"I want you to listen very carefully now. Please don't ask any questions."

"That's a bit scary, James."

"Just bear with me."

"Yes?"

"You must presume you are being followed."

"James, now this is getting a little weird."

"No questions."

"Followed by whom?"

"I don't know. You must come alone. And not a word to Anthony. There will be time for the family to digest what has happened, but not yet. Now write this down: The heart of the big apple, but a small town. Fiddle with this, assume the easternmost possibility. Go northeast on the only paved road you can. When you come to the first pastry shop, the day after tomorrow, at noon, sit in your car, and by that I mean your own car, not a rental, and I shall email you."

Martin was scribbling fast. *Big Apple . . . fiddle . . . pastry shop . . .*

"Alright. You've got my email address?"

"No."

"It's the name of my company, my name with a dot between first and last, since you're asking for some secrecy, Lord only knows why."

"You'll change it. Earth-friendly. The name backwards of the man whose memoir appears in part three of the Gallinaceous."

"Hold on. What are you talking about? You're going too fast. Say it again."

"Just remember the pigeons volume."

"Pigeons? Jesus, James, what are you talking about?"

"From the set you got when you were, I think, nine, maybe ten."

"How many volumes?"

"Forty," James recalled precisely.

"Alright," Martin said. "I am supposed to what?"

"Damn it, Martin. You're not paying attention."

"I am paying attention. But you're. . . . " He was utterly exasperated. *Calm down, Martin.* His head fluttered.

"The name of the man whose memoir it is, at the beginning of the pigeons. And then the earth-friendly server. Got it?"

Martin was writing frantically in a shorthand he could not read, even as he wrote it.

"Earth-friendly? I have no idea what you mean."

"The server. For email. Surely you've heard of it?"

"Yeah. I think I know what you mean. But . . . all this other stuff. Galli . . . whatever that was."

"Gallinaceous. That's pigeons."

"Fine. The name of the author spelled backwards. Got that."

"You do still have the collection of books?"

"As far as I know."

"Good. Then get going."

"Wait, wait a minute. James, what if all these little word games don't work? You do have a backup plan? I do not intend to travel a great distance only to miss you or reach the wrong continent."

"Margaret, no doubt, can do the fiddling for you."

"So I can tell Margaret, but not my own son?"

"Anthony is a young man, full of unpredictable emotions, impulses. He's vulnerable. And he might say something."

"Vulnerable? He's a tough kid. But what might he say? What are you talking about?"

"Not what, but to whom. Whereas your wife . . . well, this will undoubtedly involve her, no choice. The timing of your father's death was terrible. But you are to come alone. Absolutely alone, do you understand?"

"James. I need answers."

"You'll get them."

"Where are you? How did my father die? And why all this intrigue? Did my father do something wrong? Did you?"

"He did everything right. We both did. But it wasn't enough."

"Damn it, James, you're speaking in riddles."

"Go home. This is hardly the most challenging of crossword puzzles. A silly precaution, you might think. But you mustn't trust anyone. Do you hear? And you must not from this moment use your credit cards, calling cards, anything that might possibly identify you in any manner with credit agencies, banks, the police. Use nothing that can be traced. You have no idea what's at stake here. Say nothing to your cohorts. I mean it. No one. We have a serious problem. It's much bigger than the family, and you may be the only one who can sort it out. You and your wife. Your father thought so, anyway."

Martin was having difficulty breathing. "When did he die?"

"Six months ago."

CHAPTER 7

The wildlife forensic specialist—Polish, in her sixties, a walking lexicon of morose zoological oddities, and attached to IW from her genetics group at London University—had found a trail of bristly grey hairballs leading to the edge of the quay, forty feet above the polluted water of Antwerp's port. Hairballs were just one of her specialties, along with bones, horn, teeth, muscle tissue, the body particulars of hundreds of species. Spore was her stock in trade. Her medical career had veered from the individual to the many, a discipline born of mathematical probabilities and her willingness to engage in mortal combat. It might be pasteurella, anthrax, or some as yet unknown killer bacteria that would inflict the ultimate pandemic, unless she and those few in her profession were there to stop it.

The tritium foil electron capture gas chromatography device, as it was lugubriously known, was a microtech gadget that Dr. Gosha Krezlach traveled with the way most people carry iPods and laptops. In addition, she carried two large aluminum suitcases filled with the other chemical and biological tools of her trade. Airport security always regarded her with suspicion, despite her flashing a bona fide Interpol ID. The problem was her luggage frequently traveled in the same trunk as radiocarbon devices and rare animal body parts, preserved in rectified spirits and formaldehyde, or some such concoction. Residue lasted for months, got mixed up, and made her a serious risk in the minds of those who had no idea what she was really about.

Kneeling down, she shined her flashlight into the container. "Look," she said to Simon.

There, inside, were all the signs of terror and injury, a pandemonium of urine, blood, and feces. Simon had observed the evidence an hour before she'd arrived. Any large animal, thus confined, would have evacuated its bladder from stress and messed up its container. Baboons were the worst. And elephants.

"We'll run tests. I'm hesitant to speculate."

In Simon's two years of knowing Krezlach, he had not seen her so unsteady on her feet. Something was amiss.

"Any ideas?"

"Not yet. That's a lot of shit for that size container. It was scared to death." There was a light trail of dark blood, and she insisted on wearing a mask and handing them out to any other officers who had a need-to-know reason for getting close to the container. Wearing latex gloves and wielding sterilized tweezers and eyedropper, she collected samples in little vials and placed them in a tidy tray that slid into a larger receptacle. She locked it and placed it in a small carrying case.

"It'll take some time," she said to Simon.

"Are you alright?" he asked. She looked tired and nervous. By then, the pale sun had risen on a dull, drizzly morning.

"I never get used to this stuff," she exhaled with weary reconciliation. "We're losing more than we're finding."

"What do you make of this?" Simon said, pointing at the markings on the fractured exterior of the crate. To Simon, it appeared to have been tampered with from the outside, suggesting the involvement of someone on the pier who knew which crate the animal would be arriving in.

"You'd need a bomb expert, a metallurgist. I know the fundamentals, but this goes beyond basics. Not my specialty," she was quick to reply, gazing at the ruptured steel siding of the crate that had been bludgeoned with some dull but heavy instrument or perhaps rammed by a forklift.

"That's not what I was referring to." He traced what was obviously writing that had been etched into the steel with a sharp instrument, a pocketknife more than likely.

"Wait a minute." She turned the piece of steel 180 degrees. There, clearly, were the letters *CSPB*. She asked the police to take infrared and x-ray photographs of the handiwork.

Inspector Le Bon was now seated in his vehicle, speaking quietly on a cell phone. He motioned to Hubert and Simon, who came up to the car. Le Bon rolled down his window.

"There's been a murder at a museum in town, sometime between midnight and 7:30 this morning. I doubt there's a connection, except for one odd fact, apparently. The murder weapon."

Simon was growing impatient with these half-digested clues. He gazed at Le Bon balefully. "Go on."

"A sharp horn of some sort," Le Bon continued. "Or antler, maybe a tusk, I don't know."

For Simon, the connection was anything but dim at this hour. "There's a big difference," he tried to explain to Le Bon. "Horn is tissue. It's soft. Whereas an antler, which is but the outgrowth of bone, is much harder. Tusk, protected under CITES, is basically a form of enameled ivory. Like an antler, it could be used easily to kill somebody."

"I'm sorry, you lost me. Antler, tusk, horn, bone, all I know is that the night guard, having a cigarette out in the courtyard at the end of his shift, or so he says, happened upon the impaled body. The victim was an old gardener. A bit messy, evidently."

EDITIONS OF

The fyr

¿e of the commu¡

of Raphaell hythlodaye ¡
¡ge the best state of a con

CHAPTER 8

By the time Jean-Baptiste Simon, Hubert, and Inspector Le Bon arrived at Antwerp's famed Plantin-Moretus Museum at Vrijdagmarkt Square, an armada of emergency vehicles, including a fire truck, had surrounded the Renaissance exterior. It was a little after nine A.M.

Two colleagues from Le Bon's unit were on hand to escort the three men indoors, past the array of historic printing presses and the library, past the eighteen portraits all done by Pieter Paul Rubens, a local himself. This was the site of Europe's earliest and most important publishing house, where Christoffel Plantin (1520–1589) had championed every new typographical invention. Within these lustrous walls, Plantin used his technical skills to print the first Bible in five simultaneous languages, *Biblia Polyglotta*, one of 25,000 books in the collection. The museum had become the first such institution to be named a UNESCO World Heritage Site in 2005.

The men went from the luscious interior of magical cabinets, famed musical instruments, and globes on display for the thousands of tourists to see each year back out into the rain, past neatly planted rows of shrubbery and flowers that graced the small inner courtyard with its minimalist Flemish garden design, to the scene of a gruesome deconstruction at dead center.

The body of the gardener, a man in his early eighties, stood stiffly against the central stone pillar that divided two semicircular rows of low flowering bushes. Blood was everywhere. Around him, a pool of it had collected. The wind had carried some leaves into the hardening red gel of a former life. His rake lay at his feet, and a strange twisting white bone more than three feet long, resembling the kind of deadwood one finds occasionally washed up on shore, had been forced through his neck.

"He's worked here most of his life," said the security guard who had found him. "And his father and *his* father, or so I'm told."

"What's his name?"

"Jacob. Jacob Hythlodae."

"Strange name. Flemish?"

"Yes. But old Flemish," the guard said. "Old English, as well, as I understand it."

Simon examined the bone whose sharp incisorlike dagger had been thrust into the man's throat. Two feet of bone protruded from the still soft weight of the pinioned victim. It was the material of scrimshaw, which made no sense whatsoever. Only a narwhal—a very rare and endangered whale species mentioned by one of the witnesses at the docks—could have produced such a horn, which did indeed resemble that of the fancifully rendered unicorn. Now the possibility of some abstruse connection with the events earlier that morning was becoming clear, but also ever more tenebrous, confusing.

"He was shot as well," said Fabritius Cadiz, the policeman who had arrived first at the scene. Cadiz was a close friend of Inspector Le Bon's as well as of Simon's assistant, Hubert Mans. "There." He drew his finger around the entry wound in the old gardener's chest. "The bullet came second, I believe. We've recovered it from that brick pillar over there." He pointed twenty feet across the courtyard, past the gardener, through whose back the bullet had continued. There was red powder. "A large-caliber weapon. Hunters after wild boar use it throughout Europe. The bone, believe it or not, did not kill him. The bullet finished him off a few minutes later, I imagine."

"But why?" Simon wondered aloud. "That would mean, well, a kind of statement, a revenge killing. Whoever did this wanted the gardener to know he was being murdered."

"Perhaps."

"What did the gardener do?" Simon asked. "Here is an old man. He knew something, didn't he? But what? Was anything from the museum stolen?"

"Too early to tell," replied Cadiz. "The curators are inside, searching. But whoever did this was very familiar with the institution and the comings and goings within. The assailant had studied the movements of the security guards, receptionist, janitor, research staff, which is quite a number of people, and, alas, the gardener."

The crime investigators finished dusting the surroundings, photographing everything, and finally removing the gardener's corpse from its anguished stance into the confines of a white body bag, with the bone or tusk or antler—no one was certain *what* it was, including Simon—intact.

Medics trundled the body bag out of the courtyards, as Simon looked around at the Renaissance walls and repeated out loud the family name, "Hythlodae."

"Why does that name sound so familiar?" he wondered.

"They go back as long as the museum," said Cadiz. "I cannot imagine a motive for such a murder. Even if the gardener caught whoever did this in the act of trying to steal something. The bone makes no sense."

"Was it from the collection?"

"The director will know," said Cadiz.

"We'll need some DNA work," Simon concluded. "Immediately."

"But there is no doubt as to the gardener's identity," the security guard quickly interjected.

"I'm speaking of the murder weapon," Simon said.

Inspector Le Bon's phone rang. It was another investigator still out at the docks. Le Bon took down the information regarding a certain surveillance camera which had recorded two vehicles speeding away from the port, one following the other, three minutes apart, at approximately 3:03 and 3:06 that morning. The camera had recorded the vehicles' entries as well, separated by many hours, much earlier in the evening. Both vehicles could be identified by their shape.

Le Bon looked to the security guard and asked, "Does anyone on the staff here at the museum drive a Studebaker?" It was a most uncommon vehicle in this day and age. "Or a postal truck?"

"Yes, there is a Studebaker. The gardener's." He looked to the corpse. "I mean, he rarely ever drove it, a 1953 Commander Starliner. Beautiful car. He let me take it out for a spin a couple of times. I think he mentioned that it was parked a few blocks from here. At some cousin's house."

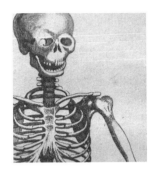

CHAPTER 9

Dr. Krezlach knew the IW lab could not handle the blood or DNA typing with anywhere near the speed that the Antwerp police were wanting. She suspected that the weapon that had impaled the gardener and the fragments recovered from around the shattered container at the port came from the same species, but it would take overnighting the elements to a wildlife forensics laboratory in Ashland, Oregon, the best in the world. If the samples turned out to be bone, the difficulty would be determining its age and the species. Bone tended to be of a mundane structure, farm-animal type, though easily carved into something that could be used as a weapon. Sometimes soft tissue remained vital within, but the only way to determine that was to disintegrate the sample with acid, a dating technique most recently applied to dinosaurs, and rarely of use, except by eccentrics hoping to clone extinct animals or Neanderthal man.

Krezlach pondered the scanty evidence, extrapolating in her mind's eye a host of possibilities. She knew that it was not unusual to hear of a buck decimating its human pursuers. It was easy to delineate horn, composed of so many successive layers of tissue, from antler. Walrus ivory, like bone, aged without much disintegration but could not easily be assayed without some recourse to molecular biology. These were the realities.

She had been through her share of archaeological samples, from ancient Norse spoons to Medieval Anglo-Saxon combs, Viking caskets made of cow bone, and a box, from the 14th century, of musk ox horn. Villagers in Renaissance Bohemia would clean bones by leaving them in ant piles to be picked over, morsel by morsel, and then they'd shape their axes and swords with the remaining materials of nature.

She had waded through all such studies, along with the mineralogy and pH of soils, to help her, and others in her profession understand what was legal and what was illegal (a threatened or endangered species or anything that could be proved as recently killed).

At Ashland, an electron microscopic analysis of the samples would determine a match. Accuracy was better than one in four million, as had been demonstrated in the case of an Alaskan poached walrus tusk some years before. The electron microscope was kept busy due to the constant need to distinguish extinct mastodon ivory from newly poached ivory before a court of law.

With respect to blood samples, wild caught parrots could be distinguished from those bred legally in captivity. The first such precedent for this type of work originated in Pennsylvania, where the dried-blood remains on a knife were determined to have come from a doe poached out of season, not from a goat, as the defendant had insisted.

Simon was eager to verify the match, but the Belgian Federal Police had jurisdiction over the murder and were not about to have a critical piece of evidence sent out of the country. If anything happened to it, it could thoroughly undermine their case. On the other hand, argued Simon, if there was a correlation between the two incidents, it could bolster their leads. The problem Simon had in convincing both Le Bon and Cadiz of this fact was the very lack of even a single link thus far. No one at the dock had come forth with testimony that had any substance.

This confederacy of indecisiveness now played into Simon's court, as he used the disarray to prevail upon his colleagues with his insistence that a policeman needed to get on the first flight out to JFK and then on to Portland, hand-carrying the horn and horn fragments in a special bag.

Le Bon, Hubert, Cadiz, Simon, and Le Bon's assistant, Julia Deblock as well as the museum director proceeded down the street, around a corner, and down two more Baroque embellished blocks, scooting past a chic pedestrian alley to the Italianate villa which proved to be as ornate as the famed Rubens House but older by more than a century. From outside, it showed only a drab-looking edifice, which betrayed nothing of the golden insides. Indeed, Le Bon's, assistant, a French graduate student in criminology, fluent in six languages and all of twenty-seven, produced an astonishing fact after a few phone calls to select nerds who populated her research universe: It was one of the oldest houses in Antwerp, dating to the first decade of the 1500s. And the family that built it was none other than the Hythlodaes.

They barged into the back, along the driveway past a "No Trespassing" sign to an ivy-covered shed. Fresh tire tracks through the mud led to the structure behind the rather enormous compound. They broke the lock to the shed. Cadiz reminded Le Bon that they had just committed two breaking-and-entries that could screw the whole case before a judge. Le Bon did not worry about things like that. He was usually spot on when it came to a veteran cop's instincts.

Sure enough, there was the Studebaker that had appeared on the security video at the entrance to the port.

It was the gardener's vehicle. The housekeeper, on learning of the news of the gardener's death, all but collapsed.

Le Bon ordered round-the-clock surveillance on the property.

"Has anyone other than Mr. Hythlodae been here lately?" The inspector softly inquired.

"No," the housekeeper said. "He never had visitors. He was such a kind man. This is unthinkable."

"Did he seem afraid of anything? Any unusual behavior of late?"

"No, nothing out of the ordinary."

"Madam, we have evidence that he drove to the docks last night, then returned here early this morning, before dawn. He didn't by chance have any large animal with him?"

The housekeeper looked at him. "What are you talking about?"

"Did he mention the docks or any animals?"

"No."

Le Bon pressed on, ignoring the fact that she kept wiping her tears with a fine silken hankie. No apron skirt. This was a well-dressed woman, maybe not a housekeeper at all.

"You have no idea why a gardener, who we have ascertained actually owns this . . . ", he paused, gazing at the austerely rich furnishings in the entranceway, "this mansion, would drive off in the middle of the night, come back, and then head off to the museum only to be murdered?"

She hesitated, then restated a final, "No."

"Do you know anyone who works for the postal service?" The second vehicle had been IDed as a French, not Belgian, postal delivery truck. The video enhancement had even revealed a dented front right fender. Neither of the two vehicles yielded identifiable license plates.

She shook her head.

"Do you mind if we look around?" said Le Bon. He peered past the hallway into a room chockfull of evident treasures, a library, sculptures, musical instruments, and paintings, none of which, Le Bon noticed, seemed to hold any obvious interest for Museum Director Edouard Revere, a fact of some peculiarity, he thought, given the "gardener's" position. Le Bon then took his cell phone in hand on the pretext of checking messages but, in fact, taking silent video of the contents on a wide shot. He entered a second and third room, each more opulent in its way than the last, holding his cell phone in a video-capture mode. He knew there could be evidence lurking, fingerprints or objects that might be removed in the gardener's absence.

Le Bon climbed the stairwell and continued his documentation in rooms upstairs when the housekeeper answered a phone call. She listened and murmured, "Yes, sir. Of course," then turned the phone over to Revere. "It's for you," she said.

Revere took the phone. After a pause, he merely nodded, "Um-huh." And then handed the phone to Le Bon. "He wants to speak with you."

Le Bon knew at once that there would be a problem. It was a lawyer for Jacob Hythlodae, informing the inspector that he would need to obtain a search warrant to enter the property. That he had no right to question the housekeeper without a lawyer present, and so on.

Who called the lawyer, and when? Le Bon mused.

"Thank you, madame. I am sorry for your loss. I expect we will come back. We all want to find out who did this terrible thing to your employer and, I imagine, your friend." She thanked him.

Le Bon fixed his gaze on Revere as he paid his own respects to the housekeeper. Revere's succinctness could only be read as cryptic, Le Bon thought.

Outside, Le Bon placed a call to run the gardener's details. His driver's license had expired decades before. He was born in 1923. Title to the property was vested in a trust comprised of Hythlodaes across Europe, who obviously had turned over their legal affairs to the lawyer to whom Le Bon had just had the pleasure of speaking. This was no cousin's house, exactly, but the gardener's own. A mansion owned by a gardener who had kept his great wealth hidden from those on the outside. *Why would a man of such financial means be content to engage in menial labor for his entire adult life?* Le Bon wondered.

Not even the museum director who had employed Jacob Hythlodae for so many years, knew—or was willing to admit knowing—that Hythlodae was enormously wealthy.

"There's something else," Julia Deblock declared. "The name, like the house, dates to approximately the same eponymous debut."

"What does that mean?" Le Bon asked impatiently. His young assistant was always casting about for imponderable phrases and terminology. He assumed she thought this clever, an edge up on a criminological vocation. Simon and Cadiz looked up from their cell phones, where they had been working over the bureaucratic details of an exhausting night and a morning that had proved even more disturbing for the normally tranquil Antwerp.

She proceeded, "Raphael Hythlodae or –daeus, ring any bell?"

The three men frowned. It did not, although Simon *did* remember something . . .

"Wait a minute. A literary character?"

"Actually, a real person," Deblock went on. "From Thomas More's *Utopia,* published in 1516. The man's name was none other than Hythlodae. There were other spellings—*day, daeus.*"

Le Bon looked to the museum director. "Surely you knew of this?"

"It is no secret," Revere replied. "We all had to suffer through it in Greek *and* Latin as students." Le Bon and Simon both sensed that he was holding something back. The museum director's manner about this affair was growing increasingly strange.

Julia continued. "He was described by More as a weather-beaten man who had traveled the world and actually *been* to Utopia, lived there for something like five years. Book One is basically an edited transcription of Hythlodae's own observations as he relates them to More. And guess where they had their little discussion that would become the source material for one of the most famous books published in the Renaissance? Right here, I imagine, at the house of Hythlodae, though More said it was in his own garden. The point is, the whole encounter took place in Antwerp."

"What does that buy us?" Le Bon grumbled, not half as intrigued as Simon.

"I have no idea," Julia Deblock replied, "except that *Hythlodae* means 'angel' or, according to the Greek, a person who talks nonsense."

"Nonsense," Le Bon reiterated. "Well, that's helpful."

"Now I remember!" Simon chimed in. "The Greek meaning was the ironic part, just like *Utopia* itself, which means, in Greek, no such place, right?"

"Depends how you pronounce it. *Topia* means place. *Ou* means 'no,' but *eu* means good. More was an intellectual giant who played with language, politics, satire, and meant to take up the notion of governance, good and bad."

Le Bon was in no mood for all this. He had not counted on a dissertation from his underling and had several things on his mind other than Greek etymology.

"Utopia," Deblock concluded, ignoring her distracted boss, "pronounced like *Eutopia*, was indeed a paradise, and the Utopians lived in a pure state of nature, unlike the vast majority of Europeans."

"It was a fantasy," Cadiz claimed cynically. "I read it."

"Yes, but the Hythlodae family was no fantasy," Deblock pointed out.

"Mademoiselle Deblock, we have one or two things to do this morning, as opposed to this tiresome fishing expedition."

"I just think there might be something very interesting in that house," she declared.

"That's why I filmed everything I could," the inspector replied.

"What are you thinking?" Simon asked, more than a little curious. By now he had no doubt that there was a connection between the murder and the escaped animal, whatever it was.

"Well, the book, *Utopia*, refers to a certain map," Deblock replied.

Revere broke in suddenly, "We have the map. It is part of the most famous atlas ever published, by Abraham Ortelius, one of the icons of our museum collection. There are no secrets. Thousands of tourists each year gaze at it. In fact, it is the least artistic production of all the maps in the atlas, which was published in 1570, called the *Theatrum*. It also happened to be one of the best-selling works of its time. There are no secrets, gentlemen. Rather, hundreds of best-selling editions."

An awkward silence fell over the group. As a policeman, Simon could not help but wonder why the museum director was so insistent that this map was no secret.

"So where was Utopia?" Simon asked.

"Nobody knows," Revere replied. "Does it really matter? It was a political satire. Henry VIII was executing twenty thousand thieves a year in England. Can you imagine? Gruesome times with no respite. And as I'm sure you know, More did not exactly ingratiate himself with the king. By refusing to acknowledge Henry VIII as the Supreme Being in England, if you will, he paid with his life. All his efforts, on a personal level, were in vain, as it turned out."

"But some scholars have pointed to Norway, at least the sparsely populated

Norway of More's time," Julia explained. "More provided clues."

"And others insist it was a city called Amanote, meaning 'dream-town,' somewhere in the New World," Revere said.

"Yes, it is possible," Deblock added. "Raphael Hythlodae had been to America with Amerigo Vespucci, or so says Pieter Gillis, another character in the book and a well-known resident of Antwerp."

Simon knew that all was not as it appeared. Revere was too calm. He seemed strangely unmoved by the murder of a man who quite obviously enshrined as much history as his museum. Not to mention the fact that he was an employee and probably a friend.

Revere, perhaps sensing Simon's unease, volunteered an insight that gave all of them slight pause, something he regretted saying the moment he uttered the words, "The map and its positioning of Utopia are more interesting for what they leave out."

"Meaning what?" Simon finally asked.

"Never in the book or on the map itself is there a suggestion, for example, of Brazil, a logical choice in those days, given the view that it was a vast continent of unknown species and noble savages. Or alternatively England herself, a geographic ruse that might have afforded the author some brownie points on the political home front."

Simon did not yet know what to make of Revere's oddly slippery manner.

"Do the letters *CSPB* mean anything to either of you?" Simon asked, looking at both the security guard and Revere, and then to Mademoiselle Deblock.

CHAPTER 10

By the time Martin arrived to meet Margaret for lunch, he had already let his secretary, Alicia, know to put all meetings on hold for the next week. His explanation was fashioned from the most plausible of scenarios: first dibs on a major estate soon to enter the market on account of some death in somebody's family. He delivered the message with the cold, businesslike opportunism that had made his firm so successful.

Margaret was just wrapping up a discussion with the principal curator of the exhibition. More than 100,000 people had come to view the manuscript illuminations and other art objects, with just one week left before the exhibition would be taken down. These were unprecedented numbers for a small institution lodged somewhere between "gallery" and "museum." This newfound celebrity was largely Margaret's doing.

Margaret was Flemish and had obtained her doctorate at Oxford in Burgundian art history, with a dissertation that focused on what she described in the accompanying catalogue as "a history of imagination in wilderness." Though not yet fifty and looking more like an ageless thirty-five-year-old sultry actress, she had already been likened to such past giants as Lord Kenneth

Clark, Siegfried Gideon, and Erwin Panofsky, all formidable forces in the art world. A social historian of the Renaissance, she knew musicology, comparative literature, and the minutiae of iconography from a dozen countries. Moreover, she was expert in several old languages—from Dutch, French, and Italian to Church Russian and Greek. Her German, Portuguese, and Latin were decent. Margaret Olivier could have held her own at any European dinner party in the 14th, 15th or 16th centuries. Yet she had refused appointments at the most prestigious universities to remain an independent consultant, whether for museums, auction houses, or—predominantly—her own husband's company, aptly called Olivier's.

Her ability to cut to the marrow often demolished the competition. She could invariably provide her husband a twenty-four-hour turn around time of estimates with potential clients. She would examine digital images of an estate and price each object, historic element, sculptural detail, or painting on the wall with an exactitude and market realism that were frightening. She had written eleven books (she could type in excess of one hundred words per minute) and had published nearly two hundred academic papers, with titles such as, "Campin, Bouts, and the Brothers Limbourg: the Impact of Great Bibliophiles on the Landscape Miniatures of the Flemish and Dutch Renaissance." In short, Margaret Olivier was a freak. Her long auburn hair, striking dark eyes, and *Venus of Dresden*-like curves endowed her with the beauty of a rash and sexual misfit in the body of an unabashed but professional prodigy.

For his part, Martin's law degree, coupled with training at Sotheby's, had admirably prepared him for a career driven by the continual supply of old dusty estates ("romantically neglected," as their advertisements would describe them in magazines such as *Country Life*) throughout England and Scotland. His firm specialized in whole estates, meaning the land, the mansion, and the contents of the house. That might include such riches as rare book libraries, garden sculptures, tapestries, a vast range of antique furnishings, as well as works by Old Masters.

Martin was persuasive when negotiating with a grieving widow or overwhelmed grandchildren. Why exhaust yourselves grappling with the vicissitudes, endless appraisals, assessments, indemnification papers (lest a firm find itself commending a painting of contested authenticity), the myriad commissions and menacing tax ramifications on an entire estate's contents, when Olivier's could provide an all-inclusive service that guaranteed the highest prices in the real estate *and* art worlds with the least resistance or complication?

He had sold dozens of Grade 1 listed palaces, castles dating to the 13th century, and one unprepossessing, run-down estate that contained within its dank confines an orgy of surprises: not only seventy-five acres of never-before-cut forest but also a gallery of paintings that included a Rembrandt, a Constable, and an oil portrait of William Shakespeare of unknown authorship.

Margaret and Martin headed out of the museum in Chelsea to their favorite little bistro around the corner. Martin's driver, Max, waited for them in a valet space at the museum.

"Something bizarre, no, that's not it . . . something actually terrible has happened. I'll tell you when we sit down."

Margaret assessed the irritating bundle of traveling instructions with her characteristic alacrity. That was Margaret. "*Coeur*, heart; *Big NY* equals big apple. Corbigny. No doubt about it. You never told me your family farm was actually in Burgundy. That's absurd! I mean, Burgundy, for God's sake. I probably know the place."

"He always mentioned eastern France. It just never occurred to me."

"And your father never mentioned anything more about it? That's so bizarre. He knew I did my Ph.D. on Burgundian art." Her frustration had long been sublimated. Martin's father had always preferred to ignore her line of work and for that matter, his own son's as well. She never knew why. Edward was a scientist but not a traditional one. He never published. He never gave interviews. Why was he famous? For discovering a few new species of birds, which he refused to name or permit to be named in his honor? He was loath to describe anything about them, actually. Or give up their whereabouts. Margaret always thought him too *precious* for words—a modesty that was hiding something. She just couldn't put her finger on it, and she had stopped caring.

What she did know was that he had remained remote, despite the eccentric birthday gifts. Edward's one wife, Martin's mother, had perished in some exotic jungle. Margaret and Martin had been dating for all of a month when it had happened. She remembered the sensation that this was a lonely, strange family. Martin never mentioned a funeral, never shared even a single photograph of his mother, never discussed what had happened. Days then weeks passed. She looked in the London *Times*. There was no obituary column anywhere, just a huge blank.

"It's an English thing," Martin said, distracted, hopelessly wondering himself what had happened.

And now, that same sensation all over again.

"He always said it was a dump. A former presbytery, a run-down farm, some wild land that was confined, legally bound up with French. . . . I don't know what. Too much trouble. You know my father."

"You're the most knowledgeable rural real estate agent in England, or I used to think so. And you're telling me you never even expressed an interest in seeing your own family property?"

"It's Uncle James', mostly. I mean, Dad hardly ever went there."

"How do you know?"

Martin didn't actually have a clue. As far as he knew, his father had spent most of his time in the field, doing biological research in faraway places. But maybe that was all some peculiar ruse, a cover-up.

"Anyway, we'll know soon enough. I'm just going to stop at the house, pick up a few things, and leave. James insisted I drive."

"You're driving to Burgundy? This afternoon?" Margaret said, somewhat astonished.

"Well, not exactly," Martin continued. "Max will drive."

"But I thought you said James demanded you come alone?"

"He did. But as you can appreciate, I'm not comfortable driving on the right side." Margaret, no great admirer of her husband's distracted driving skills, made a funny little noise of agreement. "I'll call you tonight," Martin added, "when I know more."

CHAPTER 11

_y_ nilp@earthlink.net.eu

In his twenty minutes at the house, Martin had found William Jardine's forty-volume *Naturalist's Library,* with the particular volume on pigeons and its short introduction by way of the *Memoirs of Pliny,* written by the son of a man who would die from the sulfurous fumes of Vesuvius the day after it had destroyed Pompeii. Whatever the connection, Martin had gotten the first part right, at least.

Now the question was whether he was waiting outside the right pastry shop. Or in the proper country. It was noon. He sat in the back of his BMW 740, tinted glass, iPhone in his hand. Service. But not a word from James Olivier. Nothing.

Suddenly, the village was pounded by a clanging to the angels—the acoustic ferocity of a shelling. Bells from a nearby *eglise,* but still no email.

"Shit," Martin exhaled, at eight minutes after twelve.

"Maybe I should leave you alone, sir," Max suggested.

"This is so fucked!"

"I'd say so, sir." They had just driven some five hundred kilometers. The navigation system made it very simple, of course, but the traffic was terrible. Tens of millions of tourists going in and out of every region in the country. Summer in France, but it was drizzling and cold here in the Bourgogne. Somewhere near Sens, the weather had dramatically taken a turn for the worse.

They drove slowly through the town, with its typically uneven hybridization of post-World War II drab streets lined with mundane shops, including a salon de coiffure, a tax office, the more recently built train station, no TGV stop here, and in the small old town center, a fromagerie and a boulangerie. Up a chestnut and lilac alley lay the local cemetery. A canal, with curving ponts of old brick, wound its way toward a row of mountains discernible in the distance, covered in forest. Above the quietly drifting watercourse, each house had its little flower box, the occupants fully in bloom.

"Max, go get yourself a coffee. And while you're at it, those chocolate croissants looked good. I'll have two."

Martin sat staring at the iPhone. His Wi-Fi free-roaming connection to system orange was operational, but nothing was coming through.

"There is no backup," he said aloud. "Damn it!"

Suddenly his iPhone rang. It read: "Anonymous caller."

"James?"

"I asked you to come alone." The phone went dead.

From James' perch, a large screech owl flew out of the partly opened window.

Martin pressed Dial Caller.

Nothing. It rang and rang. No message.

Well, at least I know I'm in the right place, he thought, stepping out of the car and peering in every direction.

Max returned with coffee and croissants.

"Get in the car," Martin said. "We're being watched."

Max did as he was told, at ease with the instructions. He sat loosely before the steering column, quickly opening the glove compartment with his left hand to verify the position of a certain weapon.

"We wait," Martin exhaled.

A nearby church, its foundation built atop 3rd century Roman ruins, contained an eighty-three-foot-high clocher, or bell tower, from which someone who had access, a key, or close friendship with the curate could view the entire village unseen.

A panorama not only of the village but of 360 degrees of splendid patchwork to every horizon was visible. There lay a small corner of the Bourgogne, a tired land littered with ceramic shards, painted beads from cultures that had migrated back and forth between Champagne and the Jura, the Marne and the Sea. Charcoal relics radiocarbon dated to nearly the moment in time when some person or persons sat pondering a campfire, Bronze Age memorabilia, a rich Medieval strata of passing personalities, beautifully fashioned clasps, the odd remaining walls of other towers. And, of course, famed burials, like that of the primeval princess of Vix, crowned in a golden diadem, found resting in her cave, and a vase, the oldest ever turned up in Western Europe. Menhirs at Epoigny, a Roman temple on Mont Dardon or the ancient villa rustica at La Grenouillère.

And somewhere nearby were once peoples known as Helvetii and Aedui who'd been pursued by Caesar's armies. James knew all about them.

James, sixty-seven years, a slight tremor in the left hand which held the cell phone, binoculars in the right, could divine sure enough that Martin had, indeed, been transported by a man who could only be the driver by his liveried appearance and well-trained mannerisms. It added a complication, but one that James would have to accept.

He let dangle freely around his neck the 40x binoculars, and with his right, steady hand, he dialed the text message:

"Can you trust that man with you?"

"Absolutely," Martin typed in response, relieved at last to be in touch with the whole reason for this spontaneous and morbid expedition into a country that had, surprisingly, held little interest for him.

There was a moment's pause, then Martin's iPhone vibrated. Martin answered, noticing that Max kept his eyes down, taking care not to look in the rearview mirror.

"Absolutely," he reiterated. "He's been my driver and security guard for years. I vouch for him completely."

"All right, then," James finally volunteered. "Rolling terrain. Are you in shape?"

"You're joking?"

"No joke, Martin. Your driver will take you to a broken bridge no later than two hours from now. . . . "

And, he went on to leave precise satellite coordinates.

"But how?"

"There's a program on your iPhone that will translate. It's not that complicated. Even I can figure it out." James went on, explaining about the broken bridge, the various water levels this time of year given the huge amount of rain, going on foot, wading across the one possible narrows, then 2.7 miles to the edge of a meadow, deep clover, poppies, even orchids. He was to beware of fast-moving boars ("you won't hear them coming through the dense groves of chestnuts"), and that's where Martin was to stand, waiting.

"I thought I was coming to the house?"

"First the meadow. A necessary precaution."

"James, what the hell is going on?"

"I'm sorry, Martin. You'll have to trust me on this one."

"Trust you? I haven't heard from you in half a lifetime, and now I should trust you?"

"You haven't exactly reached out either, you know. It works both ways. But never mind that," he said nervously. "This is bigger than both of us. Much bigger."

"And I just stand there? For how long?"

"At approximately 3:30, with your left arm fully extended, just stand there."

"Left arm, you say?"

"Yes, left arm fully extended, not upward, not down, but horizontally. Quite important. Wear an overcoat. And a glove."

"I don't have a glove."

"I'm sure your driver has gloves."

Martin only then realized that he had to do what he was told or go home. He felt a dull resignation overtaking him.

"I'm standing in a meadow at 3:30, my left arm extended."

"Horizontally."

"Why am I standing in a meadow with my arm extended, wearing a glove?"

"Do you know what a falcon looks like?"

"I would not know how to distinguish a falcon from an eagle from a vulture, if that's what you mean."

"She'll know you. She will be carrying a handwritten message in her right talon. Take the slip of paper. Stroke the bird's neck in gratitude, gently. That's how it has always been done. Then raise your arm, which is her cue to fly away. The directions will be in that piece of paper. And one last thing."

James knew the conversation had gone on way too long. "If you have any cause to believe that you are being followed, you are to abort the whole deal. And do be careful with the boars. They're everywhere."

"How did he die, James?"

"I can't tell you that. Not now."

CHAPTER 12

M artin stared out at the cold, rain-drenched countryside of Burgundy as Max drove him to a place matching the satellite coordinates they had managed to compute.

A few minutes after Martin's vehicle had disappeared from the central plaza, James Olivier, still standing hidden in the corner of the bell tower, rang up a number on his cell phone.

"Lance, I need Eyos there in precisely two hours. Figure twenty more minutes before you toss her."

As he prepared to descend the eleven flights of narrow, spiraling stairs, built of local stone in the late 16th century, his cell phone vibrated. James thought it was Lance calling right back.

"What?"

"Hello?" a trembling voice called out.

"Who is this?" James asked, ready to hang up at once.

"James, is that you? It's Edouard Revere."

Along a lowland swath of the hilly Morvan, with its old Roman vineyards, limestone cliffs, Celtic ruins, and Pleistocene caverns, Max and Martin sped past partly worked fields of bright yellow rape and crumbling walls of mossy stone. The wine from this part of the Bourgogne was unavailable except for the occasional three-star restaurant to which some Frenchmen would drive for hours just to taste les ducs de Bourgogne, gastropods, the Géants, particularly—broiled, served up with chopped shallots, anise liqueur, pine nuts, Dijon-style mustard, or any of another fifty ways that the Burgundian snails, *Helix pomata*, were prepared.

France, with its more than 500,000 square kilometers, one million years of *Homo erectus*, followed by a few dozen millennia of *Homo sapiens* history, of troubadours and conquerors, and the stubbornness that enshrines every village with its potagers, or backyard vegetable gardens, and their inevitably delicious by-products, was certainly not unappealing, Martin thought. At the same time, all this beauty to which so many of the world's tourists flock now seemed to Martin's mind a dreaded confusion.

Max suddenly screeched to a halt, the car spinning halfway around.

"Jesus!" Martin screamed.

Two riders on horseback had crossed the road in the middle of a turn. Max had been exceeding the speed limit by double. The BMW's braking system, one of the best in the world, and Max's own unusual skills staved off disaster. The road was as slick as ice. The two stallions reared frantically, the lead horse front-kicking at the vehicle, resulting in a significant dent on Martin's rear passenger door. But no injuries.

The French couple was screaming, and Martin's French was not up to it.

"I'm so sorry. You're alright, it appears?"

A spasm of insults and counter insults ensued until finally the couple, walking their horses to the other side of the road, remounted and trotted off away from the highway.

"Take it slower," Martin demanded, his nervous system frayed to the bone.

"No worries, sir. It's back there, anyway," the driver good-naturedly agreed. He turned around, driving very slowly, on the lookout for tenacious outdoorsmen. Finally, he left the two-lane paved road for a dubious-looking muddy clearing that went into deep forest. He had passed the all but invisible entranceway two miles before.

"You sure about this?"

But before Max could confirm, the friendly English-speaking woman's voice on the navigation system said, "Continue straight. In half a mile, you will be arriving at your destination."

The muddy clearing grew dense with foliage. Tree limbs caved in from all sides. Suddenly the road ended, and before them moved a fast-flowing creek, much swifter and deeper than James had indicated.

"Oh, great," Martin thought, getting out of the car, rolling up his pants, removing his jacket, and tying his shoelaces together so he could toss his shoes over one shoulder. It was 2:07. He had just enough time, assuming he did not get lost.

"You wait here," he told Max. "Stay out of sight. I expect to be back by five or sooner. Oh, and watch out for big mammals. Pigs with tusks."

"I'll do that, sir."

Martin picked up the largest stick he could find, and presently he arrived at an improbably fast-flowing tributary.

You must be kidding! His chest throbbed. He could not see any possibility of getting across without drowning. He probed with a stick over the edge of the embankment as instructed and eventually found a section possibly shallow enough. He stepped down with difficulty, the water hitting his knees. He then proceeded further, up to his thighs. The force was pulling him. He fought the stream, found higher rocky ground underfoot, and kept pushing. Now a kind of sandbar emerged, and his feet sank deep into it. He was stuck, suddenly aware of the very real possibility of getting marooned, and he thought to call out for Max.

Martin reached out with his stick toward the higher ground and boulders, and he extricated himself enough to move another foot farther, then another and another until he reached the far side. It had been all of twenty, twenty-five feet, but it had seemed a near Mount Everest of expenditure. This city boy was not exactly up to such misadventure. Martin wondered how the elder James could possibly manage this terrain and for what looming reason he had been sent here.

Martin climbed out over the sandy ridge, pulling himself up by the thick roots of a plane tree, sat down to catch his breath. He was sopping and cold. The rain increased.

Standing back up, he peered forward into the dark forest, then walked on until he eventually disappeared into a deep grassy ravine that angled uphill towards the unknown.

CHAPTER 13

Julia Deblock arrived at police headquarters in downtown Antwerp joined by an elderly gentleman in his priest's frock coat. They walked passed Julia's own cubicle, where she had been working for the last fourteen months, straight to her boss's closed door. She knocked twice, then entered.

"Those four letters, *CSPB*. I think they refer to Hythlodae," she announced.

Le Bon looked at the older man with her, whom he seemed to recognize, but he could not be certain.

"This is my uncle, Father Bruno."

"Call me Leopold."

The inspector looked quizzically at Julia, then stood up and shook her uncle's hand from across his inordinately messy desk.

"Paul Le Bon. Do I know you?"

"Yes. We met about twelve years ago. I was a parish clerk at the time when a man entered the church, said some things, then tried unsuccessfully to damage an important painting, before taking his own life."

"*The Descent from the Cross.* Then he used a knife on himself. Very unusual case."

"The case is closed. We try to forgive and forget," the priest said solemnly.

"As I recall, there was something else."

"Precisely," Julia Deblock declared. "Which is why I thought it would be worthwhile for you two to reconnect."

"Go on?" Le Bon said.

"Julia suspected something. Smart girl," Bruno said. "Though she is too young to remember what happened that day. It wasn't the first time. And as I now understand, it will not be the last."

"You've lost me."

"This Mr. Hythlodae," the priest went on.

"He's in the morgue," Le Bon said curtly. "They're going to open him up tonight. Did you know him?"

"Not personally. May I sit down?"

"I'm sorry. Of course, please. Something to drink?"

"That's fine," Bruno said, waving off the temptation of a coffee. He was nursing a recent revelation from his doctor—a blood-pressure reading of 180 over 130—and trying, by the look of it, to somehow skirt the delicacy of what he had to convey, and just say it. "Julia mentioned that there was an incident out at the docks here in Antwerp last night. And that the letters *CSPB* were scrawled on a piece of metal at the crime scene."

"Of what interest would that be to you?" Le Bon fixed his steely grey eyes on the priest, not sure yet whether to be annoyed that his assistant had divulged confidential information. She must have had a reason to do so.

"No one in my position would be unfamiliar with those letters."

"How is that?" Le Bon asked.

"*Crux Sanctii Patris Benedicti.* The Cross of our Holy Father Benedict. Saint Benedict."

"Meaning what?"

"It comes from the Medal of Saint Benedict, undoubtedly the most important and, if you will, the most unconditional indulgence that the Church can accord another at the time of his or her death."

"I remember," Julia started. "So many stories about the old days when you could buy an 'indulgence' from the Catholic Church. If, say, you were an adulterer, you could buy an indulgence that would instantly wipe away the sin."

"That's right," Father Bruno replied. "The medal cleanses its bearer at the moment of death. On a par with that of the Virgin herself."

"How much are they?" Le Bon grinned.

"The letters *CSPB* we only understand from a manuscript composed in 1415. The death that is conferred by the medal is referred to by the theologians as a Holy Death."

"*Eius in obitu nostro praesentia muniamur.* May we be strengthened by His presence in the hour of our death. A fundamental relationship between the faithful and their God. Saint Benedict lived in that spirit on Monte Cassino throughout the late 6th century, near Rome. When he died, he was swallowed by the light. There were witnesses. He also voiced a number of curses."

"Curses?"

"Exorcisms. Nothing complicated, mind you. I mean very simple and direct statements. Be gone, Satan, for example."

"A Holy Death," Le Bon repeated. "Superstitions. Nobody really . . . "

"Oh, yes. Some people do believe. In Mexico City there are now at least twenty-two chapels devoted to an ancient Aztec deity, Mictlantecuhtli. . . . I can't quite pronounce it, I'm afraid, but we know that an entire cult is emerging devoted to the same sort of deity. Not just in Mexico, but also in the southwestern United States, and a few places in Europe, as well as Turkey and North Africa."

"These are Benedictines?"

"No . . . well, we don't really know. Possibly criminal elements, drug dealers, using voodoo or bad mojo, they have various names for it. Trying to fight fire with fire. Magic. Hocus-pocus. The Catholic diocese would prefer, for now, to think of the followers as confused. They call her La Santisima Muerte, Holy Death Goddess. And they have created images of the skeleton of the Virgin Mary."

"Turf warfare between gangs exploiting church relics and deep-seated beliefs, and probably the gullibility of people related to the victims," Deblock added.

"OK. What's the connection to a dead gardener in Antwerp this morning, where no letters were found?"

"Are you sure about that?" Father Bruno asked.

"Please excuse me one moment." Le Bon picked up his cell and called Simon, who had spent the remainder of the morning at the Plantin-Moretus Museum questioning Director Revere and waiting for his staff to come up with any missing items. Guards were searching every room, every corner of every wall, the maps, particularly those of the *Theatrum*. There was nothing to dust. Nothing out of order. So far, not one item could be said to be missing.

"Did you find those same four letters anywhere else?" Le Bon asked him.

"No," Simon replied. "We've looked at everything."

"Wait a minute, Jean, I'm going to put you on speaker phone. This is Father Leopold Bruno, my assistant Julia's uncle. She invited him to my office because he thinks he may have some idea about the crime scene last night or a motive."

"Father, meet Jean-Baptiste Simon. He is Deputy Director of the Interpol Wildlife Division. He's investigating both incidents. Tell him what you know."

"Hello, Father," Simon said.

"Did you check the man's belongings?" Bruno inquired.

"A colleague is going through his things as we speak. Is there something in particular?"

"Ask him if the man was wearing any amulet or anything of a religious nature."

"He had a centime-sized coin in his wallet, along with some currency, a few twenty-Euro bills. No ID of any sort, but a photograph or two I can't really talk about."

"But you're sure it was a coin? It wasn't oval? Did you read it?"

"No. I don't remember if there was anything to read. But I'll tell you what, that's easy to resolve. Those items are all here inside the museum at the moment. Give me five minutes. I'll call you back. "

"We'll be here, Jean," Le Bon said.

Simon walked down a corridor to where the investigating team had placed all the evidence in plastic bags, including Hythlodae's wallet. Cadiz and Hubert were methodically making a list of everything they had collected. Later, they would move all the bags to the forensics lab in downtown Antwerp, where Dr. Krezlach and Le Bon and the entire western European IW team were based.

"Hubert, where's that coin that was in his wallet?"

Hubert found it immediately and presented it to his boss, wearing gloves.

"Who has the magnifying glass?"

One was forthcoming. Simon removed the oval-shaped object from the plastic bag, held it up to the light, then examined it under magnification. The oval was no coin, and it was old, most of its engraving rubbed off. He could see *ux . . . ra . . . ihi lux, nun . . . co . . . t . . . x.*

On the backside were tiny smudges, nothing legible. The coin, if it was a coin, Simon thought, must be several hundred years old. He could ask Revere if he knew anything about it, given the museum director's familiarity with old things, but he then thought it best to leave that alone for the time being.

Simon removed his cell phone from his pocket and called Le Bon back, still holding the strange oval between two fingers.

"Here's what it says, hold on a minute." Simon had Hubert hold the oval while Simon held the magnifying glass to read the letters back to Father Bruno.

Bruno crossed himself. The *ihi lux* was an instant giveaway, confirming what he already suspected to be true. He said nervously, "*Crux Sacra Sit Mihi Lux. Nunquam Draco Sit Mihi Dux!*"

"What does it mean?" Simon asked.

"I Pray that the Holy Crucifix Should Serve as my Sunlight and that the Dragon Never Serve as my Guide."

"I've heard stranger," Le Bon said.

"No, you haven't." Father Bruno's glance at his niece told her that her intuition had been correct.

"So what does this have to do with anything?" Simon asked.

"He didn't have time to grab hold of it," Bruno speculated.

"What do you mean?" Le Bon asked.

"To have clutched it to his heart might have helped."

"Helped? Helped save him? What?"

"This is difficult to explain, theological, but of enormous import."

"I'm afraid you've lost me, as well," Simon added. "This thing is the size of a penny."

"Yes. I know. Still, it could have saved him."

"No, Father. Not in this instance. The murder involved a large weapon. A penny-sized . . . "

Bruno interjected, "I am referring to what happens to him now."

"Yes. Of course." Simon understood that part—heaven and earth and the in-between. What he didn't understand was what those four letters had to do with the victim or what relevancy they might pose to a missing large ungulate, possibly an endangered species, now more than likely dead, and a gardener who had turned out to have been enormously wealthy and was most certainly dead.

"CSPB refers to *Crux Sanctii Patris Benedicti*. The Cross of our Holy Father Benedict. Patron saint of hermits and monks, of the whole of Europe, of agricultural laborers, temptations, witchcraft, poisons, and people at the time of their death. The person who left those four letters on a metal crate had something very important to say, to protect, to bless," Father Bruno declared. "He carved or etched those letters to protect a soul and proclaim a Holy Death, as opposed to one that had been granted to the Devil."

"When you're dead, you're dead," Simon said. "I've seen too many corpses to think otherwise."

"You don't believe in God, Monsieur Simon? Or heaven?"

"I do, in fact, Father. I am also a Catholic. But in my profession I have become increasingly disappointed with God. There are too many innocent victims, particularly among other species. Religion has not sufficiently explained this problem, not to my way of thinking. But this is not the time to get into that. Perhaps sometime over coffee. For now, I need only to know one thing. What can you tell me about our murder victim that we don't already know?"

"As I told you, Saint Benedict was associated in church history with poisonings and other forms of dying. We think of him as the patron of the dead," Father Bruno said. "His own death has been formally characterized as Holy Death. That is a critical combination of words, if you will. How to die with virtue, how to transform murder, suicide, and the natural decay that kills all things into something divine. That's where the cult of Benedict assumes universal proportions, and where my dear niece, Julia, seems to have put two and two together."

Julia Deblock now said what she had been waiting to tell her boss, and Simon as well. "I looked closely at the letters and wrote up all the possible combinations. It is an anagram. Anyone could figure it out easily. Holy Death equates with Hythlodae. Although Sir Thomas More declares that Hythlodae was Portuguese by birth and the anagram is English, there is no doubt about it," she said. "These are not coincidences, but clues that were meant to be read by someone."

CHAPTER 14

Holy Death, Simon reiterated to himself. Hythlodae didn't seem like the typical conspirator. But then, what was he?

He put the oval coin, as he still thought of it, back into the plastic evidence bag and took his assistant, Hubert Mans, aside. "I want every major sting that has gone down in the last twenty years checked for this phrase. Have you ever come across it?"

"No," Hubert said.

Nor had Simon. "We must ascertain the name, address, phone number, and occupation of every member of Jacob Hythlodae's family. And I want IW agents stationed around the clock at whatever port in the Emirates was to have received that shipment. Get the manifest, speak to the harbor master, and find out whose bill of lading correlates with the crate in question."

"I did. First of all, it turns out to be Dubai. And the company involved is a subsidiary of one of the cousins of the sheikh. Total immunity. We have nowhere to go with it. Sorry, boss."

"They're signatories to an international security protocol."

"That's for suspected terrorist activities."

"For now, we don't know *what* was in that crate, and we have no reason to exclude any possibility. I know we have Hans in Dubai. Let him check it out and get back to us."

Hans Maybeck was a German scuba diver who had one of the better jobs in IW. He played the perpetual tourist with his adventuresome wife and four kids. They were always on holiday in the Emirates at the Jumeirah Hotel on the beach. He could tell you where every Damani gazelle slept beneath each Sodom's apple tree, from Bahrain to Qatar, and he knew which cousin of which emir was keeping illegal dugongs in his swimming pool for personal amusement.

Hans would meet his informants at any number of popular nightclubs in Dubai, at bowling alleys, discos, in the Satwa heart of town, where chai was taken informally, or along Dubai Creek at night, or sampling aromatic tobacco (sheesha) at a coffeehouse.

Where it got a little crazy was when the royals of Oman or Yemen got into the sport, going out on dune buggies along the Hajar escarpment in search of endangered wild cats, the scimitar-horned oryx, or a leopard for their illegal collections.

Simon had not gotten a single answer from any member of the museum staff that shed the slightest light on why someone would have wanted to kill Jacob Hytholdae and in such a manner.

He examined other maps in the collection from the late 16th century, along with municipal documents pertaining to the Hythlodaes, as well as Gillis. What was surprising was their later obscurity, given the fanfare of so many subsequent editions of *Utopia*.

In fact, there was no mention of where Raphael Hythlodae was buried, when he died, or what happened to his family members. A letter from the painter Hans Holbein, another friend of Sir Thomas More, referenced him, but in connection, strangely, with "a new bird."

Just as Simon was giving the sleeve, with its rare letter, back to a member of the staff, he received a call from Dr. Krezlach.

"I had not counted on such a day as this," she joked. "Sometimes we'll go for weeks with nothing to do but read."

"What is it?"

"Chronic wasting disease. Not just in a deer. A badger, possibly a dog."

"You're joking."

"They say it appears to have skipped between species quickly, although, as usual, the World Health Organization is not releasing some critical data. But local authorities have traced the disease to two deer near your hometown of Dijon. I've been asked to go there, pitch in, and collect some blood. They're understaffed. Seems to be the order of the day. Whatever it is, it's spreading everywhere. I just wanted you to know that your case will have to wait until I get back. So sorry."

CHAPTER 15

E yos was certainly not your everyday variety of falcon. As her name im-
plied (to those who know something about falconry), she had presumably been taken from a nest somewhere in Greenland or Iceland as a chick,
then hand raised. The largest of all falcons, she was a gyr, grey to grey-brown,
the upper portions of her flight feathers darker, her undersides verging toward white, particularly along the ends of her primary feathers. More so
than any others of her kind—the red-footed, peregrine, Merlin, and Eleono-
ra's—Eyos was enormous. She inhabited her menacing body with grace, or
so it appeared to Martin Oliver, who stood uneasily some forty feet beneath
the hovering bird at the anointed spot.

The seven-kilo avian swooped down, rose, then landed gracefully on Martin's gloved hand. She wore two minute golden bells. Tied to her talon was a
slip of paper, which Martin removed gingerly. They stared at each other.

"Hello," Martin managed.

The bird peered intensely and shook her head once, splashing cold water
from her wings onto Martin's face. He raised his right hand to stroke her

neck feathers. She let him. He then raised his left arm, hoping she would take the cue. She did not.

Martin's arm was feeling the weight. *What do I do now?* He slightly panicked.

She started to move toward him. *Oh dear.* Martin tried, stupidly, to back away, forgetting that she was attached to his arm. But with a gyrfalcon approaching, logic is not easily predictable. The bird walked all the way up his shoulder so that the weighty creature was at his face. She touched Martin's face with her enormous beak, first on his left cheek, then his right eye. Martin remained motionless.

Oh dear! The bird was totally in control, could do to him whatever might be on her mind.

Then she leapt off, landing in the meadow, and immediately started up his leg, the talons digging into his calf muscle, then his thigh, approaching his crotch.

Martin lurched. But the bird would not give up her search.

And then Martin realized what she was after—the remains of a chocolate croissant, still wrapped in a piece of newspaper, stuffed in his pants pocket. He reached down, withdrew it from his pocket, and before he could toss it, the bird had it in her beak. She hopped back down on to the ground and delicately proceeded to take the remaining chocolate only. The bread did not interest her.

She cried for more and flew back onto Martin's shoulder. None of this was in the game plan.

Nothing was, particularly her preening his curly, black, receding hair, which had evidently acquired its share of sticks and leaves and two ticks during his hike. She carefully relieved him all of the biological debris.

Back on the gloved portion of his hand, she looked him in the eyes with an intensity he had never seen in his entire life, then turned and looked upward. Martin took this as a sign. He tossed her, and she took the toss, flying off over the forest and disappearing at last.

Martin breathed a huge sigh, sat down amid buttercups and marigolds, and opened the note. It gave a whole new set of arcane-sounding instructions. But this time, they led to a house.

Martin then did what he had absolutely been forbidden from doing. He placed a phone call to Margaret, giving her the name of the closest village and landmark and explaining precisely where he would be in less than five hours—assuming he didn't get lost and the water levels in the creek had not risen any higher, and he could even find the exact spot that enabled him to get across in the first place and find Max and the car.

"James has taken elaborate precautions to keep this whole thing under wraps. The location is absolutely hidden," he said.

"Your father was murdered. And James doesn't know who did it. Or maybe he does, and he's afraid of saying," Margaret surmised.

"It's more than that. It's the location itself he seems especially paranoid about. I have no idea why."

"Maybe your father was killed there. If so, the chateau would become a crime site. Overwhelmed by police. That's one huge invasion of privacy, and you know how your family is."

"Still, you'd think he'd want the murder of his only brother solved."

"Yes. One would think so, but he has waited six months. That makes your uncle a suspect. In fact, he's already broken certain laws, you can be sure. And you'll be equally suspect if you don't report all this to the authorities."

"Not until we find out what has really happened. I'll call you tonight. In the meantime, find out where the hell this place is. You know the region, I don't. My iPhone is on silent mode. Send text messages. Tell me what you find. I have no idea what I'm getting into."

"Where are you now?" she asked.

"In a meadow. And for the last ten minutes, I've had a giant falcon on my arm."

"A falcon? Martin, you don't know the first thing about falcons."

"You're wrong. In fact, I had her eating right out of the palm of my hand."

"Sure you did."

And he proceeded to read to her the instructions Eyos had brought to him.

CHAPTER 16

James had by necessity sent instructions to Martin leading him via the circuitous route from Corbigny to the house. In fact, there was no *easy* way to get there. The big old mansion, or chateau, as James still thought of it, was the last window on the world. His brother, Edward, had perceived it that way as well.

There were no public road maps to this house, no signage or institutional plaques leading to what was both a fort and chateau de plaisance with its ancient winding wall of nearly seventeen miles and numerous seigniorial architectural features. Many chateaux throughout France enjoy mention on the major thoroughfares, of interest to tourists on holiday. But not this one.

Visitors had come, on average, less than once every twenty years, beginning in the early 15th century. Directions were given out on the most excruciating need-to-know basis. No map contained the chateau. No reference to it had ever been promulgated. It drizzled there almost continuously, but no one who didn't live there would know about this freakish microclimate. And the nearest neighbor was countless miles away.

James reached the house in forty minutes. He punched in a code that opened the first of three ancient sets of gates. Each had electronic pads and were keyed into three video surveillance cameras that were no longer functioning.

Eight months before, someone had messed with the system. Edward had tried to fix it himself, which was the only way, really. The amperage had become attenuated along the length of the electric wire. The sectors no longer transmitted data as they had throughout the 1980s. Both telephone and radio information had been scattered. Broadband did not yet exist in the area, and even if it had, a minimum of one bar was needed if a signal were to remain viable. There were very few areas within the estate that yielded even one bar of signal strength for a cell phone or any other electronic device. And those were the obvious places: hilltops, towers, any clearing or gap in the forest that provided a visible distance, enough of an opening to *grab* signal strength from the nearest microwave tower, which happened to be about seven miles away. Even satellite technology was spotty. Iridium telephones functioned only in the rare opening of canopy.

A few cameras had been toppled in one of those many extended storms that come in during the spring from the Atlantic. A combination of factors made it difficult to keep the system intact, but the most problematic was the fact of Edward's death. He simply had not lived long enough to finish the necessary repairs or modernization.

James hadn't a clue in that department. He was a zoologist of the old school, specializing in nearly every animal and insect. He also knew one or two things about the forest. Like his late ornithologist brother, Edward, James never published. Nor had their parents nor their parents nor their parents. Indeed, Martin's quarterly real estate update *Olivier's* sent to his several hundred clients was the first time in generations that an Olivier had dared to put anything in print. Edward had not approved. In fact, he had been horrified. Martin had not taken the hint, despite more than a decade of clues.

Martin, who now reached the first gate after driving two hours—James had sent him and his driver the long way—clumsily spoke into the intercom.

"It's me."

James opened the gate electronically from inside the house. That function still worked. James appeared just inside as the gate, ten feet high with impenetrable walls of rusted iron and ancient bolts, swung open. He was clad in blue denims, gumboots, and a cotton pullover.

James looked closely at the driver, then at his nephew and after some pause said, "That's alright. Drive in, put the vehicle right over there." He pointed to a muddy area.

Martin got out of the car, and then Max parked the vehicle as instructed. Martin extended his hand to James.

James embraced him. "Let me look at you. My, but you have aged a little bit!" He had not seen his nephew in twenty-five years.

Martin smiled and returned the compliment.

James continued to stare affectionately at his nephew. *He looks just like his father!* he thought.

Then he took Martin's hand and placed a small silver medal in his palm. "Your father wanted you to have this."

Martin looked down at the plain silver oval with its slender silver chain and read aloud four letters engraved therein: "*CSPB.* What does it mean?"

"It's the Medal of Saint Benedict, Martin. Edward carried it for good luck. Let's just say Saint Benedict exerted a distinct influence on your father. We found it in the forest. He'd lost it on the fatal day."

"Saint Benedict? But my father wasn't remotely religious. I don't understand."

"Of course you don't," James said, leading him and Max into the house.

CHAPTER 17

Ten minutes south of Dijon's main train station, in a low-end industrial yard, three men arrived in separate vehicles and assembled in a nondescript condemned warehouse whose back entrance was lost in a maze of fenced-off dead ends and scattered remains. Once, a metal fabrication business had succeeded for a few years in this corner of the city, followed by a cemetery for junked automobiles, which were slowly sold off as scrap.

The long-dead body of a twelve-year-old North African male hooker had been found naked and partly eaten by catfish in a side canal a mile away. A pipe bomb had destroyed a gas station in the middle of the night. Trends argued for the area's abandonment. Despite new environmental regulations (a mayor of Dijon had become the first environmental minister of France), the area had decayed into a hopeless state of weeds, broken tarmac, abandoned abattoirs, barbed wire, and long-empty factory-unit remnants, as revelations of chemical waste proved too problematic even for developers of unwanted land to take an interest.

Gouge de Bar arrived by motorcycle wearing a rucksack in which he carried a small plastic folder containing a set of photographs and a poor reproduction of a page from the public library that was itself a reproduction of a manuscript from the abbey at Citeaux. It contained a map.

He arrived at the same time as one of his accomplices.

"Berndt," de Bar acknowledged. Berndt had driven a dusty Volvo station wagon of no particular distinction. The license plate was Swiss.

A third vehicle, an old regional postal delivery truck, was already alongside the building.

Berndt led the way inside.

A large man named Raoul Fougeret was seated at a knotty pine table examining a firearm. Behind him were several large steel cases. The interior was otherwise boarded up, abandoned, and filled with dust-covered metal, rubber, and ceramic debris that no one in fifty years had bothered to claim.

Raoul sized up de Bar through the weapon's cross hairs. A small laser pixel caught him on the cheek.

De Bar stood looking at him dead on, with an unfazed, crazy grin. They were close friends.

"Put it down," Berndt said angrily.

Raoul lowered the weapon nonchalantly. "You're late."

"And you are one royal idiot," Berndt said.

"I silenced the witness."

"You've compromised the whole operation."

"That's bullshit."

"The target escaped. The rest was personal. Now they know. Everybody knows. "

"I've got six former mates lined up. They're all placed and ready to go in."

"How much do they know?" Berndt asked.

"Wild animals. That's all they need to know. They've done this sort of work for years, and across much harsher terrain. Africa. Middle East. Columbia. I know them."

Raoul was seething. Berndt, who circled him, walking slowly, could not possibly understand. Yes, it was personal. But it also went back centuries.

Berndt knew he needed these two crude assassins, de Bar and Raoul, the latter actually believing himself to be descended from Burgundian knights who had once defended a monarch before falling out of favor.

In actual fact, Raoul was the direct link to Abdul's family, by intermarriage many generations before, and to the steady flow of euros. He and de Bar had worked together in the Persian Gulf, smuggling dugongs; in England, stealing rare breeds of sheep; in Brazil, it was a Spix's macaw as well as a rare albino bushmaster—one of the two deadliest snakes in the western Amazon—bound for a collector in the Canary Islands.

After Jimmy's death, six months before, de Bar and Raoul had not managed to cover their tracks with anywhere near the meticulous care they should have, and they knew it. They had dumped Jimmy's body, gored by what at first had appeared to be a Cape buffalo that charged from out of the rain in dense forest at forty miles per hour, into the back of Jimmy's Saab. De Bar had not seen the animal coming. Neither he nor Jimmy was ready. They should have been, after eleven years wrangling on big-game hunting ranches across Angola, Mozambique, and South Africa. But a Cape buffalo with horns that seemed to spread eight or nine feet had not been on their minds that night. And in retrospect, de Bar was pretty certain that it was no known bison.

After that night, de Bar did some Internet hunting in libraries in Paris and London. He was pretty certain what it was, after reading various descriptions and seeing an image of an actual re-creation.

"Latifrons," he insisted. "*Bison latifrons*, thought to have gone extinct ten, fifteen thousand years ago."

A suggestion of such magnitude did not surprise Raoul. First of all, he knew that a similar creature, the wisent, had managed to survive in several Eastern European zoos and breeding preserves. More than 3,500 now inhabited Bialowieza National Park, as well as areas in Belarus, Lithuania, Slovakia, and Russia. Moreover, this particular estate was chockfull of its own remarkable microcosms, about which he was entirely circumspect, even with his own co-conspirators.

Raoul had his reasons—dynastic delusions—and had not hesitated to kill others that stood in the way. He had no need to divulge this information to his on-again, off-again partner, Berndt, whose temper was unpredictable, but more important, who was never to be privy to the essentials of a relationship dating to the time of Saladin and the near conquest of Vienna by the Ottomans. Raoul had a mighty motive, albeit a perverse and twisted one. It was his legacy he was fighting for, he believed, and the fabulously wealthy Abdul, the young Porsche prince, as he was thought of by peers, had checked him out (in terms of an Arab connection) and liked the sound of it.

"Find the beast and you shall have your kingdom," Abdul had told Raoul.

Abdul's own private zoo was only part of his motivation. Notwithstanding his nation's high marks for compliance with international wildlife protection, particularly its efforts to reintrutduce ungulates and the Arabian leopard to their native habitat, Abdul's particular circumstances of wealth and privilege had long seduced him into an underworld of high risk intrigues. He bred endangered species, then sold them off to cousins across the Persian Gulf. And he consumed experimental fluids and powders of rare, threatened, or otherwise extinct animals and plants the way others took B12.

Raoul had already gone by himself to the southwestern corner of the estate. It was he who had disabled the video surveillance. Raoul knew things about the history of the property and where the true value lay that neither of his colleagues would ever know, if he had anything to do with it—information passed down from his own father and grandfather, who shared the same burden of disenfranchisement from the ultimate glory. They had not managed to do a damn thing about it. Times were such in the past that it was simply impossible to counter the forces arrayed in defense of the estate.

But World War II had changed certain characteristics of the social environment in Burgundy, giving Raoul new munitions and ploys. He also noted the essential decay of the ancient manse itself. He had detected no more than three persons inhabiting the chateau. And now one of them was presumed to be dead. Another was quite elderly. The third person was an unknown, but he was only one. One man, and an awesome treasure, locked somewhere in that house. Raoul had quietly, obsessively calculated the chances of finding it; strategizing with a steady focus. A treasure that even Abdul knew nothing about.

The sequence of events, as Raoul had long planned them, had gone without too many hitches. After letting some time pass, a caution demanded by Abdul, whom Raoul also knew it prudent to oblige, things had gone much, much better, at least until the very last.

They had easily found the breach in the wall, which had been fixed only amateurishly by *someone*. He penetrated several hundred meters into the rainy interior and tracked down their prey with the aid of infrared scopes, heat-seeking binoculars, and a lure culled from medieval bestiaries and greatly enhanced by application of more modern perfumes and food additives, a narcotic that gave off a penetrating aroma, particles of fructose that could be detected at a level of one-per-billion molecules by any mammal. Big cats could detect the perfume Obsession from a quarter of a mile away. A certain cosmetic, sold on many roadsides in Gabon and the Democratic Republic of the Congo, attracted elephants and whole troops of baboons from a much farther distance.

Though almost overwhelmed by unexpected eyes, hovering forms, entire flocks and herds, and solitary monsters, they still managed to seize the one creature, not thirty meters in from the breach in the wall, tie it up, and get out.

The animal could not move. It was transfixed by the drug, and its powerful limbs were tied in a manner rendering any kicking impossible. More important, the animal did not expect what was coming. Call it innocence. It had no fear, exhibited no proclivity for flight whatsoever. But the effects of the drug were unknown on such a beast, whose metabolism had never been the subject of inquiry, indeed, whose very existence had never truly been accepted, other than in mythic panoramas involving virgins and religious allegory.

Abdul, however, did not doubt its existence. He had grown up in a forty-thousand-square-foot family compound of atrocious taste, row upon row of caged living trophies in the inner courtyard. The hybridization of rare creatures within the middle of Dubai had been the stock in trade of his father's considerable fortune. That included the *Oryx leucoryx*, whose last known progenitor had been captured with the aid of a helicopter and a net, and a dozen certified thugs in Land Rovers racing across the dunes of the Rub' al Khali, the no-man's land of Saudi Arabia, back in the late 1960s. The oryx had been bred with other desert ruminants, and Abdul's family now had the only secret breeding station in all of the Persian Gulf for this supposedly extinct antelope.

They had gotten the one—a brilliant stroke of intuition, planning and luck. But *one* was only half the story, a useless anachronism without its mate. Whom to blame for the loss of the female? That was the question plaguing Berndt, who suspected some surreptitious agenda on the part of Raoul. Berndt had not been there that night, but the rendition of events, as described by both Raoul and de Bar, suggested that something was amiss, or did not add up. Raoul attributed it to the presence of an unexpected, expert hunter who prowled the estate with bow and arrow and seemed, however incredibly, to be on a first-name basis, as it were, with beasts. Some gamekeeper who mingled silently with the hyenas and bison, could direct their stampedes, and move with impunity among large predators.

That was Raoul's explanation.

"They've got an African tracker in there, I'd stake my life on it," de Bar argued.

They had gotten the male trophy away and into the truck. They had gone back in to catch the mate, when Jimmy was killed. With stampedes all around them and a skilled hunter seeking his own revenge, they had no more taste for continuing their raid. They had hurt, probably killed one of the defenders. They also knew this estate was ripe for the picking. They would return soon enough. But for the time being, it was all they could do to get Jimmy into the trunk and sequester the vehicle a few hundred meters off the road by turning on the ignition and forcing the gas pedal down with a wedged limb of a broken oak tree. They watched as the Saab sank partway and then was jolted by the swollen, sluggish forces at work in the braided river. There was a dark purgatory of currents, a kind of moving quicksand that dragged the vehicle off toward an unknown destination amid a labyrinth of marshlands and canals.

Now, Gouge de Bar seriously wished he had not panicked, running the scenario over in his mind again and again. Although buffalo, particularly swamp buffalo, were among the most dangerous of all animals, certainly as frightening as mambas, he knew how to stop them. A machine gun.

"We now have the map, surveillance photos, GPS points, and nets with enough tensile strength to hold anything. And we know she's in there."

A coughing spasm gripped the forty-something athlete. De Bar swallowed a dollop of sputum while putting his rucksack on the table and removing the plastic envelopes.

"You sick?" Raoul asked.

"No," de Bar said.

His eyes and head burned, but he preferred to ignore it.

Berndt, who had been a Dutch Special Forces agent in the Persian Gulf, where he first had met de Bar and Raoul, realized that their team of mercenaries had little time left to go back, track down another male and female, and capture as many other rarities as they could. Each one translated into major dollars. He knew the place was teeming with animals—not your everyday variety. And Abdul and his friends were willing to pay whatever it cost.

This time, however, there would be more precautions at the port. Berndt's suspicions were working in an amphetamized high gear. He could point to a dozen areas where the team had gotten sloppy. Either that, or somebody on the inside had cut a better deal with a few of the dockworkers. Raoul alleged that the culprit was a gardener by day. Berndt had his doubts.

Raoul, who had been so confident about the whole thing, placed a ticking clock on the entire operation with the murder of the gardener. The police could put the pieces together at any moment and trace the murder to him.

Because of the weather, they could not even determine how large this private zoo was or what was really in there. Only that the ancient Roman wall stretched over four successive valleys, some fifteen to twenty miles in one direction and another three or four at an angle. The interior, Raul caculated, must be something like fifty square miles of dense forest, one of the largest remaining freeholds in the Morvan country, with a chateau secreted away in the southwestern corner. Raoul was certain there were no more than three and possibly only two occupants and no visitor that their surveillance of six months had revealed. Whoever lived there had not involved the police. There was an obvious reason why, which Raoul understood.

"Killing the gardener was a mistake," Berndt restated for the record.

Raoul glared at him and then shrugged and turned away. *I had to do it*, Raoul Fougeret thought. He remembered with satisfaction walking silently up to the man whose back was turned. Raoul grabbed hold of him with the bulk of his 220 pounds, then—certain that Hythlodae saw who it was that exacted justice, his own justice—plunged the horn which had belonged to his own family for centuries straight through him, pushing it harder and harder until it had gone all the way through the throat. Amazingly, the action had not proved sufficient to actually cause death. An additional bullet had been necessary.

None of them have the spine for this sort of business, Raoul had thought, as he moved away from the museum, skirting security with easy expertise and driving away.

There were few others to worry about. The Hythlodae and Olivier families and their scarce allies were scattered in a diaspora of disinterest across Europe, holding down respectable jobs, prominent positions, with no talk of their ancient Order. They drove automobiles, carried briefcases to work, managed banks, and worked in hospitals. Their service to the Order was symbolic. They were unarmed, untrained, and unfamiliar with the territory—except for the one archer, most likely a man for hire. The most senior members of the Order who still remembered the secrets conveyed by their great-grandparents, who had remembered from *their* great-grandparents, knew only of a rural Old World, a time of nostalgia, a Golden Age. This much Raoul could gauge by the broken-down condition of the chateau and the lack of comings and goings through its main gate. These fragmented offspring had time on their hands and the accumulated wealth to afford the delusion that they could make a difference in a world that had changed significantly. Most of those left were old men who could not bench press fifty pounds if their lives depended on it.

The gardener, also an old man, had been of a different caliber. His murder would send a message that Raoul hoped might render their upcoming foray uncontested. Raoul was aware of the fact that one of the chateau's inhabitants was English. He had put that much together after months and months of watching, waiting, and taking his morning newspaper from a nearby town frequented for basic services by one James Olivier.

Raoul had tried to find out anything at all about this man. But he was not discoverable. His life was a huge blank. No secret bank accounts. Googling his name yielded no assistance, only an avalanche of others with the same name—professors, actors, authors. Not the man in question. And locals could offer nothing of any substance. He was older than seventy years, a farmer of sorts. Knew his birds. Never shaved. Drove an old car. Bought few groceries. And that was the extent of it.

When Raoul first took out the surveillance cameras, he saw the two elderly men, one of them attempting to fix them, the other holding a ladder. He knew his combatants, or he thought he did.

"We'll meet in Paris. There is a safe house. Checked for bugs. Noisy. Crowded. We'll all assemble. Day after tomorrow at midnight. The plans need to be confirmed. By Thursday, we go in," Raoul declared.

Both Berndt and de Bar were anxious to get it over with. Neither of them had counted on human corpses.

And neither of them knew what Raoul Fougeret was actually planning.

CHAPTER 18

"First, let me help you with your things. Your bedroom is up the stairs, then down the hall to the far right. I trust it will prove comfortable. Bathroom en suite," James said, leading his nephew up the winding marble stairwell to the premier étage, where room upon room spanned what, to Martin's rather expert observations, must have surpassed twenty thousand square feet of dilapidated grandeur. He had sold similar estates in the U. K., from Kent and Sussex to Norwich and the Lake District, but none this old.

"Just how old is this place?" Martin asked, ascending the stairs.

"The foundations date back to before the Roman armies, well before. Later, in the early 10th century it was an important monastery. As for the property itself, land is land. Rather eternal, I would say."

Martin threw his things down on the enormous Louis XIV bed. A single tall, narrow armoire from the Revolution (it was said people used to hide in them) stood slightly at an angle along the wall. The armoire was seriously in need of repair, though still bearing the original hardware. Martin knew it at a glance.

He then slipped into the bathroom to relieve himself after nearly three hours—a bathroom that had not been equipped with anything more modern than those fittings and exposed plumbing particulars from the late 1920s, although the tile work and bathtub were spotless and in perfect condition.

As he repaired back to the corridor, he noticed that the walls were rather bare. Lush silk curtains covered the windows but only a few photographs and the odd book.

Downstairs, the same. Martin could not help but wonder at the frugal trappings in room after room. The exterior had promised an absolutely astonishing fortress—a castle as grand or grander than anything he had ever laid eyes upon.

Once they were seated comfortably in the library, James offered Martin a cup of tea, which Martin declined. He could tell that James was somehow studying him, procrastinating.

"Not exactly a farm, is it?" Martin began, breaking the ice.

"Ah, yes. We do call it that, from time to time. It is not a farm in the true sense, obviously. And there is no point drawing attention to oneself by calling it a chateau. Especially in this part of the country."

"What's going on, uncle? Why all these antics? What happened to my father?"

"Yes, of course." He *was* studying his nephew. He saw many of the same gestures that Edward had used, the same voice, solid chin, sculptured features, a rough quality, though, with an unshaved face and a sense of restlessness. But how restless? *Can he be trusted?*

"History," he began, "has dealt a fatal blow to most biological corridors in France that might allow for unmolested mammalian migrations," James began, eyeing his nephew for slack eyes or a bewildered expression.

Martin didn't blink, though he had no clue what his uncle had just said.

James continued, "The Morvan, despite its own turbulent history, in which your family played a significant part, managed to vouchsafe this one microcosm, and thank God for that."

"James, I studied law, interned at Sotheby's. I'm not a biologist. You're losing me."

"Right." James withdrew a pipe from a small box on the table, added a mixture of Lebanese sweet-smelling tobacco from a pouch in his pocket, and lit it.

"Do you smoke?"

"Not anymore."

James watched as philosophical smoke rings rose toward the gold moldings on the plastered ceiling, done by some eastern European craftsman centuries before in the manner of a flower's inflorescence.

Then James began. "Lad, what I'm about to tell you may seem all but impossible. And now, the impossible is in serious trouble."

"Go on."

∿

Max Hardiman was sitting in a spare salon three rooms away down an enormous mirrored corridor, with a glass of Scotch in his hand, admiring the walls of the strangest mansion he'd ever seen, and he'd seen more than a few driving Martin around to hundreds of estates throughout the United Kingdom. This one was different.

He looked out the large floor-to-ceiling windows and noticed something moving, coming out of the forest, on the inside of a kind of green moat between the chateau and a wall that stretched in all directions, over hills, disappearing into the wood.

What the hell? Max stood up, holding fast to his Scotch, and walked very quietly towards the windows that formed a twelve-foot, maybe fourteen-foot-high double door. It was some kind of animal, a big one. He stared at the beast with a sense of fright mixed with enthrallment.

"Oh, shit!" He cried out, moving backward. The animal had seen him and was now moving fast towards the chateau.

An elephant!

The closer the leviathan's eagerness brought him, the larger it appeared to Max, who tried to vanish in the back of the room. He dropped his glass of Scotch on the floor with a shattering haste as he made for the exit, stepping into the corridor.

"Don't move," James warned, having seen the approaching creature from a window in the library. He had proceeded at once, with his utterly bewildered nephew in tow, to the rescue.

"What is that?" Max stammered.

"Her name is Alice. She's an elephant. Quite tame, as a rule."

"An elephant?" Martin had a few seconds to mull on every National Geographic and Animal Planet image he'd ever seen. "You sure about that?" He was peering at the beast, which now stood a mere ten feet from the fragile crinkled-glass veneer that was the window, the door in its Gothic-looking frame, where Max had stood. The giant seemed overly curious, almost playful, and at ease in its surroundings.

"To be more precise, a woolly mammoth," James volunteered.

A mournful trumpeting, almost a wail from outside, resonated through their bodies . . .

James shook his head sadly. "That is the sound of loneliness, I'm afraid. Her mate died." James looked at them and then smiled. "Come. Let me introduce you."

CHAPTER 19

Hubert Mans and Julia Deblock spent four hours searching every newly integrated Central Image System and Interpol database at the supercomputer processing center in the basement of an unprepossessing 1840s compound in downtown Antwerp.

Spellings, families, locations—any connection whatsoever that might link pieces of known information. A Namibian named Jimmy Serko had made it four times onto the list kept by the WWF in their Washington, D.C., office, TRAFFIC. The same name appeared on the manifest kept by the equivalent of the harbor master in Dubai. On further checking, Mans and Deblock discovered that Jimmy Serko was associated with a dummy corporation in Amsterdam, one of the highest-ranking cities in the world for doing business. Easier, less restrictive than Switzerland, it always had been a center of commerce, both legitimate and not. If Rembrandt were alive today, Interpol agents associated with Mans would say, he'd have been jailed for multiple counts of aiding and abetting the trade in endangered species.

What's more, two other Hythlodaes had died in recent years. A Yardling Hythlodae's body had been recovered from a dumpster in the

Montmartre—two bullet holes. Felix Hythlodae of the Utrecht Hills (the second-highest mountains in Holland, exceeding one hundred feet) had been run over two years and three months before by a truck whose license plate was traced to the Serko Corporation. More digging in Antwerp had revealed certain patterns common to this emerging dummy corporation. Dutch police subsequently confirmed that the corporate credit card expenses by one Jimmy Serko—purchases of rope, stun guns, tranquilizers from Romania, and netting—had been made off the Internet from a hashish café along the Herrengracht Canal. Hardly your typical company, even by Dutch standards.

American Express had also confirmed enough particulars to validate that Serko Corporation was a pass-through for smugglers, and Jimmy Serko seemed without a doubt to be the point person. Every credit card corporate fraud department had his name on its hit list.

"Look at this," Mans said, drawing Julia's attention to a string of disparate, unconnected credit card purchases in Rome, Hamburg, Manchester, Sofia, Windhoek, and Dijon.

"That's a bar tab. And another."

"An ATM machine fourteen minutes after the third drink order. Eight hundred in euros," Mans said. He had a hunch.

"A hooker?"

"If that is a hotel and he placed a phone call to the Trois Ducs, then yes."

Within twenty minutes, an Interpol email provided an image from the bank security archived video from the ATM transaction.

"White. Late forties. A positive ID."

Two hours later, a local associate had interviewed three women. One of them confirmed that he was the asshole Afrikaner, "a short fuse, and a certain tattoo a woman never forgot."

"Even one who'd gone down on eight men that day. A dragon on his pecker which, when erect, spat fire. Jimmy Serko."

A *dragon*? Simon speculated. He had now assembled members of his IW team, including Hubert Mans, in Dijon. Le Bon had lent him Julia Deblock.

But then, Serko had stopped using his credit card. No more cash withdrawals. WWF had lost him. Interpol had drawn a blank.

Then a match surfaced from a routine weekly missing-persons report filed in Johannesburg. A Mrs. Karoo, maiden name Serko, claimed to be the mother of James Serko.

Interpol made the match eleven days after Serko had screwed the hooker on the west end of Dijon. They just hadn't had a reason as yet to circulate the information. It was progress, to be sure, but on a suspicious hit and run and four unsolved smuggling cases that had been downgraded in terms of priority. Until now.

"He made a mistake," Simon said, taking notes, "when he used the hotel valet service. We got him."

The valet remembered the man, remembered the car. A 2003 Saab.

"They have video in the garage," the valet said. "But I don't know how long . . ."

Within minutes, Simon had the new tech administrator for the hotel on the phone. The administrator had planned to erase all the tapes after a year, like many of his peers at the finer hotels. Then he had thought the better of it and put them in a storage unit in the basement. It would take a few hours, that was all, to find the video from the night in question.

When he did get his hands on it, the Saab was identified, its license plate number, beginning with NL, the Netherlands, captured for twenty-eight frames, approximately one second.

CHAPTER 20

James led Martin and Max outside. The mammoth, Alice, watched them approach. Her tusks cast long late-afternoon shadows across the 14th century brickwork of the courtyard.

"Alice," James said softly, "come say 'hello.'"

He extended his hand with the palm turned upward. After a moment, during which both Martin and Max seemed to be holding their breath, Alice raised her trunk, almost waving it in their direction. Slowly, blowing large bursts of air, she moved toward them, each step surprisingly graceful and deliberate. Martin and Max stood completely still. Alice stopped in front of them. Ten thousand pounds, a monster of unfathomable poise. Martin thought of some nature show he had seen with his son once, about gorillas, or maybe it was dingos, and that one should not look them in the eye because that could be construed as a challenge. Alice seemed to waver before him now, huge and shaggy and as uncertain as Martin what to do. He could smell her musty odor and almost feel the heat and moisture of her breath as she moved her trunk near him, around him, but not touching him. He tried not to look her in the eye, tried to bow his head before her massive presence, but he was unable to. He found himself peering up at her, gazing into her deep recessive eyes, almost hidden behind curly long hair. He focused upon her enormous eyes at the very instant she met his gaze. Martin sensed an involuntary meeting of limbs, or mutually agreed contact that transcended common sense. A decorum made in heaven that made his hair stand on end. He felt as if he somehow had even reached out and touched her, although his hands remained at his side, trembling and hot.

Out of the corner of his eye, he saw Max, ever ready to protect him, ready to bend down and grab the knife that Martin knew he kept concealed in its skin-tight pouch beneath his black Brioni sock.

Martin looked at Max and suppressed a laugh. "Max, I think she's harmless."

Max nodded and relaxed a little.

"James," Martin said, "what is this place, a zoo?"

James looked at him. "Let's go inside and I'll explain. Max, if you'll excuse us?"

"Of course," Max said. "I think I'll go up to my room. It's been a long drive and an eventful day."

James and Martin left Max at bottom of the stairs. Max went up to his simply appointed chambers, a twin bed, dresser, and small bathroom with a sink and toilet. Silk draperies hung over heraldic twisting bars on the windows. Max made a thorough search of the room, looking down the three stories of limestone through the grillwork on the windows. He made a routine of such searches. Then he removed his knife and placed it under a dense paperback book on his night reading table, a history of dendrology. Just what he wanted to read.

As he dozed off, his mind lingered on that enormous animal, the pachyderm . . . *And I thought I'd seen everything* . . .

CHAPTER 21

James and Martin were seated alone in the library. James poured them each a glass from the cellar.

"Who or what killed my father, James?"

"Poachers," he said.

That much at least was starting to make sense. A strange elephant, two brothers long involved in the study of nature, whatever that meant. A farm that was really a chateau and probably a subtle ancestral tax dodge, which harbored some of the eccentric siblings' prized live animals, collected over many decades of clandestine forays into the very same exotic parts of the world that had resulted in the death of Martin's mother. So poachers had discovered their secret, and now his father was dead, too.

"And that's why you've waited all this time to say anything, for fear of the police coming here? Worry over somebody eavesdropping on our phone conversations? Concern about my being traced? But surely you have plumbers, electricians, the postal service, taxes, all of the mundane giveaways of such a place?"

James shook his head slowly, paternally, pausing as if to change his mind and end all further discussion. Martin could see that James did not quite know how to begin.

"Let's start with that woolly mammoth, Alice. Aren't they supposed to have gone out with sabertooth tigers and dinosaurs or something like that?" Martin asked.

"*Mammuthus primigenius* probably went extinct as the result of some massive disease agent, a pathogen. By 14,000 years ago, few were left. Europe, North America, other parts of the world saw their brilliant embers die out. Climate change. Human hunters. Forest collapse in some areas. A typical story that's ongoing, as everyone knows these days."

"And you and Edward? Where does his ornithology and your. . . . I don't know how to describe it, uncle, your generalist studies come in? I don't even know what you've been doing all these years, but where do you two fit into an extinct-species dissertation? Does this have something to do with our family history, this property, the death of my mother? And, if this farm were somehow spared the inclement weather or proved the perfect location for keeping alive these otherwise extinct woolly mammoths, then I'm surprised it took this long for poachers to get wind of the place."

"There is a history you do not know about. Your family history, Martin."

James leaned forward. "Here is what happened. It was the middle of the night. Poachers blew up a portion of the old wall. It is over seventeen miles in length, built sometime in the 12th, possibly 13th century, approximately the period of the chateau."

"But the locals . . . "

"They think of it as a run-down ancestral hunting lodge."

"The postman? Plumbers? Tax agents? Bakers? Nosy neighbors? There's always a question of fire, flood, road works, power lines, retirees taking up some cause or other and insistent on enlisting everyone in the neighborhood . . . ."

"There are several people who know, or who know bits and pieces. You might think of them as a family, though they are not, in the sense of any actual bloodline. 'Protectors' is perhaps a better way of understanding their role."

"Role in what?"

"A remarkable occurrence, one that I can't claim total authority over. After all, I have only lived here for a few decades. I was tested, too, you understand, late in life. As was your father."

"Tested?"

"Tested, then bound by an oath of loyalty might be a better way of phrasing it."

"One of those silly secret societies we're always hearing about."

"No society, very few people. Benedictines, men of the cloth. Men, and a few women, who also knew how to wield a sword when required. This is not a fiction, Martin. Your father was not murdered for a silly reason."

"Then what? He simply got in the way of poachers? Or was dumb enough to try to fight them off? And no sword to save himself?"

James paused, trying to think of the best way to explain something so secret, ancient, and seemingly implausible, at least to one from the outside.

"The mammoth is one of several thousand individuals. We don't even really know how many or how diverse. Neither Edward nor I ever ventured into the heart of it. We were sworn against doing so. It's a large property, though nowhere near large enough. Your father did what he thought best. But frankly his death, and other circumstances surrounding it, are why I found it necessary to bother you."

"Bother me? I loved my father. I miss him. I never understood him. Or what exactly happened to my mother."

"She made a wrong move years ago in southwestern Bolivia. It took her a few hours to die, or that's what Edward told me. She and your father were searching for some rare birds to determine how threatened they were at a certain clay lick where the macaws obtained critical nutrients or sodium. The debate still rages. She was buried there. That's what she preferred."

"A snake?"

"No. Ants. Twenty-four-hour ants, they're called. *Paraponera clavata*. Biggest ants in the world, I imagine. Horrible venom. You don't want to know more."

"Why wasn't that ever explained? What would have been so difficult?"

"Your father was not eager to draw attention to the family. And he did not want Bolivian authorities questioning him about his research. It might have gotten back to France and from France to Dijon, and then a visit by authorities to the farm. Once that happened, well, you'll understand what's at stake here soon enough."

"He could have told me."

"Yes. He probably should have. But he had his reasons."

James stood up and walked over to the wire mesh doors of fitted oak, pushed the cabinetry, which activated a turnstile, revolving the wall of the library 180 degrees. The rear of it, which had swung slowly into position, contained what appeared to be a rather extensive scientific set of works, most of them with dust jackets, a few bearing the telltale sign of bygone years, white goat or calfskin bindings with handwritten lettering.

From this assortment of several hundred works, James withdrew a Mylar envelope, approximately the size of a standard sheet of paper. An envelope within an envelope. And inside that, a sheet of paper which he held over the one light on the reading table.

"This is a leaf that had been destined for a book known as the Sherborne Missal that now resides in some institutional library or other. The manuscript was illustrated in about 1400. It contains something like 170 bird and insect species. Many are recognizable, but some are deemed by art historians to be imaginary." James pointed at one of the tiny colored figures on the page. "This bird. What does it remind you of?"

"You're asking the wrong person, uncle. I can probably identify only a half-dozen birds. A crow, a hawk, a peacock, a chicken, a sparrow. That's about it. Oh, maybe, if I'm close enough, a chickadee. And, as of today, a falcon. Beautiful bird, that one. I think it liked me."

"Yes, I think she did. Well, this is a Laysan rail. I wouldn't expect you to know it, nor most people for that matter. It went extinct on the remote Midway Atoll in the Pacific, well west of Hawaii, sometime after 1943."

"So it obviously used to be quite common?"

"We don't know. Was it migratory? Not this one. In fact, this bird in modern times had lost the use of its feathers for flight. Other rails, yes. Good fliers. And many birds have been blown by storms to continents they never knew, while others, after their juvenile stage, move out routinely to far-flung places. Climate change has always influenced migrations. But European birds never had much of an affinity with the tropics, as far as we know."

"So what's it doing in an European manuscript illumination from 1400? Midway was not exactly in the path of the first European explorers. And certainly no Vikings ever made it to the Pacific, unless Thor Heyerdahl's thesis is to be entirely rewritten."

"Correct. And here's an even more interesting question. How is it the bird happens to be doing just fine out there, beyond the wall? I know because I've seen it."

"I presume you raised the riddle in order to provide an answer?"

"Yes. The bird was here before it lost its ability to fly."

"Just like that?" Martin replied, not sure what to make of the implications.

"Yes. We're speaking of an extensive timeframe. One that is actually evolutionary."

"James, I sell real estate."

"Yes you do. Which is why you're here."

"I beg your pardon?"

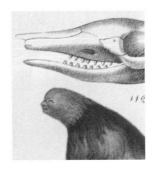

CHAPTER 22

James had provided Martin with a pair of binoculars to peer through the mist out over the wall. The rain, which had been constant for hours, had momentarily let up as darkness fell upon the chateau and its surrounding wilderness.

"Look there, see it?"

"What am I looking for?" Martin puzzled, tired from his day and this overload of bird information, back-country guessing, and the still unresolved details surrounding his father's murder. Moreover, there was an agenda at work in the heavy atmosphere of the postmortem. James had a mission that now appeared more complicated than simply dealing with a death in the family.

"Catlike," James said with a steady gaze. "Or a bit of a dog, but with stripes, there, see it!" Martin marveled at his uncle's unassisted vision.

"Yes, on top of the wall. How wide is that?"

"Three feet."

Suddenly the animal was gone, having leapt back into the forest on the uphill side, the side away from the chateau and leading into what by Burgundian standards might be thought of as mountainous terrain, hills surrounding intersecting valleys, all of which were contained within the estate.

"What was it?" Martin asked, "A dog or a cat?"

"Thylacinus cynocephalus."

"In English, James."

"Thylacine."

"Sounds like a drug."

"It is a marsupial, like a kangaroo. More like a wolf, actually."

"I've never heard of it," Martin said, undaunted by his total lack of familiarity, or even particular interest in wolves, or kangaroos.

"It went extinct, supposedly, in 1936, in an Australian zoo," James stated.

"That recently? Then how did you get it?"

"You're not following."

"Of course I am. You've got all these otherwise extinct creatures meandering around your house. I don't understand it. Either they're extinct or they're not. And if not, then surely the scientific community knows about that. You are in touch with them? Or is this some sinister experiment, a perverse *cabinet*, as they say?"

"No, lad. Nothing of the sort. If anything, the experiment is happening outside, beyond the wall, between here and Paris, London, New York, the world. Listen, I believe we owe your driver dinner, at the very least. And then you and I need to talk some more."

"That sounds like a plan, James. And by the way, just so you don't think me unmoved by the sight of these peculiar little pets running around your farm, you should know that Margaret and I recently acquired a donkey."

"A donkey?"

"Yes, for our son Anthony, really. Not your usual teenager's pastime, but we have the space where we live, and well, I'm sure you know they're in terrible straits as a rule, and this one came up at a charity we're involved with so, well, there you have it."

"What kind of donkey?"

"How should I know. Wait a minute, I *do* know. I believe it is French."

"A Poitou? Very shaggy?"

"That's the one! Nothing like a wolf, mind you. Or whatever you called it. By the way, are there still wolves in France? I'm sure there are none in England. Plenty of foxes, of course. Ten thousand on the streets of London alone. I'm quite heartened, really, by the anti-fox-hunting measures. I never did understand that one barbaric throwback among the rural rich."

James was at a crossroad with this nephew of his. How, he wondered, did someone with so meager a knowledge of natural history make half a billion pounds selling country estates? Not that it much mattered. What mattered was to move quickly. He had to trust his nephew, and there was no more time to dawdle. It was after six P.M.

Three days before, James had learned that the mayor was going to approve in principle a major development plan that could see industries and twenty thousand newcomers to the region. More specifically, a high-tech city had been touted for years as a looming possibility, offering Parisian-based multinationals a cheaper place to house their headquarters. With local tax incentives and a much better quality of life for its employees, all that was needed was the first big corporate logo to attract others behind it, and that deal seemed all but assured. James needed money fast. And someone to negotiate the offer. Someone who could guarantee anonymity.

"The outbreak of this animal disease might gain us a month or so," James had relayed to Edouard Revere earlier in the day. Edouard didn't talk. He listened. James had detected a strange clicking or staticlike hollow. He hung up. He knew someone was listening. But did Revere hear it also? James knew Revere wanted to say something but could not. But why didn't he call back later? James' phone always alerted him to a message, even if the connection was bad.

"But what kind of money?" Martin asked, as James explained over a quiet meal of croustades of red pepper, a delicate, warm soft cheese dumped in pumpkin soup with grated nutmeg and cayenne, no chicken stock, and a marquise aperitif, all taken with Max in the modest little kitchen.

Suddenly, Max leapt up, grabbing for his knife.

"He is well trained," James said with no little hint of appreciation, as he introduced a thirty-something man who had just stepped into the kitchen silently from an adjoining hallway. "Meet Lance Sèvre. He has been here for several years. Invaluable."

"Bonsoir."

Max detected immediately that Lance carried a gun in his belt, concealed by a floppy white T-shirt.

"The soup and croustades are excellent. Lance does the cooking," James said.

Lance helped himself and pulled up a chair.

"You liked the falcon?" he said with a conspiratorial naughtiness.

"No bites. That's something," Martin offered.

"Yes," Lance confirmed, nodding at James as if to say Martin must be cut from the same cloth as his late father.

Lance turned towards Martin, his eyes fixed, and spoke softly. "I am very sorry about the loss of your father. He was a great man."

"Thank you," Martin replied awkwardly.

"Martin and I have much to catch up on," James said, after sipping the last of his dessert wine. "I think my nephew and I will retire to the library and then to bed. I know it has been a long day. By the way, Max is staying in the king's annex," James said to Lance.

"Good room. Louis XIV slept in that bed when Burgundy was not French, of course," Lance said matter-of-factly, as if he had been there.

Max finished his drink. "You're joking?"

"No. But don't worry. The king was still young, prior to becoming slightly not able to hold his piss. Anyway, the sheets were cleaned since then."

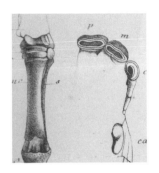

CHAPTER 23

I t was approximately 10:30 P.M. when Hubert Mans called Simon from the Interpol database-processing center to tell him the news. Simon and Chief Le Bon were sitting down for the first time all day to have a bite at a local Antwerp pub. "Police have found Jimmy Serko's car. A Saab. In a canal in Burgundy."

"Burgundy?"

"A farmer, trying to hide his geese from authorities, happened upon it. Because of that animal disease, they're making a sweep of farms throughout the region, as you know. Nasty business. The car had floated down a canal. No way to judge when, how far, or from where, although the currents and depth suggest not so far. I'm with Mademoiselle Deblock. She mentioned Burgundy to her uncle, and he seems to think it all fits."

"Fits? What do you mean?" Simon queried.

There was a pause, and then Julia's voice was on the line. "My uncle says the Benedictines are based in Burgundy."

"They were. Of course they were. Dozens of Cistercian monasteries, all over France, my dear. It is my country, as you know."

"But Burgundy remains the center. My uncle said . . . "

"Please hold on. I've got someone calling." Simon pressed his hash key and read the ID of an incoming call—Krezlach. He took the call. "Madame. I've got Julia Deblock on hold. What's up?"

"Before flying out of Antwerp earlier today on this chronic-wasting-disease business, we got a quick mass spectrometer reading on the murder weapon. It's all about carbon and nitrogen, heavy isotopes, and a diet of grass or herb. Anyway, we got some preliminary chemical analysis which is strikingly different than we'd have expected."

"And?"

"And I then called a colleague in Vienna on a hunch. It turns out our prelims match those of a certain artifact at the Schatzkammer, or Treasury, at Vienna's Hofburg Palace."

"OK? So?"

"An artifact they call the Einhorn, which means the horn of a unicorn."

"You're saying the Austrians have proof there once lived a unicorn?"

"I'm saying they have a museum with a piece of a horn that was owned by the emperor. It's covered in gold and belonged to some secret sect. A chemist analyzed it years ago, couldn't make up his mind whether it was from a narwhal or some new species. The data was logged and eventually added to an electronic file. My IW contact ran the spectrometer readings I gave him, and there appears to be a match."

"Do I take that to mean that you believe there is a unicorn out there at this moment, albeit one that is probably dead somewhere?"

"Yes. And if they could make one, they've probably made others."

"Made? What are you talking about?"

"It's called back-breeding, the reconstruction of a living extinct animal."

"How?" Simon was startled.

"You interbreed enough individuals with characteristics approximating those of the dead relative. For example, breeding together the plains zebra with the lightest stripes on the rump over generations will result in an animal closer to the quagga. And breeding the domesticated cattle with those wild, heavier ones across Slovenia will result in an animal with course hair and an extra three hundred pounds, not unlike the wild auroch, the original bulls of Europe and the Mediterranean, the ones painted at the Lascaux caves thirty thousand years ago."

"You're saying they also exist?"

"Genetic versions, yes. It takes a constellation of related descendents, enough money, land, and scientists on the payroll, or with motives of their own, to experiment until they get the right genetic conglomeration. A few zoos have gotten into this business and certainly quite a few private reserves. But usually it's about parrots, not large mammals."

"What zoos in Europe?" Simon asked. "In Vienna?"

"No. Only the Berlin and Munich zoos, but many, many years ago. It was a bit like eugenics and fell out of favor, understandably, with the fall of Hitler."

"But someone's doing it? With an eager buyer in the Persian Gulf?"

"It would appear so. The technology is not that different from the cloning of cows or sheep for special traits. We're not talking *Jurassic Park* here, but hybridizing with real animals."

"So are we looking for a secret breeding program, a laboratory, or what? There are only so many places one could hide a unicorn, right?"

"In a test tube. Among a herd of deer. On ten acres of thick forest off the side of a freeway. Hell, in the backroom of an industrial plant."

"Gosha, they found one of the poachers' cars."

"Where?"

"The Nivernais plateau."

"But that's exactly the region where the quarantines are."

"I know. I may need you tomorrow. Oh, and thanks!"

Simon pressed the hash key. "Julia, you still there?"

"Yes."

"Where were we?"

"Burgundy," she said impatiently.

CHAPTER 24

James and Martin Olivier sat once again in the modest library of the chateau, while Lance finished his dinner, drinking rounds with Max, his new buddy. They apparently shared an interest in weapons.

James had told Martin a little more about his father, Edward, and why he was such a great ornithologist.

"He discovered, easily, a dozen new species but never said a word about it to the scientific community."

"But why not?" Martin wondered aloud. "If his commitment was to saving these creatures?"

"That loyalty test I mentioned earlier."

"Loyalty to whom and for what cause?"

James took a deep breath. "Martin, our family goes back to the time of Saint Benedict."

"That's the second time you've mentioned Benedict."

"There are fewer than thirty living members of the Order of the Golden Fleece."

"The what?"

"I don't claim to know everything about the Order," James said. "Through a lot of wars, assassinations, broken promises, amid all of the transparent alliances and treaties and fleeting personalities, one thing remained true. The protection of this estate was the result of the express order by the duke who ruled Burgundy, whose daughter lived here, within these very walls. An Order that was both a decree and the perpetuation of a society that was secret in terms of its goals and the company it kept. The knights were its public profile, the handsome chivalrous do-gooders in their gorgeous getups. A PR spin. In fact, what was at stake could not be more serious. Such that kings and popes and emperors held to the secret."

"These forests? Secret? What is hidden behind that wall, James? Gold, King Kong? Or simply the fact the trees were not cut down?" Martin asked.

"That is correct. And that is something, even for an area boasting of the Morvan, the largest piece of remaining forest in France. But in quotation marks, for in France, every tract of forest over twenty-five hectares is heavily managed for utilization. Lumber, sweet beets, asparagus, wine. I think this harassment is instinctive to French culture."

"OK, so the family has this nice patch of forest."

"The point is, if you've got approximately sixty acres, you need to produce a plan for local officials to approve, a plan that maintains ample space between linear rows of planted pine or poplar, oak or maple, bearing the fruits of human intervention. And every season has its mob. Some are after rabbit, others wild boar, still others mushrooms. For reasons I am about to explain, this estate, or patch if you prefer, of nearly eighty-five thousand acres was spared such continuous manhandling."

"Eighty-five thousand acres?" Martin sat back, his brain fried momentarily by the sheer power of the value in euros.

But at the same time, he started to worry. A murdered father in France? What would the authorities think of that when it came time to settle the estate matters, which should have started at the moment of death? Panicked, he began to tally. *Taxes. Police inquiries. Fraud? My inheritance? Allegations of conspiracy?* Trapped in the French court system forever.

He removed a handkerchief from his lapel pocket and swept his brow.

"You alright?" James asked, putting down his pipe, pouring another round of sherry for both of them, taking the bottle from atop an ornate table badly in need of delicate and costly repairs. The whole interior suffered from the same neglect, Martin had noticed. Again, an obvious lack of both money and attention.

"Eighty-five thousand acres, James. That's enormous. Did my father ever take time away from bird watching to write a will?"

"Yes," James said. "The estate is divided equally between you and me. But I'm an old man, Martin. It's basically all yours, and that's the reality."

"Jesus," Martin exclaimed. "Eighty-five thousand acres. I can't believe it. Three hours from Paris. And a chateau to boot. Owned since the beginning of time. Right. So what are your intentions? I have to ask. I am a lawyer, after all. There's going to be a horrendous amount of hell to pay in the tax courts. This is not just a capital gains tax. This is a tsunami."

"We have a religious exemption."

"No way."

"But it is much better, even, than that."

"It doesn't get any better."

"Oh, not so. You see, no one is allowed here. The National Park authorities have never once rung our buzzer, despite our being inconveniently in the heart of their domain. They wouldn't dare."

"But why not?"

"Because of an edict signed many centuries ago and honored by one king, emperor, pope, and president after another. By the 20th century, the agencies in France, both local and national, concerned with energy, national parks, taxes, politics, all fell under an umbrella of silence concerning this property that has persisted from the time Saint Benedict's followers built the walls."

"How very convenient," Martin said incredulously.

"You have no idea what's at stake here. And who, in times past, has shared the burden of concern."

"Who are you talking about? Our ancestors?"

"Yes."

"James, my father and I spoke on few occasions after I went away to college. Surely you know that. And I've never had the benefit of one of those stairways with gloomy portraits on the walls going back hundreds of years and eyes following me from the canvases. I knew my grandparents on both sides briefly. Your own father, from Devon, I believe?"

"Actually, a town here, in Burgundy. He moved later on to Devon."

"Obviously not for any British tax benefits."

"That's right."

"Let's see, I also remember your mother, my grandmother. Met her on a few occasions in Wales on holiday. I know they descended from the French, English, and Flemish."

"How is Margaret," James asked, "speaking of the Flemish?"

"The same. Hugely in demand across the art world. We're alright. Our marriage, I mean. We've entirely settled down. Have a routine that seems to work."

"So your father indicated. Quite a success story from the sound of it. I heard she discovered a Rembrandt, or was it a Michelangelo drawing?"

"Both, and, of course, she's really made all the difference for our company."

"Send her my regards."

"I will. Thank you. I need to call her."

Martin pulled out his iPhone. No service.

"Shit. Brand-new phone. You're supposed to be able to reach Easter Island or the South Pole with this."

"The pigeon tower, built in the 12th century. You saw it when you drove up. There is access. Badly lit. But the only spot with cell coverage. The thing is, Martin, please make it as brief and nondescript as possible. Hang up if you hear anything weird."

"Are you serious? The same people who killed Edward?"

"Probably, yes."

"Shouldn't we be whispering?"

"Perhaps. But I can't live whispering. And you do need to contact your Margaret."

James retrieved a large flashlight, and they headed through a low laby-rinth of corridors into a small passageway that required bending way down, holding on to the granite walls and passing through a rough-hewn, ancient work area.

"This used to be a monastic refectory. Kitchen down beneath. That stair-way has been sealed off for probably eight, nine hundred years. Trap doors everywhere, and a tunnel, leading many miles away. Once, servants used it. Now we get giant hives of wasps up there. Normally, you're supposed to call the local fire department to come dispatch them. Of course, that's the last thing we'd ever do."

James noticed that Martin was suddenly not moving. He could hear the faint but colossal hum up above.

"Don't worry," James said. "It's a Triassic hymenopteran, large enough to terrorize a grown dog, but in fact, quite benign. A species of wasp, well, not exactly a wasp, more like a terrifying dragonfly, that went extinct some time in the past everywhere else in Europe. But I can vouch for them. I've never been stung."

"*. . . Don't worry. . . .*" Martin mumbled aloud.

They continued wandering along a corridor of stone and wood with countless offshoots, little rooms leading into useless cul-de-sacs, scarcely a toilet to be found in the entire castle.

"How *is* your company doing, by the way?" James enquired as they reached an old wooden winding stairwell, creaky oak, leading higher and higher.

"Uh, fine." Martin was already out of breath. "We did over eight hundred million last year in sales."

"Hold on a minute." James lifted the flashlight, revealing a series of portraits. "There you are."

Martin was chagrined. "You're joking?"

"Nothing to write home about, not these. Pretty bad paintings. And the lack of temperature control and dampness probably does them good. And they're not *all* related, or not to the Olivier family, although one of them is."

"I give up. Who are they?"

James named them as they walked past. "That's King Louis the Great of Hungary, and there, two successive kings of Spain. That one is Philip the Good, Duke of Burgundy, over there, Jean the First, and Charles the Fifth, and that's Maximilian of Habsburg."

"And the one woman or girl there? Who was she?" Martin asked, studying a painting of a gorgeous, bedecked royal who sat on a white stallion amid a sprawling wilderness.

"Mary of Burgundy," James said. "And guess what they all had in common?"

"Money?"

"Yes, certainly. But they were all members of the Order of the Golden Fleece. And the list goes on and on. What is important to know is that around 1430, a papal bull known as *Praeclarae devotionis sinceritas* made this a strictly Roman Catholic order, and that created some serious enemies. In the past, they were incapable of breaching our defenses. We had great knights . . . "

"We?" Martin asked.

"Yes, your family, dating to an illegitimate offspring of one of Mary of Burgundy's seven alliances. Not bad for a girl who died at the age of twenty-five."

"Her?"

"Yes."

"How'd she die?"

"Historical records say she fell off that horse. But we have our doubts."

"Oh?"

"More likely, she was murdered. By her death, someone attempted a huge power shift across northern Europe that might have spelled the doom of this estate. But it didn't happen, and I'll tell you why."

CHAPTER 25

The retrieval of the Saab wagon with Dutch plates was continuing when Jean-Baptiste Simon and Hubert Mans arrived at the scene, sometime near two A.M. A helicopter circled above the tiny islet of mud and lime trees in the middle of the flowing course where the vehicle was jammed by a limb through a smashed front window. The chopper trained its light on the affair, abetted by additional candlepower from the wild shore, where four police vehicles and a half-dozen armed cops waited and urged on two scuba divers who were overdressed, all things being equal.

The vehicle lurched through the hot glare of lights, pulled by the winch on an SUV, eventually reaching the shore. A few onlookers and one fisherman watched, with nothing better to do at this time of night. A canal barge passed by, carrying a half-dozen Russian insomniacs, tourists who had been drinking on their deck chairs, consuming cheese and crackers and caviar. They assailed the captain of their overweighted boat with rude commentary, complicated by the police, who shouted at the captain above the din of the vessel's loudly puttering engine to keep a wide berth. A local man riding his bicycle with a baguette in newsprint cast a passing glance and then vanished in the late-night mist. Burgundy kept its own hours.

The waterway had been one of the big projects of the 1820s, part of the effort to lift the local economies by tying the Rhône to the Rhine. Simon recalled his own love affair with the rivers, having grown up in their interlinking worlds where he and his young schoolmates would skinny-dip. He had heard the stories of the resistance fighters hiding out in those dark forests on either side, woods and rocky steeps said to be so wild that not even a goat could survive. He smelled the pungent night air, and it brought back all his wondrous upbringing.

"They seem to be enjoying themselves," he muttered to Hubert, referring to the Russians, now having disappeared in the growing fog.

As the police converged on the vehicle with their flashlights, they all smelled the same telltale odor.

"Open it," Simon said, the sleeve of his jacket over his mouth and nose. Hordes of strange wormlike creatures wriggled out of the trunk with a kind of urgency.

"Fuck!" the officer who opened the trunk said, as he reeled away from the now exposed rear of the vehicle.

Simon twisted his flashlight over the back of the smashed metal heap and peered in on the mostly devoured corpse, smothered in evacuating maggots. The chest cavity still held flesh, however, hanging from the partially exposed ribs.

"What is that?" Mans uttered.

"A person, I think it's safe to surmise," Simon said. "I need gloves!"

He received and fitted two white plastic gloves on either hand, then removed a rolled-up piece of leather, approximately eight centimeters in length, from the jaw. Simon then unfurled the leaf of papyruslike scroll on which were the remains, in ink, of Latin words. A French officer stepped forward to take photographs.

"What is that? Can you read it?" And Simon tried to pronounce the unpronounceable: "*Itentur n rnum? Itentur n ernum?* Hubert, get Mademoiselle Deblock on the phone. Tell her I need to speak with her uncle right away."

CHAPTER 26

James and Martin had reached the topmost portion of the tower. James leaned against a portal that gave a view of the storm with its erratic swells and perturbations. Dark clouds exploded in rain or sleet one moment, then went cold, windy, and grey the next. They were close to the ancient wooden beams of the attic overhead The slate work, redone in the early 1960s with its thousands of tiny, neatly fitted dowels, vented the wrath of pelting raindrops. There were some leaks, drops of water splattering on both men, and on countless nests being sat in.

"Martin, long ago there were great generals to defend this property. Men with names like Antoine de Croy, Pierre de Bauffremont. Once they were celebrated. But presently, we have only myself and Lance. And a few others across Europe."

"Across Europe?"

"Yes. But they are old. Retired. And I am hardly a combatant. It's difficult enough these days just getting up these stairs to make a damned phone call. Lance is something else again. But he is only one man and, in fact, an ecologist by training."

"And I'm hardly what you'd call a militant," Martin said. "It sounds like what you need is a security force, or a private army even, to defend this place. Are you asking me to help you sell part of the estate because this is all so overwhelming to you now?

"Martin, now you must listen very carefully. The Oliviers would never, could never sell this estate. This land is not ours, not really. We're merely privileged stewards for our brief time here. A privilege that confers severe duties. And the land is more valuable than any of us can comprehend. I'm talking about buying, not selling."

"But that's exceedingly imprudent. You want to buy *more* land? How do you plan to protect yourself financially, to protect the estate, if you already refuse to deal with the authorities with the land you have now? Progress itself is probably the greatest threat of all. There are bound to be intruders. A new freeway nearby, at some point in the future. French imminent domain cannot be pretty. A hundred other possibilities leap forward. You can't keep it a secret forever. And what's the point of doing so, anyway? And what about bringing those responsible for killing my dad, your only brother, to justice?"

"Justice. Yes. That's precisely what I'm talking about."

"You're losing me."

"The poachers are the sum total of the modern world, and they outnumber us. Of course, Edward misread the signs. So did I, I'm sorry to admit. But Lance did not. He was just too late."

"And outgunned, I would have to conclude."

"That is a major concern. And quite frankly, I do not know what we're going to do about it."

"What are you hiding from? Why *not* turn to the police? What other choice is there?"

James suddenly felt tired, burdened by so many months and years of hiding, anxious to unload that burden and confide in the man he prayed might offer them a way out.

"There is one thing we can and we must do," James began.

"Which is?"

"We need to buy the adjoining property. You can't see it, of course, even if it weren't raining. It's way over there, past three ridgelines and roughly one hundred square kilometers." He pointed in a general direction. "I'm not worried so much about an outbreak of avian flu, or even global warming, though I'm worried for the world in general, obviously. But these animals living here have seen it all, genetically I mean, developing every evolutionary immunity.

It's modernity that most concerns me. And that freeway you mentioned or, rather, speculated upon, that's the sort of thing that could trigger the death knell. Already terrible events are in motion. A whole development, to be precise. That's the problem we face. That's what I'm talking about."

Martin understood at once. But did not know exactly where his uncle was preparing to go with this.

"It has to be done without fuss. And it can't be the Oliviers who are doing the buying. I may be a recluse, but a few people do know me and our last name, including the nearby mayor. Every hunter and farmer and real estate agent in every town and village from Mâcon to Auxerre would find a reason to object. The French, needless to say, are testy, especially when it comes to land. They'd be all over us with questions. The British tax authorities as well. That cannot happen. There must be no publicity. No debate. No visitors are allowed here, Martin, except by invitation only. The purchase needs to be done quickly, quietly, and secretly, with no margin for error, no room for the other buyer coming up with a higher offer."

"That's all doable," Martin weighed in. "But how much money do you need?"

"I am guessing somewhere in the neighborhood of a billion euros."

"You have eighty-five thousand acres and you're telling me that's not enough? How do you rake the leaves on that amount of land? Weed, prune? You're not a kid, James. These animals. Alright, so they're rare, maybe the rarest ever. But eighty-five thousand acres, why, that's the size of a national park."

"A *national park* is a meaningless phrase, Martin. Meaningless in terms of protection. The measure of true protection, scientific protection, is everything, and we barely have it."

"Well, how many animals are there?"

"Not sure. No idea, in fact."

"Not very scientific, James."

"No. I think you already know that your father and I have our own ideas about the role of science. Edward was a strong believer in the noninvasive approach. No testing. No harm. No trespassing. Minimalist. Most scientists find that a nonviable method of obtaining new data. Edward and I happened to disagree with them. That's why we dropped out, vanished. Never published. What was the point?"

"I'm not the one to debate the ethics of science with. You know that. My father's been killed, you've ignored the police, which is surely a crime, and you've stored up all this terrible anxiety, which is now *my* anxiety and *my* complicity. And now you're telling me, on top of everything else, you—*we*—need a billion euros. Borrow against the land. Land is what, five, ten thousand an acre? A wine grower would pay more, I imagine. That's close to a billion right there. Sell the damned paintings in the stairwell. Take out a loan on this joint."

James stood up and walked toward the top of the stairs with a slow, lugubrious gate.

He turned and stared balefully at his nephew. "Martin, call your wife."

"Frankly, at this stage I'm not even sure what to tell her."

"Ask her if she's ever heard of Engelbert of Nassau."

CHAPTER 27

Mans sped on wet, windy roads through the fog toward Dijon, with Simon studying a map by his flashlight in the passenger side.

"What's with the goddamned cell coverage around here?" Mans asked, making a wide swerve toward the canal as he tried to read his phone.

"Perhaps you'd like me to drive?"

Simon tried the number on his own little RAZR, with its orange service brightly lit up. He threw his partner a condescending look that Hubert recognized as the mark of a true Frenchman.

"Yes?"

"Hello, is this Father Bruno? It's Inspector Jean Simon. Julia gave me this number."

"What time is it?"

"Sorry about that, but I need your help."

"Another corpse."

He wasn't asking but assuming.

"Yes. But. . . . "

"And there will be others."

"This one had a message hidden in the body."

"What did it say?"

Simon read from a notepad, "*Itentur n rnum.* Something like that. Some letters missing, I'm pretty sure. They got wet. Another spooky riddle."

"The letters were handwritten?"

"Yes, and stuffed in the jaw of a corpse."

"And you have no idea who the dead man is?"

"He was in the trunk of a suspect's vehicle."

"What kind of suspect?"

"International poaching ring. But that's just for your ears."

"I see."

"Does it make any sense?" Simon pressed.

"Yes. I think it does."

There was a pause as Father Bruno tried to calm his breathing. For years, he had been on a nightly dose of Niaspan for his clogged arteries, and it sometimes gave him slight hot flashes. Now they were more than flashes.

"It is Latin, of course. A statement believed to have been uttered by Christ, ending with *precipitentur in infernum.* I believe those are the words that you found."

"That was good."

"Latin was the most successful, logical language ever devised. I'm surprised police aren't encouraged to study it."

"What does it mean?"

"It is a curse, used by the Benedictines as well. 'Take him down to the lowest depths of Hell.' Followed by, 'Devil be gone.' "

CHAPTER 28

James and Martin had returned to the main house. James had shown Martin to his quarters.

"I hope the mattress is alright. No one has slept in that bed for six months."

Martin looked up at him. "This was my father's room?"

"Yes. Nothing has been changed."

Martin glanced around, taking in the familiar array of used scientific books and odd paraphernalia. What he did not expect to see was a small picture of a saint on the wall.

"Benedict," James said, "a little sketch by Hans Memling. Done, I was assured, in 1482, five years prior to the painter's oil of the same subject at the Galleria degli Uffizi, in Florence."

"1482 . . ."

"Yes. The year our relative either fell off her horse or was assassinated or both."

"You're joking? That's a Memling, an *original* Memling?"

"Yes. Edward was very partial to it."

"But it must be worth a bloody fortune," Martin said, tempted to touch it with his finger. There was no glass protecting the elegantly framed portrait.

"That's alright. Touch it. It's never been appraised, of course. Nothing has here."

"You mean there's more?"

James stared into space.

"One billion euros worth?"

"Have a seat, lad."

Martin took his shoes off and sat gingerly on the bed, knowing his father had last put his face against the old goose down pillows. He spread out, thinking back, in the dim light of a forty-watt bulb, to the last time he was with his father at a book fair in Saint Albans on the outskirts of London. His father had insisted on going into the church, the oldest and, as far as Martin knew, just about the only Catholic church in all of England that had somehow managed to flourish. He remembered something of the story of the martyred Roman soldier who would later be canonized. But not much else. Nor did he pay attention to his father's apparent devotion to the legend.

"The sellers are looking at the long-term value of a corporate village," James began.

"Corporate village? I'm sorry. What?"

"Martin, they're no dummies. I know them. Rich farming families out of Sens. They have their own illustrious history and would have you believe that they were once the leading family in the center of France.

"These three families from Sens, southeast of Paris, have some high-minded notions about their antiquity and the value of the several thousand acres they own over there, past the three mountain ridges you can't see from here. There has been local mention of some Arab sheik or other who is dying to get his hands on it and invest in French industry out here. We must get that land before it is fragmented, turned into an industrial park. A human population explosion next door, with its freeways, airport, and overpasses would be a disaster of biblical dimensions."

"That's rather extreme, isn't it?"

"No, it is not. The buffer is absolutely critical."

James could see that his nephew doubted the whole enterprise.

"You're skeptical."

"James, investors expect a return. Where is the return? Unless, of course, you're planning on selling the Memling, or the very forest you mean to protect. Or doing business with the poachers. Why not get the French military to simply protect the place? For free. You're tax exempt? There is huge historical currency, World Heritage status, all of that. Scientists, surely, would rally around the estate. The World Wildlife Fund, the National Trust, or whatever it's called in France, a special police unit. I mean, why fight possibilities that would cost the Olivier family nothing? What's the problem? Alright, so you're justifiably worried about modernity. But the government is not going to be unreasonable. They protect the Louvre. It is a national treasure. No one is going to steal the *Mona Lisa*."

"It *has* been stolen. It went missing for a week in the 19th century. And her celebrity and streams of millions of tourists are not exactly what one would wish for the rarest parrots on earth. Every scientist would have a different opinion about what to do, standard operating procedures, what was most important, what kind of research to undertake, which genes and DNA to preserve, and how to spend the taxpayers' money. A nightmare. Worse, a disaster of intrusiveness. Martin, there is a hell of a difference between a museum and what I'm talking about. I had hoped you would understand that. Tell me that the fate, not only of this family, but of this . . . this garden is not in further jeopardy?"

Martin got up and walked to the window. He gazed out over the chateau grounds. Suddenly, he glimpsed another strange if somewhat smaller creature, seen by the dim lights that shone as the one remaining security system intact around the periphery. It wandered like an old man, hunched and stout, through the grassy verge that led to the back of the chateau.

"What is that?"

"That?" James came and joined him at the window. "Ahh. That would be a dodo, *Pezophaps solitaria*, or *Raphus cucullatus*, as it was also described. They probably originated among the Mascarene Islands, possibly Rodrigues, not far from Madagascar. Or the nearby Mauritius. She'd normally be asleep at night. I've thought to turn the lights off. Terrible annoyance, I realize. But we think it a necessity."

Martin stared in half-awe, trying to recover some remembrance from childhood or from a book. And for just an instant, his heart began to melt with the strange sense of familiarity. It had to do with his father. Somewhere far back at the first moment, a chime of recognition he had held dear but had lost, until just now.

"Are you alright?" James asked, a twinkle in his eye, recognizing the glint of dreamy romance.

"I don't know if I've ever actually seen one of those."

"Probably not," James allowed, smiling wearily.

CHAPTER 29

At a private lodging in Paris, on the fifth floor of a building that housed an all-night disco at street level ("illegal clandestine soirée" was the local name for such rave clubs), eight men assembled at midnight. The sounds of the rock music and of the hollering that accompanied the chaos down below emanated for several blocks throughout the 9th Arrondissement. A long line of pale-faced creatures waited to be admitted to the underground haven of throbbing music, dance floor theatrics, and who knew what else. This building was perfect for muffling the goings-on sixty feet above, in one back apartment where Berndt held court with a group of mercenaries he had never met, with no last names.

He scrutinized the six men Raoul had brought onboard, all allegedly his trustworthy poachers from past operations throughout the world.

Raoul, however, had not yet arrived, and Berndt was beginning to suspect a problem.

"Check outside," he said quietly to de Bar, who started toward the stairwell. At that moment, Berndt's cell phone vibrated, and he answered.

"Yeah?"

"I'm twenty minutes away. There's been a slight change in plans." It was Raoul.

"Go on."

"Have you seen the news?"

"No."

"This disease thing is everywhere. Something more than bird flu. They're not saying, but the Bourgogne is surrounded by medics and cops. It presents a difficulty."

"Then we wait," Berndt said. "A month, two months."

"No, we can't wait," Raoul went on, driving toward Pont de Bercy. He had seen the news on a TV in a bar an hour earlier. "The police are moving in large groups through the countryside. They could find Jimmy's car. Or much worse. And then the prize is gone. We need to move tomorrow."

At that same moment, the local newspapers in Dijon were printing news that would land on every doorstep within a matter of hours, headlines that read of "Grippe de TSE" and of a general disaster: "La confirmation de la présence du virus . . . ."

Every doorstep except that of James Olivier. He had no doorstep. He received no paper, no deliveries whatsoever—which is why he felt a particular jolt of panic in the middle of the night when the old buzzer on the outermost wall sounded an alarm.

Martin could hear the commotion from where he lay half asleep. By the time Lance had gotten to the huge iron door, Martin was standing, looking for the first solid object that might be used as a weapon, just in case . . . .

"James?"

"What is it, Lance?" James cried out.

"It's me, Edouard," a voice wavered in the storm.

CHAPTER 30

A light sleeper, Margaret Olivier woke the moment she heard the phone ring. She put down the phone after approximately three minutes of speaking with her husband. He had made it brief on account, he said, of the possibility that someone was eavesdropping.

A penny for your thought ... arriving at the number of letters of a certain donkey's name ...

Martin was catching on.

Although it was not yet four A.M., Margaret's brain was racing. *Engelbert of Nassau. It couldn't be ...*

And the clues, so unlike her husband to be anything but conventional. A penny for my pensée? Penny? Dime? Di ... Dijon airport. No. He said penny ... money? Uh, coin? Cointrin! Of course, Geneva's international airport, where they'd made love wildly at a five-star hotel after a successful Christie's auction Margaret had consulted on, many years ago. Overlooking the lake. And Mont Blanc on a clear day.

"I love you," Martin had uttered again and again. "I'm a rainbow trout ...

a black swan dipping into the still waters," he murmured playfully beneath the Egyptian cotton sheets. So perfectly free and easy, free of intervening years that had been stuffed with formality, English ways, of idiotic restraint. And he fell asleep beside her, curled up at peace. She couldn't remember that they'd made love very often since. And that was being generous, she reflected. Busy lives had usurped the easiness of their early romance. Everything seemed to conspire against it.

Nine letters. Nine A.M. She got on the Internet. There was a standby-only flight leaving Heathrow at 6:15 A.M., arriving precisely at nine A.M. She'd just make it if she had left the house two minutes ago. Heathrow had become so difficult. The security. The lines. No time to think about it. Rain jacket. Hiking boots. Hurry. No water bottle or perfume or gel caps.

Geneva's airport was approximately one hundred minutes from the property, at a reasonable clip.

∿

Once at Heathrow, Margaret left her car with a valet service they used, ran to Austrian Airways, removing her shoes, her ring, her watch ... running. Only to be told the flight had been oversold. They were announcing a free round trip anywhere in the European Union if someone would give up his seat. Five bookings in excess.

"A thousand euros, cash, right now!" Margaret suddenly exclaimed in a loud voice.

"Madame, you can't do that!" chastised an airline official.

But she could and did. Someone already in line had heard and capitulated to the offer. An ATM machine happened to be handy, and one thousand euros poorer, Margaret had a confirmed seat on the direct flight to Geneva presently boarding.

CHAPTER 31

Revere looked at James, both men standing beside Lance at the entrance to the chateau.

"They've killed Jacob."

James stared at the words, leaning feebly against a corroded pilaster on the inside of the doorway, beside the entrance to the cloakroom where Lance removed Revere's sopping overcoat.

"And the animal?"

"I fear the worst."

Suddenly Martin appeared, wielding a brass candelabrum, presumably prepared to do combat.

Max appeared as well, descending the stairs from his own part of the chateau in his pajamas.

Revere shot a glance at James' troubled associates.

"Edouard, this is my nephew I told you about, Martin Olivier. That is Martin's driver, Max. Martin, Max, this is Edouard, an old friend from Belgium, unexpected, I'm afraid."

Martin lowered his weapon.

"Is everything alright?" Max asked. The visitor had the body of a soccer player with a drenched tousle of red hair and unshaved face. Max could see at once that he was extremely agitated.

"Into the library, gentlemen," James directed.

"Max, could you excuse us?" Martin asked.

James interceded, "No, that's alright, we may need him."

James, Edouard, Lance, Martin, and Max took seats in the round, ornate, rather naked room. James noticed Martin looking up at the single motto on the wall, shining in the play of reflections that quietly dazzled the interior.

"That is an old engraving of a servant to the royal Pepin, Eustache, later canonized," James said. "He'd been hunting stags, raised his bow and arrow and, just before delivering a fatal wound, perceived Christ crucified between the antlers. He thereafter resigned as a hunter to become a protector of the beasts instead."

"Nice. Now, who killed your friend? The same people? The poachers?" Martin pressed.

"I told you he didn't just do real estate, but trained as a lawyer," James explained to Edouard. "What will you take?"

"A double malt, whatever it is," Edouard declared.

To Martin, a good double malt signified revival, recovery, hope. "I'll have one as well, thank you." Max remarked that he was on duty and passed.

Lance headed towards the bar.

"Make that three of those," James added, then turned toward Edouard. "When and by what means did they get to Jacob?"

Martin noticed the slight glance of light off a tear that had welled in his uncle's eye.

"Last night. Sometime after he'd managed to liberate the animal. They left him in the garden of the museum, crucified by a horn."

"My God . . ." his voice trailed away.

"But the police, surely they're all over this?" Martin said.

James' look of despair lent urgency to the query.

"Yes, that's how I spent my day," Edouard replied.

"What if they followed you?" Lance suggested.

"No. I drove for hours, alone. The Antwerp police were gone by early afternoon, more interested in Jacob's house, not that they'll find anything. And the museum's map collection, which, of course, should prove even less fruitful," Edouard assured them.

"What the hell is happening?" Martin asked James.

Edouard looked across at him, past a three-hundred–year-old globe and a badly pockmarked writing desk from the 17th century, rain sleeking hard against the enormous windows to the west.

"James, how much have you actually told your nephew?"

"Not everything," James admitted.

"What about his wife? We need her."

"Martin will be leaving soon for the airport in Geneva to pick her up."

Martin shot James a look. *How did he know?*

"Remarkable acoustics in these walls," James volunteered. "I couldn't help but overhear."

"Max, are you alright to drive?" James asked.

CHAPTER 32

I t was just after five A.M., when Fabritius Cadiz managed to reach Simon
   and Mans, who were on the outskirts of Dijon, driving toward a Best
Western hotel where the two men had planned to spend a few hours getting
some shuteye, a hot shower, and a round of fresh coffee.

"We've got an approximate on the trace," Cadiz said.

"How approximate?" Simon asked, speaking into his cell phone.

"Well, you know Burgundy, so this will probably make sense to you," the
Belgian policeman, speaking from headquarters in Antwerp, went on. "The
problem is not entirely clear to us. There's tremendous interference. Revere
must have driven into a series of canyons."

"There are no canyons."

"Well, mountains."

"The highest is about three thousand feet."

"Then the bug is defective."

"Just tell me what you're seeing." Simon himself had placed the little transmitter under the back of Revere's car before leaving the museum earlier in the afternoon.

"The satellite is picking up steep gradients."

"What's the nearest town?"

"Château-Chinon."

"Go on?"

"Twenty-one kilometers due north. That's what it's showing. But there is a twelve, thirteen percent margin of error."

"And the vehicle has stopped?"

"Yes. An hour ago. There's no town anywhere near. Looks like the national park." And he conveyed some coordinates.

"Thanks, Fabbi."

"What did he say?" Mans inquired.

"Turn off at the next exit. We've got to head back in the direction of Nevers and then figure it out. Though I have a hunch."

"But that's at least an hour or more. We need gas. And I need coffee."

Simon studied his map of the Bourgogne. Revere was somewhere in the vicinity of Montsauche, in the region of the Lac des Settons, between the Rivers Yonne and Cure, both near flood levels at present due to all the rain. It could be no coincidence, he realized, that Serko's body was found where it was. The area was wild—the wildest in all of the Morvan, as the region was known. A complex portion of the central massif that took up some twenty percent of France, with combes or valleys of granite and porphyry, of ancient habitation but little modern activity—and this explained why it was largely parkland, said to be without periphery—and caves, in some cases a mile deep, painted by the ancients.

Simon's grandfather was a Morvandeau, and *his* father. Both spoke the ancient dialect, the so-called Sologne-Bourbonnais patois.

Something else now started to fall into place as well, but Simon needed to call his father just to be sure.

He placed the call, knowing his dad's habits, those of a farmer's. Early riser.

"Mom? It's me. Where's dad?"

"In the milking barn. Is everything alright?

"Yes. Sorry to call so early. Do you remember that story Grandpa used to tell, about the monastery where he learned to paint?"

"Of course. A Cistercian abbey with huge grounds. But he couldn't paint if his life depended on it. That's why he took up farming."

"But where was it?"

"I never understood exactly. On the way to Prémery, south of Tannay. But why?"

"Routine investigation. Are you guys outside the quarantine?"

"For now. But it is terrible. Your father does not do well with stress, as you know. His ulcer erupts."

"Just stay away from the open markets. I've got to run. Love to Dad."

"Wait, I thought you were going to Greece with Sylvie and the baby?"

"So did I."

Simon then placed a phone call to Father Bruno.

"Father, I'm really sorry. It's me again, Jean Simon. What can you tell me about a Cistercian monastery northeast of Château-Chinon? Not far from the regional park?"

Bruno had half expected this. He had been up all night, in part on account of this persistent inspector, but also because he had been doing some figuring on his own. And the worlds were perilously colliding, the one concerning those very monks this policeman was now evoking from the beguiling mists of the Middle Ages. The answer was cloaked in one of the most bizarre and elusive mysteries he had ever known in his life as a man of the cloth.

"I know the one," and he conveyed to Simon the kind of explicit directions that all the high technology back in Antwerp had failed to deliver. Simon gave Mans a queer look as he took a few notes with his right hand. This Belgian prelate appeared to be uncannily familiar with the geographic points of interest.

"It ceased to be a monastery nearly a thousand years ago."

"What happened?"

"The earliest royal families of Burgundy acquired it."

"And today?"

"Today? Why, I think it is just forest, ruins. I don't know of anyone who has ever been there, not in my lifetime. Come to think of it. . . . " Father Bruno *had* thought of it, the minute the murder at the docks had involved wildlife as well as the Benedictines.

Simon sensed a frustrating hesitation on the part of Bruno that he had not detected in any of their exchanges earlier.

"How large was the monastery?"

"It wasn't the monastery itself but the surroundings."

"What about them? Large enough for wild animals to roam?"

"Legend says so, yes."

Bruno had feared to come out with what had been on his mind for many hours, in his gut for several years. He read newspapers avidly, stayed abreast of all the scientific bad news. He was no ordinary member of the Church.

"Be careful," he finally announced, almost a command.

"Of what?"

"Have you ever read the poet John Donne?"

"The English poet who said 'no man is an island.'"

"And who also wrote, 'Serpens fixa Cruci si sit natura, Crucique A fixo nobis Gratia tota fluat.'"

"Your Latin again."

"Donne's. He wrote it in Latin to his friend the religious poet George Herbert."

"What does it say?"

"'Crucify nature then, and then implore all grace from Him crucified there before.'"

"That's your translation?"

"James Russell Lowell's. Mine is slightly simpler, and if I told you it concerns the end of the world, would you believe me?"

"I might." Simon was tired of wading through hesitancies and the damned rain and fog, dead bodies, riddles, and satellite margins of error. But Bruno was no dummy, and the connection to nature and, by implication, all wildlife held a special metaphoric significance for the deputy director of the IW Secretariat. "How did the poem end? In English, please?"

"'To you, who bear his name, great bounties deal.'"

CHAPTER 33

Three bogus courier service trucks, one French postal truck, an old van, a bakery vehicle, and several SUVs, spaced more than three miles apart, moved silently through different boulevards of Paris late in the rain-splashed night, taking various routes toward and beyond the Portes d'Orléans, Dorée, d'Italie, and de Choisy. Raoul was in the lead postal delivery vehicle, Berndt followed up in the rear driving the rural bakery truck. De Bar drove with the leader of the team in a van, the others scattered in assorted unwashed SUVs, all communicating on Blackberries.

They carried between them an arsenal of nets, cages, powerful tranquilizers, ropes, hooks, and other supplies sufficient to relocate approximately twenty small mammals, fifty birds, another fifty amphibians and reptiles, and at least two very large beasts. If anything went wrong, they also had enough rounds of heavy firepower to defend themselves against even a stampede of nasty creatures, or worse. Their munitions would see them through the wall. Hand grenades, large wire cutters, rubber boots and gloves, watering sprays for deactivating any electric trip wires, special infrared helmets with real-time computer-controlled heat-seeking readouts, walkie-talkies, and several shoulder-launchable missiles gave them the comfort that even an opposing SWAT team would have little chance of stopping them.

They had water bags for amphibians and cool compresses to keep any traumatized animal alive. Special small coolers, padded crates of several sizes, and various injectibles for reviving stunned mammals, bringing them back by degree without inducing shock, filled the back of the SUVs. They were not interested in paws, furs, or feathers. No trophies. If the animals weren't alive, then they were of no use.

Raoul would handle cover on the chateau side, Berndt the eight kilometers to the northwest, on the far outside corner of the property. De Bar and the six ops—Ops 1, 2, 3, 4, 5, 6, that's how they preferred it—would go in through a new section of wall that they would open up. They would make their way into the forest in three groups of two, staged in steps: two forward, two center, two rear, a relay method that most of the team had used in Botswana two years before and in several of the thirteen new national parks of Gabon eight months before that, so as to send live captures back out toward the waiting vehicles. The pit viper had died. All the other live captures had been successful.

They would go in only as far as necessary to find any of the creatures on their list, net them, haul them in, and send them toward the rear.

They had a checklist from Abdul, outlandish though it was. And they also had instructions from Raoul to basically grab whatever was feasible and had never been seen before. He felt confident. The opposition was no longer an issue—two old men, illegitimate heirs in his mind, and one well-trained hunter.

And one of those two old men had presumably been killed, or certainly crippled in the last assault.

The rain all but guaranteed success. Out of nine surveillance days, it had rained, or drizzled ninety-seven percent of the time. Deep cloudcover, as low as a hundred feet. Visibility, twenty meters.

Since the group had specialized in poaching for something like a hundred years between them, having tallied over 1,400 exotic species of birds, mammals, reptiles, and amphibians, they were highly prepared for making the kinds of snap judgments needed in their profession.

In any case, Raoul contemplated, as he drove silently out of Paris in light traffic, he had nothing to worry about other than the next twenty-four hours. Even if things went badly, by the time it all went down, he would have obtained the *real* prize and have left the country, his future secured.

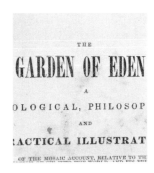

THE

GARDEN OF EDEN

A

OLOGICAL, PHILOSOP

AND

ACTICAL ILLUSTRAT

OF THE MOSAIC ACCOUNT, RELATIVE TO THE

CHAPTER 34

The rain continued to pelt the chateau. Leaden rainspouts and gutters overflowed, the smell of tannin and sulphur in the air. There was thunder, and lightning hit in repeated flashes. Winds howled through the forest.

Martin sat in the library with James and Edouard. Max had gone up to his room to get ready for the drive to Geneva.

Lance had gone to the tower, according to James, to "check on things, what with all the rain, and the leaky roof."

"When were you planning to tell him?" Edouard finally asked, breaking an awkward silence that had settled in.

"You're right. It's time."

Martin looked at him expectantly.

James suddenly found himself undone by a swelling of emotions.

"Would you prefer if I told him?" Edouard chimed in.

"I'm alright." James took a swig of his drink and a deep breath.

"Here's the thing, lad. These eighty-five thousand acres or so, they are not just another forest."

"James, we've been through this."

Far above, where rafters and slate nails buffered against the outer world and rain converged along runnels of decorated stone, distant screeches told Lance, who stood beneath the roof, that out there, amid his grid of covered microphones clipped to trees, there was a perceived terror in the night. The tower looked out over the ranges, serving as a line-of-sight transmitter, a newly equipped wire threading its way up the enormous limestone, which received acoustical hootings of griffins and roars of other upset beasts.

Moreover, to enable him to delineate specific howls from mere white noise, Lance had installed a computer translation system, which he had developed while finishing graduate school. The small screen's x-y coordinates blossomed and subsided with scratchy fill, a phosphor series of mushroom clouds reacting in heights and depths to each incoming elocution. A flock of birds broken up with fear, a herd of racing chamois troubled by their detection of an intruder, howler monkeys racing across a canopy to defend their young. Lance detected, against a background of wind through aching trees that stood their ground, accustomed to centuries of turbulence, and thunder and sheet lightning in the heavens above, a chorus of the frightened and the vulnerable below, which shot through him with a fury.

"You have heard of the Garden of Eden, of course," James began.

"Alright, so?"

"What is the Garden of Eden to you, I mean?"

"James, it's nearly five A.M. Skip the philosophy and tell me what's on your mind."

Edouard threw James a look. James nodded.

"Martin, I've been trying to say to you is that, well, this *is* the Garden of Eden. It is the secret that the Olivier family has kept for generations, for many centuries. But a secret that preceded us by tens, hundreds of millions of years. Unless you take a literal reading of the Bible, in which case it is only a few thousands of years. The prophets were poets, not scientists. And they took liberties with chronology, which is why there are so many calendars, so many astronomical revelations, symbols, even with respect to precise dates of Homer, Moses, Christ. Ten, fifteen thousand years ago, glaciers swept across Europe, as they did North America. The ice retreated, changing ecosystems. Countless species throughout the world went extinct because their habitats were transformed more rapidly than they could transform themselves, their choice of plants and insects, their metabolisms. From Siberia to what is now

Ireland, creatures both large and small vanished. And a few human types, as well. There were also hyper-diseases that ensured that those species that had originally survived also succumbed. Not all of them disappeared, of course, though most did. And then Homo erectus, Neanderthal, Cro-Magnon man, big-time hunters added to the chaos, chasing down huge numbers of remaining large mammals. There are caves, even in Burgundy, filled with primeval artifacts. Corpses of hundreds of horses driven off cliffs, then eaten, just thirty miles from here."

"James, where is this all leading to? I have to confess, I am exhausted."

James shared a melancholy look with Edouard. But both men felt no choice than to persevere with this obviously slow learner.

"Alright, the point is, during the last several thousands of those years, the pressures intensified. I'm sure you are aware of the fact that humans have accelerated species extinctions by something like ten thousand times more than what is called the natural background rate for extinctions. Your own father devoted his life to understanding what was happening."

"To be perfectly candid, I had no idea. I know we have a big problem. But I never really cottoned to numbers, unless there was a dollar sign riding on them."

"Oh, there is, lad. There is. These eighty five thousand primeval acres are all that's left of the time prior to the glaciers."

Martin started to reply, but then something hit him. Perhaps it was the conspiratorial twinkling of eyes, as if they had slipped him a mickey in one of countless drinks he'd consumed in the past several hours. He felt dizzy, and the whole room seemed, however slightly, to shift. And the conversation grew somewhat fuzzy around the edges . . . *Irish elks, sabertooth cats . . .*

" *. . . the great auk, a Labrador duck,*" Edouard added, "*and passenger pigeon, okapi and aurochs, bullockornis and unicorns . . . .*"

"In fact," James carried on, "as pressures mounted in the 18th and 19th centuries throughout the world, from Madagascar to Peru, from New Zealand to India, this monastic haunt, revered by those entrusted with the secret, protected by the Knights of the Order of the Golden Fleece, became the last refuge on earth."

"Large enough," said Edouard, "wild enough, consistent enough since time immemorial to host this overflowing of abundant need. Animals, insects, flowers in a state of crisis. All took refuge here. There are no birds endemic to Europe, not counting the Madeiras. But here, across this biologically-sinecured estate, well, a different story entirely."

"So does the Vatican know about this place?" Martin wondered out loud, exasperated by the sheer scope of what he was being told.

"There was a pope who visited," James began. "Some five hundred years ago. During lunch, a hippopotamus scared the shit out of him. It only wanted to horse around, as only hippos can. He excommunicated the hippo and for good measure placed all of the other wild creatures here on the Papal Index, as well. Not that anyone paid attention. We are one heresy the Vatican finds it easy to ignore. Although I should add that a 19th century pope forbade Catholics to provide sanctuary for animals under the notion that humans were superior and should not waste their time providing any measure of comfort for lesser beings, because it is official papal doctrine that all other animals, besides humans, have no souls. They cannot be saved."

"But that's just crazy?"

Edouard chimed in, "Actually, the Greek Orthodox Church most recently equated human-induced extinctions with sin. Biblical sin. That was a huge step forward."

"Yes, more akin to the thinking of some of our notable guests in times past," James added.

CHAPTER 35

For years Margaret Olivier had lived and breathed within the alluring uncertainty of the manuscript collection owned by Count Engelbert of Nassau, a member of the Duke of Burgundy's inner circle and one of the wealthiest citizens of Bruges during the late 15th century. When Martin had mentioned his name, without any other information, she assumed he had stumbled on one of the books. If so, a fortune would be involved.

"We'll be landing in just over an hour," the copilot announced as the aircraft lifted to twenty-three thousand feet, heading out over the English Channel.

Margaret opened her laptop and began to ripple through images from her dissertation years before, refamiliarizing herself with a world she had given up for lack of new materials to devour or new opportunities, by her reckoning, for breakthrough research.

The images, from nearly fifteen years before, now struck her with all the same stunning originality and power as the first time she had encountered them. She admired the dozens of "Masters" that had made 15th century European manuscript illumination the most exciting, mysterious, and sought-after of all Renaissance art forms.

In the 1400s, the great illuminations were for nobility, kings, and empresses who acquitted their conscience by commissioning the greatest artists of all time to paint private prayer books. Called *Horae*, the plural for hours in Latin, a work in this genre came to be known as a Book of Hours.

But it was not just royalty that owned such books. They were also mass-produced in cheap renditions, the way the Bible and Marco Polo's famed book were manufactured in hundreds of editions. And it all happened just before Gutenberg showed up. By the 1470s, the first printed book in Rome, *The Letters of St. Jerome*, began to be typeset along with other works, including the famed *Navis Stultorum* or *Ship of Fools*, and the heyday of the great hand-painted books in Europe would start to wane. With printing, Margaret argued in her thesis, certain secrets locked in the physical juxtaposition of painting and literature, words and pictures side by side, disappeared forever.

The secrets. . . . Her mind reverberated, going back to a time just before she had met Martin, when she was living in an apartment at Oxford, teaching graduate seminars, and traveling throughout Europe on faculty research grants.

Some of those secrets were contained within the very notion of "Master," which was the equivalent of "unknown." Artists like those anonymous giants bearing names such as the Master of St. Francis, Master of the Jerusalem Chronicle, of the Barberini Panels, of the Visitation, the Resurrection, the Prophets, and, most exquisite of all, in her opinion, the Master of Mary of Burgundy, an artist whose identity had never been solved but who was responsible for a *Book of Hours* unlike any that had ever been painted.

She stared at four images from one owned by none other than the man Martin had cryptically named, Count Engelbert. Martin had said nothing else. He knew nothing else.

"Why do you mention his name? What? What are you holding back?" She had pressed, without getting an answer.

Margaret knew that prior to the count's possession of the priceless manuscript, Mary of Burgundy herself was the proud owner, and if not Mary, certainly her son, Philip the Fair. Mary, after all, could afford anything during the four years she "owned" the largest kingdom in the world, half of Europe, with its capital in the Netherlands. Art historians had looked to Alexander Bening, or his son Simon, as the actual painter. But Margaret was unsure.

Disputes among art scholars raged over numerous questions of style, attribution, or better yet, authentic authorship and the provenance or gene-alogy of ownership.

Margaret was one of that select coterie of individuals considered the cho-sen ones, historians who could be trusted with a single fragile piece of paper in their gloved hands, a single sheet worth tens of millions of dollars. She knew all the owners or institutional directors from personal experience—the Huntington Library in Pasadena, California, the National Library in Madrid, the Print Room at Berlin, the Holkham Hall of the Earl of Leices-ter, the Czartoryski Museum in Kracow, the British Museum, the Musée Condé in Chantilly, and, of course, the great libraries at Oxford, Vienna, and Paris.

A famed ornithologist, while traipsing through Peruvian jungle, had dis-covered a new neotropical bird species by simply hearing it utter a note. It is said by observers that he knew at once the species had never been encoun-tered, yet he did not ever get a glimpse of the bird itself. Margaret was like that with some periods of art history. A single sketch, ignored by other his-torians, had spoken to her of Raphael, and she had been right. A painting of Saint Anthony from Cuzco, circa 1750, never cleaned, she determined was concealing something, a conclusion she had reached in three minutes, not with black light or any other technical means. Once again, circumstances favored her intuition. The work had surfaced in a dimly lit portion of an antique shop in downtown Rio, bearing a strange, encrusted backside and a single signature, illegible. But the manner of ink and the fine stroke remind-ed Margaret of something. She had seen the same on the back of a Giorgione at a castle in Liechtenstein. Again, she proved her argument, a painting be-neath a painting, and tens of millions of dollars passed hands as the upshot.

She had twenty minutes before landing, ten minutes before they would ask passengers to turn off all electrical gadgets. Margaret raced over the keyboard, typing in notes for herself: Sort out anything new on Engelbert-Bodleian Library, Bibliothèque Nationale, Getty, Morgan; download all pertinent images from the *Codex Vindobonensis 1857*, Vienna; check all new commentaries on saints' days, the Blessed Sacraments, confessions, sorrows, contemplations, any new data on borders, optical illusions, trompe d'oeil . . .

She took a cup of coffee, then set it down as the plane's progress was sud-denly marked by lurches. She grabbed hold of her seatbelt, glanced at her iPhone, and then proceeded to shut down her Apple.

As the jet descended toward Geneva, the Alps becoming clear, Marga-ret's mind focused, not on the bumps as they passed through gigantic cu-mulous clouds, but rather on a very different three-dimensional space, the one she had explored for her Ph.D., the one that artists such as the elusive Master of Mary of Burgundy had actually invented in the service of various meditations. These musings had focused upon nature, paradise, culminating in a new reverence for landscape whose supreme palettes were indebted to all those moments decreed as holy, or representative of Christian piety, the seven times of prayer throughout each day, from matins and lauds to vespers and compline. They were of the labored Hours of the Cross, of the Virgin, and of those countless nuances associated with death and burial. These treasures were the beginning of nature painting. Christianity had transformed perspective and aesthetics into a total celebration of animals, forests, and flowers, turning the very rose into the most popular romance in the history of the human heart and a humble garden into a realm of moral and philosophical epics.

But Margaret also knew that there was a certain hopelessness to them by this time, at least for the scholar. The art world had no more major manuscripts to be discovered, or that was the consensus, based on a conspicuous absence of major works turning up at auction during the past three decades. The same could be said, of course, of Rembrandts or Giorgiones.

So, she wondered, *what on earth had her husband found? Or, better yet, inherited?*

CHAPTER 36

Jean-Baptiste Simon and Hubert Mans were approaching the outskirts of Château-Chinon, rising nearly fifteen hundred feet above sea level, on a kind of a pass in the mountains. The window wipers on Mans' Renault sluggishly cleared the accumulating sleet.

"I've never seen such weather in France. It's summer," Simon puzzled aloud.

"Global warming," Mans replied, matter-of-factly.

Their driving route continued through areas Simon knew well—the Bibracte, the volcanic landscape near Beuvray, and the forests of the Resistance. It was the oldest region of Burgundy in terms of human occupations, wars, and dramatic scenery. But it seemed unfamiliar on this morning, when the dawn had yet to reveal itself amid such freakishly poor weather.

Near the old towers of the Porte Notre-Dame, they pulled over into a parking lot, and Simon placed a call to Le Bon.

"I need you to track the owners of a certain monastery. Father Bruno said it had been abandoned for a thousand years." And he conveyed coordinates and other pieces of information.

A sleepy, somewhat cranky Le Bon replied, "Nonsense. Somebody is always paying the taxes."

"Exactly."

"I'll get back to you."

Not two minutes after ending the call, Simon's cell rang back. A number he did not recognize.

"Yes?"

"Jean? It's Hans."

"Where are you?"

"Dubai. We had Abdul, for about forty-five minutes. A raid at his compound early this morning resulted in a fucking horror show. You would have puked. We're talking dozens of CITES violations. And something else. . . . I don't even know how to describe it."

"I'm listening."

"I've sent a dozen images of it to Krezlach's colleagues. But I believe it is a mammal nobody knew about. A new species, or one that was thought extinct for a long, long time. A bit like that wild dog they found in Maine, part dingo, part something else."

"Where's Abdul now?"

"His people have him. Diplomatic bullshit. But there's some trade agreement cooking between Dubai and the French. I think this could prove embarrassing. We'll get him back."

Simon closed his cell phone and then wrote something in his notepad.

"You see that?" Mans said.

Simon looked up from his notes. "What?"

"A fleet of courier trucks and SUVs."

The vehicles had joined into close formation once well beyond the peripherique around Paris.

"They're already gone, down around that corner. And all heading into the Morvan. That seems odd, no?"

"Yes, it does. Follow them. But they mustn't see us."

CHAPTER 37

"Martin, you do understand?" James pressed. "Not one cage, no human intervention, but the real deal. As it has always been and so remains to this moment."

"I thought the Ark was atop Mount Ararat. Made of gopher wood. Some Christian expedition from Texas claims to have found it. And what about the Deluge? And the original couple?" Martin's fatigue grappled with skepticism. "And the serpent? The apple tree? Satan? The Old and New Testaments? What you're saying not only defies science but every religion. And what about Brazil? Suriname? New Guinea? Surely there are wilder, far less disturbed places? Why else did my parents bother going to South America if that were not the case?"

"I'm sorry, Martin. Too many questions. Not enough time in the world to do justice to them," James answered patiently. "All I can tell you is this, the Ark exists. But it is not a boat lifted by floodwaters to the summit of a mountain in Iran. The story of the ark is a metaphor. But this chateau, this obscure forest in the Northern Hemisphere, this is no metaphor. The deluge, well, consider what happened after the Ice Age melted. The sea levels rose. As for an original couple, twenty miles from here, we know of Pleistocene burials with later human materials. It's just impossible to unsort it all. But there are parts of the property to which no one, to our knowledge, has ever been. The so-called Wild Child of Aveyron lived here, in the remains of the monastery, before wandering into town. They never traced him. Although Napoleon knew the truth."

"Napoleon was here?" Martin should not have been surprised.

"Only for a night. He was informed that soldiers were not welcome in this place, and he accepted the verdict, luckily. He ventured no farther than that grassy clearing you saw when you arrived. Not even van Eyck, Brueghel the Elder, nor Buffon went further than a few hundred meters. The list of visitors is rather impressive, if highly selective. By invitation only, you can be sure. But what you must understand is that few people, to our knowledge, have ever gone beyond that wall right there."

"What about you and my father?" Martin asked astonished.

"From time to time, whenever there was a good reason to do so, yes. Lance has studied it. So did Edward. But not all the way in."

"But what's really out there?"

"We're not sure. A center, perhaps the source of a certain spring and, quite likely, a very special tree. But these are speculations based upon instinct, imagination, and a certain bias that is akin to the world's spiritual subconscious. The monks that once inhabited the ruins beneath where we now stand no doubt trekked farther than was necessary. But their curiosity did serve, in the end, to instill a sacrosanct legend within the Brethren. Someone has been there, we know."

"Been where? James, these riddles are just too annoying."

James glanced at Edouard, who looked away, ashamed in a sense that this all had to be articulated at such an eleventh hour, as if left to colossal chance and the uncertain consequences of doing so.

"Let's put it this way," James continued, "there *is* something out there of enormous importance, countless rare species, that is a fact, but until such time as there may be a necessity of venturing there, we have always preferred, as have the majority of those before us, to live and let live. Noninterference. In Sanskrit, *ahimsa*. Lord knows there has been more than enough human interference with the natural order of things. No mouse or fox or rabbit has ever been slain here. No chicken served up between two slices of bread or mutton in a stew. No Charolais steak. The fact is, these quarters have always hosted, how shall I best put it, herbivorous modesty?"

"So you're vegetarian. Please don't rub it in. I'm quite the lover of steak, if you don't mind. Although you'll find plenty in common with both Margaret and Anthony, half of whose chums are downright vegans. I don't know what's come over people."

"Well, there is also the issue of original sin. We have no reason to be a burden. The animals live in peace. Why stress them out, let alone kill them merely for food or fur or tamper with things we don't understand? The painters who came here were painting what they saw, from real life. We've become entirely cynical, I'm afraid, in a matter of a very brief period of time. Those on the outside, I mean."

Fair enough, Martin reckoned. *But, van Eyck? Brueghel?* It was the dream, of sorts, that he had fashioned as a child, growing up mostly without his father, who sent strange, wonderful letters home from far-flung regions of the planet. So exotic was that dream, in fact, that Martin had erected his own fabulous kingdom and actually dwelt there, along a babbling brook in rural England, surrounded by picture books, rare works of natural history. And *Peter Pan*, exquisitely illustrated.

But after his mother's death and a stint at a strict "public school," as the British uniquely label them—a private upper-class boarding school, in fact, with little monsters in school uniforms—that kingdom had simply ceased to exist, receding somewhere far off into his untouchable interior. A realm that grew so faint one dared not share it any longer. And, whom with?

Until the very lack of familiarity drove it away. By the time of law school, these memories were of childhood merely and unsettling at best.

The spell was suddenly broken as Lance moved quickly from somewhere outside into the room. "We've got company!"

CHAPTER 38

"Where are they?" James demanded. Martin noticed for the first time that James' right hand was shaking. A Parkinson's-like tremor.

But it was also clear that James had been living in dread of this moment.

"From the sounds of it, farther north than before," Lance said.

"Right. You're heading up, then?"

"Yes, and Max here has offered to help."

Martin looked to his chauffeur with a mixture of concern and pride. He knew something none of the others could know, unless Max had divulged some of the details of his illustrious past to Lance. More than merely driving people around, Max had been a Royal Marine Commando sharpshooter, a sniper with the kind of seniority that either guaranteed you'd be killed in combat or you'd retire for a higher-paying civilian job, which is why he'd gone into private security, first in Ecuador for an oil magnate, then London.

"I'm fine with this," Max volunteered. He withdrew a cold-steel Bowie knife from a sheath near his ankle and a .45-caliber Colt with nine bullets in the clip from under his vest.

Max smiled. "If I even hit somebody's pinky with this, they'll be on the ground."

"What's your shoe size?" Lance asked. "You'll need boots. It's muddy and steep."

"I've got running shoes, a 9-millimeter Glock, and an M16 in the trunk."

"We like that."

Edouard glanced at James, who was staring out at the unending storm, a tempest far worse than usual for this time of year. "James, what are we going to do? You know the Brethren are willing to cough up everything they have, the Hythlodae Trust, worth easily fifty million. Before coming, I computed the contributions from the others, and it adds another twelve million or so. But that is a far cry from a billion."

"Edouard, we have to find the book," James declared resolutely. "And I'm praying Margaret, whom I've never met, can help us. I believe you know her reputation in the area we're talking about."

"Yes."

"Right. Daybreak is coming. Martin, I assume your BMW has a navigation system, because the roads from here to Geneva are a bit tricky, at least the first fifty miles, especially in this weather. But you need to hightail it to the airport and get back here yesterday."

Edouard sank back into a large cushioned chair, embroidered with silk from Italy sometime in the 16th century, frayed and probably ridden with worms.

"Book?" Martin inquired. "What book?"

CHAPTER 39

Father Leopold Bruno entered his church for matins, praying alone before a 17th century statue of the crucifixion and a large fresco of *The Agony in the Garden,* by a disciple of Bellini. There was Christ praying at Gethsemane beneath a full moon, three disciples silhouetted nearby, amid stark mountains and rocks blanched to the intensity of white marble by the lunar light. A wilderness scene of perdurable lament, cast off into the dark south-facing wall. Few visitors to the church ever stopped to look at it.

Bruno had been up all night. When not speaking by phone to his niece or to Jean-Baptiste Simon, he had been searching through the musty archives deep beneath the nave. Something had clicked in his mind.

Rummaging through dozens of old documents attesting to loyalties, oaths, consecrations, and bequests, he searched for one file he had remembered hearing about. It had only flashed through his mind an hour or so earlier, like some terrible revelation.

"You've never heard about it," the Father before him had uttered on his deathbed many years before, with a smile that was not meant to comfort or disturb. "I have told no one, until this moment."

"What, Father?" the then young Bruno had inquired gently.

"There is a letter, dated 1766, in that wretched dungeon of ours. Locked in a box. Someday, when you are my age, have a look at it."

The priest had extended his hand. Bruno took it in his own, only to discover a tiny gift, the first time he had ever seen one, the Medal of Saint Benedict, on a lighter-than-air silver chain.

During the few seconds Bruno had spent studying the Latin on the medal, his predecessor had lapsed into a morphine-induced coma, and he was dead by the following morning. Smiling. Blissed out. Colon cancer had been the diagnosis. His last words had been that strange incitement to visit a wretched dungeon, his bemused confession.

It was the kind of drama one does not expect. And Father Bruno *had* forgotten, until this night, clasping the medal to his chest on the thin sliver chain he had always worn since that day.

How could I have been so eager to explain it? His mind ricocheted with a horrible regret. He had been to a conference of priests in Mexico City a month before and had returned to Antwerp full of uncertainty. His own Benedictine vows, the spate of murders throughout South America involving, somehow incredibly, Saint Benedict, and then the call from his niece about the gruesome murder right here in his own city.

He had not stopped to think it through, so full of himself, his grasp of Latin, of history, of literature. And, he admitted to himself, he wanted to impress a niece from whom he had been estranged for years. More precisely, he had been estranged from Julia Deblock's mother, his one sibling, Dora, who always believed her younger brother Leopold would be a great writer or philosopher. Not a slave to dogma, as she thought of it from the moment Leopold had dropped out of university and entered a monastery near Ghent. And then he had risen in the ranks until he commanded his own church in Antwerp.

They had hardly spoken in years.

How clever he'd been, for all of twenty-four hours or less, giving out clues like chocolate kisses.

Only to discover that he may well have betrayed his entire Order, or worse.

He crept with a flashlight through the dank bowels of his church where no administrator had bothered coming for years. It was a cavernous wild, a dungeon just as the late Father had described, bolted shut, containing row upon row of skulls and documents, dating back four centuries, that pertained to every previous congregation, donor, absolution, conversion, birth, and death. Rarely had Father Bruno been asked about its contents, and only once in his tenure had a descendant requested a certain certificate of minor importance.

The first long tier contained file cabinets, filthy glass cabinets stacked with loose bindings, stapled wads of receipts in moldy folders, smothered in dust, amid cobwebs littered with stricken flies. *One of these days, somebody has to get in here and clean it up,* he thought, frustrated by the disarray.

Two rats scurried into the darkness.

Some bones, they looked like chicken, moldered in the open. *Disgusting,* he thought. On to the next tier and the next. Heaps of administrative books filled with nothing more than bookkeepers' records, dating to the beginnings of the church in the Renaissance.

And there it was, sitting on a table, overwhelmed by other paraphernalia and chaos. A rusted metal box.

He found pliers and attacked the corroded antique lock. It snapped with little effort. A blank, plain envelope. He used a knife to carefully slice open the top portion, preserving the seal, a magnificent oval of carnelian wax that had withstood the centuries. Stamped upon it was a round shield, all of a quarter inch in diameter, and surrounding it, an eagle with two distinctive heads, their wings ready to set sail. In their talons, two royal scepters, two swords.

Toison d'Or . . . the Golden Fleece. A knight with a shield in the form of a unicorn . . .

And there was a letter, in dark blue ink, written in French:

> *Cher Père,*
> *Tous les animaux naissent librement,*
> *pourtant vivent partout asservis.*
> *Excepté ici, au centre du monde.*
> *Je vous suis endetté.*
> J. J. Rousseau Dijon, 1766

Au centre du monde. . . . Now he remembered.

Days in his cell meditating, studying, preparing for the priesthood. And always the tantalizing if unspoken possibility, a shared belief among the wretched, naively hopeful novitiates, that paradise existed, not just for those who were blessed in the next life but here, now, in this world. Rousseau had gotten it right in his Social Contract and, the year before that, in a single confessional letter unknown to posterity. Not just man, but all the other animals, born free, were everywhere in chains. His fellow Benedictines had acted upon that grim reaper pervading the world ever since the Fall, had taken steps to protect all that was original and pure, at the very center of goodness, or so went the rumor. . . . A place somewhere in eastern France. . . . Rousseau had evidently been there.

And just two hours before, he, Father Bruno, had surrendered the location to Inspector Simon, like an absolute fool.

"Dear Lord!" Father Bruno murmured in panic, staring at the Christ figure.

"What have I done!"

CHAPTER 40

Mans was racing to catch up with the suspect fleet of vehicles when his Renault spun out on a mud-drenched soft shoulder. The lightweight vehicle stuttered, then flipped, as it sideswiped a parked dumpster and, traveling thirty miles per hour, smashed into an oak tree.

A silence, fused with steam, and the heavy downpour that probably protected them from any resulting fire or explosion greeted the wreck, out of which both men crept away.

"I'm sorry," Mans uttered rather pathetically.

"You OK?"

Both men had sustained minor bruises. The old vehicle was not equipped with air bags, but their seat belts undoubtedly saved them.

Simon called Le Bon about their situation. Le Bon had already obtained information pertaining to the monastery and had alerted the nearest French police station to dispatch backup. Many gendarmes in the area were still mopping up the scene of Jimmy Serko's recovered vehicle and body. But Le Bon had managed to drum up a few others, and they would be traveling, necessarily, the very road on which Simon and Mans had just taken their spill.

"Here's the lieutenant's cell phone number. I'm looking at the map now. They should be minutes away."

Le Bon wasn't wrong. No sooner had Simon proceeded to dial than two police vehicles, their sirens blazing, could be heard coming up the road from the east. Simon grabbed hold of a flashlight from inside the remains of Mans' vehicle and stood at the side of the foggy highway.

Two police cars raced by, nearly missing the scene of the accident.

Both vehicles swerved, then crept in reverse toward the two rather embarrassed survivors.

~~~

Max and Edouard tried unequally to keep pace with Lance, who moved rapidly up the winding slope along the inside of the wall, all three men loaded down with weapons. Lance knew they had very little time to reach the particular set of pitfall traps, dug during centuries past and each large enough to bag a person, if they wanted to gain and maintain an uphill advantage and be able to look down and see the interlopers.

Edouard, more accustomed in the last few years to a desk job and official functions, was least able to keep up. "Wait," he cried out, gasping for air. His ribcage smarted with the speed and anxiety of their rapid progress.

Max, on the other hand, was fast, and possibly even more studied in his ability than Lance. Max seemed back in his true environment, South America, where he had once survived a face-off against would-be assassins in a jungle. Max had killed quite a few assailants in his day.

Twenty minutes up the mountain, they achieved an overlook. Lance studied the thousands of acres before them with high-powered binoculars. The fog and rain gave no purchase on a view.

"This is bad," both Max and Edouard heard him say, just as several animals moved somewhere nearby. They could hear large branches breaking out in the darkness, and creatures nervously trotting through the underbrush and then the sound of an entire herd running.

"Les sangliers," Lance said. Wild boar. "Possibly red deer and swamp buffalo with them. They like to hang out together."

Their sudden agitation told Lance what his eyes could not yet detect: the boar had sensed something. Now their heavy grunting confirmed it.

All three men checked their weapons and proceeded toward the inside of the long, sinuous array of traps.

Inside the chateau, James had retrieved a precious box from a vault hidden in the rear of a clothes closet in a seemingly closed-off portion of the house.

Now he returned to the library, sat down beside Martin, and opened the box.

"That's the book?"

"Not exactly." He withdrew the thin manuscript, crisply bound in 16th century cobalt morocco, with oval garlands of embossed gold and precious jewels embedded throughout the gilded covers and spine.

Martin opened the book, aware of the fragility of all old manuscripts, particularly their spines, but especially so given the apparent importance of this one.

The book was only a few pages in length.

"But it's just signatures."

"Yes. A kind of legend."

"And no dates. What is it?" Martin could not make out a single name at first.

"Our guest register, or what I would prefer to think of as a primer, if you will, beginning in the 12th century. It's been rebound, although not from overuse. Too much moisture, I'm afraid."

"I can't make them out. Who are they?" Martin asked.

"See that, an F? Yes?" James pointed.

Martin examined it. "That would be an R?"

His uncle nodded.

"Francis?"

"There, very good."

"A French king?"

"No. Saint Francis."

"You're joking?"

"And this one, Jan van Eyck, and there, his brother Hubert."

Martin glanced at the row upon row of inscriptions, dozens and dozens of names. Scanning down, he could make out a few of the signatures: Shelley, Beethoven.

"Beethoven?"

"Yes." James could now see the expansion of consciousness overwhelming his nephew.

"In no particular order?" Martin asked.

"No. We believe there are reasons for that. Knowing your wife's reputation as a scholar, she should have no difficulty recognizing most if not all of the names. Here. Hold it tenderly. There is no copy. Show it to Margaret. She'll have time to examine it on your drive back."

Martin looked at his watch, just coming on seven A.M. He stood up.

"Actually, the name Margaret needs to consider, in addition to Engelbert of Nassau, is this one."

James pointed to one particular signature amid many on the first page, "Lodewijk van Gruuthuse of Bruges. He was one of ours."

"Meaning?"

"A knight of the Golden Fleece. He owned a huge library. Which today is a small treasure house of tapestries, paintings, and books."

"You said *primer*. Primer for what?" Martin enquired.

"These visitors didn't just sign their names and leave. The real treasure is something else."

"Go on?"

"A second manuscript, the substance, not the signatures. And, I daresay, far more valuable. That's where the billion dollars has to come from, I'm afraid."

"Paintings? Music?" Martin was addled, calculating, trying to get it right, and James was in an obvious hurry.

"Most of the visitors contributed something, a painting usually, but also the odd written or musical refrain, each one executed while visiting the chateau and, in the case of Beethoven, perhaps Vivaldi as well, we believe, sometime afterward. There are no dates affixed in this book. I think everyone appreciated that they had had some kind of timeless experience, shall we say. My grandfather said it was approximately two hundred pages, 150 odd paintings or, rather, manuscript illustrations. Later, two entire scores are said to have been added to the manuscript: Beethoven's Ninth and Vivaldi's *Four Seasons*."

"You're really serious?"

"Actually, we have evidence to believe that Vivaldi's fame derives in part from his time spent here at the chateau. But that's only our theory. The same with Buffon, possibly Darwin, we're not sure. But we know of countless new species here, never before documented except in paintings, particularly those of Savery. Saint Francis wrote a prayer. Giotto, in turn, painted Saint Francis kneeling here at the chateau, near to the wall, speaking to a large flock of winged cows, the kind you see at Chartres in stone. We have two live ones here, and Swedish sea eagles long gone from Europe by Francis' time; one survived here. Each visitor was sworn to secrecy, knighted, made part of a family. These were not Masons or Knights Templar but something else entirely. A community of artists each of whom had seen something he would not otherwise have believed existed but for the truth of the chateau. An orchid that blooms in the night, once in a thousand years. Species thrive here side by side in a communion just as Isaiah had imagined it. Paradise paintings precisely modeled on the original, right here, in our backyard. Breughel was here briefly on his way back from Italy to Antwerp in the early 1600s. It's possible Rubens met him here. We don't know how long Hubert and his brother Jan Van Eyck stayed, but Savery spent many months."

"How do you know that if there are no dates in the guest registry?"

"Because of the number of paradise paintings he did based on the property. So many different views, animals, plants. Even the chateau itself is represented in a work that ended up hanging in a museum in Vienna. Most of the species profiled had long been deemed extinct. But more than the mysteries of nature, each visitor here had a religious experience, it may be assumed. Well, more than assumed, if you want my own personal opinion. From experience, I should add. Fra Angelico, for example . . . there, that's his signature. There are those who would argue he spent a month here. Whereas Rembrandt came for only two days, sketched furiously, and was gone."

"And you've seen this book? Held it in your hands?"

"I'm afraid not. My grandfather and his predecessors knew it intimately, however, and he's the one who told both your father and me about it. We grew up hearing of various intrigues, legends, even tales of how the book had been stolen not once, not twice, but many times. There are those who would kill for it, Martin. Napoleon possibly tried. And the Nazis scoured every museum in Europe looking for it. The book is not just a book, as you surely can now appreciate. It is the future."

"The future? What do you mean?"

"Your great-grandfather told us that it was, in essence, the final work of the most important trilogy ever written."

Martin tried but could not grasp the meaning.

"There was the Old Testament, the New Testament, but not, until the last entry in this book, was there a Future Testament. And those privileged to have taken part in this remarkable, and I dare say timeless, piece of habitat were themselves prophets, their collective efforts the same kind of cumulative wisdom that we attribute, for example, to the authorship of Ecclesiastes, a work I personally believe as having been achieved over time."

The words set in quite heavily. A *future* testament? Martin felt sick, laden with horrible excitement.

"But James, surely . . . I mean, we can't *sell* such a book?"

"Not at auction. No open market. That's not even a consideration. No. Frankly, the world is not ready for such a book. I never intended any such thing. Rather, a discrete, trustworthy exchange. Where we are assured of its safekeeping. We have one or two museum directors in the Order. But they do not have the resources to acquire it. Few museums do. We've even thought of some consortium purchasing it—all close family friends. But there is not enough money, nor are we eager to draw attention to our plight. If I sound a little desperate, nephew, I think you can now understand."

"You're adding more and more contingencies. Finding a buyer will be difficult enough. Trusting him? You must be joking?"

"You've got to get going," James said. He was not prepared to have this conversation, not yet. There were other stipulations, complications, problems of ethics, and problems of a more practical sort. "You don't want to keep Margaret waiting, and we have a lot of work to do."

"So where's the book?"

And his heart began to sink when he caught the sad frown on James' face. "That's the problem. You see, your great-great-grandfather turned the book over to a relative at the palace I referred to, sometime in the middle of the French Revolution. I don't know any of the details except to say our ancestors clearly knew that such political tumult posed the first significant threat in centuries to the precious work. Apparently the book had been breached—written about. A certain visitor could not keep a secret—we never knew who it was, but something had to be done to hide the manuscript. We are told it was taken by the monks at Cluny, good friends of the family. But monks are not very good at hiding books. They read too much. However the security measures were conceived and the integrity of the guest list and the manuscript itself preserved, it was felt that the book would be safer in a palace, protected by obscurity, and one or two locks and keys. As it turned out, that assumption was dead-on. Cluny was laid waste to, as you probably know, at the end of the Revolution."

"I hadn't heard, to be quite frank. But moving on, what about this palace in Bruges you mentioned?"

"Yes. Well, actually, as of the 20th century, that palace is a museum. It's on the tourist circuit."

"And you've been in contact with the Oliviers still living there, who are in possession of the manuscript?"

"No."

"Right. But there *are* Oliviers living there? And you're *sure* they will want to give us back this priceless book?"

"No. There are no other Oliviers. And I have no idea how we're going to pull this off."

"This is looking better and better."

Martin sat back down on the couch.

"Tell me you at least know where within the palace, this modern-day museum, the book is hidden."

James was not quick to volunteer any such certitude, which took yet more wind out of Martin's already flopping sail.

"Your great-grandfather said it was probably sequestered in a vault at the Gruuthuse, 220-odd years ago. I am betting that it is still there."

"You said, *probably*?" And he repeated it with near anger, "*Probably*? You mean you don't know if it's even *at* the museum?"

"There is a chance it was stolen before it could be safely brought to the Gruuthuse. How am I supposed to know? There was never any written confirmation, if that's what you mean. You can appreciate that even by the late 18th century, the manuscript had the power and prestige of the ninth wonder of the world in the palm of one's hand. Much like the grail."

"Uh-huh. In a vault?"

"Or a box. Or perhaps more deceptively simple yet, in the vast library. Just another book. Obvious, but totally obscured."

"Somewhere in a museum? The ninth wonder of the world in an obvious box. James, are you daft? Surely my father never went along with any of this?"

"Your father spent months at a time lying out there in the grass, gazing at dodos. That's all he cared about."

"So you're saying he didn't care one way or the other?"

"Precisely. I think he figured it was in safe hands, somebody's hands, and didn't really want to get involved. He was a poet, a scientist, and, politically speaking, a man without a country."

"Alright. Let me just understand this. It's maybe in a box, possibly an obvious box, at some museum in Bruges. Assuming it's that simple."

"Actually, it's not that simple."

Martin smiled. "Of course not."

"It was relocated once, possibly twice, to England, we are told, via Vienna, maybe Elba, and, well, merely theory mind you, Saint Petersburg."

"But it was returned to Belgium?"

James looked away, unsure, feeling rather ill and dismayed. He had had too many contingencies to rely upon in this matter. And it was all beginning to cave in around him. Not least, the fear of assassins coming for him.

He glanced at a suit of armor in a corner, scarcely noticeable between two dark armoires. The steel overalls of the grandmaster himself, Emperor Charles VI, after he had set up the Toison d'Or in Vienna in 1713, after years of turbulent, forgettable history—a battleground claiming members of the House of Habsburg, the Spanish, the Dutch, the French. Twenty-four knights originally, before they grew in number to thirty, and their sovereign, the grandmaster. Whether in Burgundy with its cabal of descendants honoring the Golden Fleece or in Savoy where the Annunziata held sway, the fealty and secrecy were the same—houses of loyalty to an ideal.

But the chateau and all that had happened to make it so were of a different realm entirely. Biology had changed everything—history, nation states, and the meaning of modernity.

There was no warrior's skeleton beneath all that heavy chain mail, the kind visible as early as the depictions of Beowulf or in the Bayeux Tapestry. A helmet, hinged, borne by a gorget, chin guarded, with a slit for an ocularium. And in his hand, protected by steel gloves, a sword not typical of the region but of Scotland. Known as a claidheamh-mor, heavy enough to require two strong wrists, well-toned muscle, experience in the field, capable of killing anything. James would never be able to lift it.

Which is when he remembered the shotgun in the armoire to the right. *Or was it the left?* The weapon should be loaded. Lance made certain of such precautions.

"What is this?" Martin had noticed a seemingly impenetrable mishmash after all the signatures—a jumble of curious notations, meaningless, in several languages, including Greek and Latin, combining various shorthands with numbers, unfamiliar words, seals and crescents bearing the family titles of some ancient genealogies.

"Clues," James sighed resignedly. "Encoded messages."

"To what? Or whom?"

"Possibly to nothing. Personally, I suspect they were invented to throw any thieves off track. Understand that the Revolution threw everything off balance. The whole world was up for grabs, one might assume. The poet Wordsworth said somewhere that the French Revolution was a heaven. But only for a few days. Then the Reign of Terror began. Your ancestors dealt with an emergency in the only way they knew how. Rather clumsily, I think. But we have the benefit of hindsight. Unfortunately, they did not leave any precise road map for their own descendants."

"Well, that at least adds some uncertainty, doesn't it? Why make it too easy?"

"But then again, given that the first line is French, you'll notice, *Plus est en Vous.*"

"There is more in you?"

"Correct. That was a motto belonging to Lodewijk van Gruuthuse. I'm not sure what to make of it. I pray it is no red herring. Or that my great-grand-father was not somehow mistaken or fooled. Gruuthuse is our only logical hope. And the primer and key are certainly proof of the Olivier patrimony, if any such be needed."

"So what do we do, James? I'm not entirely optimistic, I'm sorry to say."

"Go pick up your wife."

"What about the intruders?"

"Lance has taken every precaution."

Martin could easily sense the fragility in James' assertiveness. He might be in terrific shape, physically, from all his days spent doing natural history work out in the "garden," but he was, nonetheless, an old man.

"That's not entirely reassuring."

"There is a grid of deep pits up there. Spikes inside. No animal has ever fall-en in because Lance keeps the perimeters well marked, with various scents, urine of muskrat, mostly. It has universal characteristics. Who would have known?" He let sail a rather rakish grin. "And Lance has stashed enough fire power to take out a whole battalion if need be. And there are others to help him."

"Who would that be?"

"Some huge ungulates and carnivores."

"Of course."

James looked away, almost apologetically. He realized how bizarre it all must sound to his nephew.

Martin didn't know what else to do but accede to the fantastical pos-sibility that James was not entirely insane. "Alright. I should be back here by noon. And then we'll all go to Bruges together, avoiding Paris."

James went to the wall of books, withdrew one of them from among hundreds—Martin could not actually see *which* one, he wasn't particularly interested at this point—and behind it was something taped. James pulled off the tape and revealed a small nondescript key, an old one for sure—small, rusted from lack of use.

"We have this."

"Very good. Explain?"

"From generation to generation, our family has owned it. I believe it must go with the primer. It's the master key."

"Assuming it *is* the key, and there is a friend of the Olivier family still in place at this institution, then it should be simple, right?"

"I'm hoping for as much."

"And certainly there is a known list of Knights of the Golden Fleece, with our family history intertwined, that would include this museum?"

"Yes."

"Then pick up the phone, tell them we're coming to retrieve what is rightfully ours."

"Not a good idea, Martin. Who knows what power plays may be lurking or what bozo might now be in charge, ignorant of or indifferent to history? Your father was killed for that book."

"For the book or by poachers, which is what you said?"

"I don't know, to be quite honest."

"I see."

"I think a surprise visit has its advantages, don't you?"

"I suppose so."

"Good, and we best bring a photograph of the chateau. Here." He opened a drawer and handed Martin a small black-and-white image, probably taken decades before. "And your ID," James thought to add, silly though it sounded. "And I'll have mine, not that I've needed it in decades."

Martin was boggled by the layers of uncertainty. He was having difficulty grasping any logical game plan with which to combat the absolute strangeness of this quest he now found himself destined to play out, when just two days before he was not the least focused on France, assassins, history, endangered species, a dead father, and, allegedly, the greatest manuscript in history, which just happened to belong to him.

"Worst-case scenario, this picture of your great-great-grandfather with his signature across it . . . " he withdrew the image from his own wallet and gave it to Martin, "should provide the added proof we Oliviers are who we say we are." James then handed the antique key to Martin for safekeeping.

And then, as an afterthought, James added, "If it is the master key, at least it'll open the front door to the palace. That's a first step."

CHAPTER 41

Margaret was waiting curbside. Martin was only twenty minutes late. If not for the navigational system, he'd have missed Switzerland altogether.

"Are you alright?" she asked, placing her briefcase and laptop in the back.

"I've not slept since I saw you."

"I got a few hours. Let me drive."

"You need to study this."

Martin placed the "guest register" in Margaret's lap as he drove away from the busy airport, swaddled in fair and summery sunshine, a colossal relief.

"What is it?"

"Just open it."

She stared at the first page, then uttered, "No way . . . ." Martin caught his wife's eyes widening.

The two police cars that rescued Simon and Mans had originated in Nevers, where a leading school for car racing had given the two cops at the respective wheels a particular flair for the death zone, as Simon now thought of it. Simon and Mans rode with the policeman in the lead. His partner followed in the second vehicle.

"One hundred sixty is too fast for this road," Simon uttered in a nervous dialect that revealed he was of Burgundian stock. Unfortunately, the policeman at the wheel was from Normandy and hadn't a clue what Simon had just said.

"Let me remind you, we crashed because there is ice on the road, comprenez-vous?"

The gendarme slowed down, noticeably irritated. Sunrise had broken through the storm, and the narrow winding highway glistened in the bright light.

A postal truck passed them in the opposite direction. It took Simon a minute to register something.

"Turn around! Hurry!"

Mans figured it out as well. "That's the second vehicle from the dock. The postal truck with a dent!"

"I don't want to alert them," Simon exhorted.

Both police vehicles came to a stop. The drivers were out of their depths, not having a clue what the hell was going on. "What do you propose?" Mans said, both he and Simon visibly on the cusp of what they knew to be the answer.

"Where are we, exactly?" he asked the gendarme behind the wheel.

The cop pinpointed their whereabouts precisely on a map that offered far more detail of the Bourgogne than Simon's. Now Simon could put Fabbi's coordinates, and the information provided by Father Bruno, in far better perspective. There was the wilderness and there the location of Serko's wreck. And there the remains of some large compound. It all came together.

"We need serious backup. This is it. You catch up with the SUVs. I think I have a good idea where that postal truck is headed. What is that?" he asked the gendarme, pointing to the faint outline of structures on the map. The map legend made no reference to it.

The gendarme shook his head. "A farm, maybe."

"Not a monastery or the ruins of one?"

"Je ne sais pas."

Simon asked the gendarme to join his colleague with Mans in the other vehicle while he pursued the postal truck.

But first he called Le Bon and explained what was happening.

"Basically, we need everything they've got."

∿

Martin's forehead ached with a blinding migraine. He knew that his uncle was at great risk. That the Oliviers had been charged with protecting the most important secret in . . . his mind failed to find the proper superlatives . . . or greatest hoax . . . but Margaret began to spell it out as they approached the verdant, storm-wracked Mâcon, the southern tip of Burgundy.

"Assuming this document is authentic . . ." Margaret said.

Martin, forgetting his earlier doubts, took the innuendo personally and exclaimed, "But of course it's authentic." He'd *seen* a dodo, after all, a ten-foot-tall mastodon. Not to mention a lovely little Memlinc.

"The point is, *this* collection of signatures, in itself, has no comparable . . . I mean, not even the signatories to the Declaration of Independence, the Magna Carta . . . ." She was fumbling for analogies. "It's priceless."

"Who do you recognize?"

"Nearly all of them. The greatest lineup in Renaissance history: Petrus Christus. Gerard David. Jan van Eyck. Rogier van der Weyden. Hans Memlinc. Rembrandt. Dieric Bouts. Michelangelo, for starters."

"Michelangelo?"

"Yes. Oh, and so many more. Martin, this is the most precious document in history. Again, assuming it's real. But how could it be? And more important, what is it?"

"What do you mean?"

"I mean, why did they sign it? There's something missing, something it must refer to." She held the book to the light as they traveled fast on the main freeway leading northwest from Geneva. "Why are Saint Francis and Fra Angelico, Giotto, Roelandt Savery and Jan Brueghel the Elder, Jean-Jacques Rousseau, Claude Lorraine, and the writer, Bernardin de Saint Pierre, all signatories to the same four-page manuscript? It makes no logical sense."

She looked at her husband and sensed at once that he was withholding something. She knew that look.

"Martin? What aren't you telling me?"

CHAPTER 42

The net was shot at 3,200 feet per second, trapping six gorgeously green parrots all at once where they perched in an ancient grove, hunkered down in the cold sunrise. Their miniature flock reacted too late to the powerful gunshot.

"Gotchya!" the heavy-breathing man grunted.

With deft and brutal motions, he hauled in the first of many trophies to come: *Conuropsis carolinensis*, the most recent parrot to have gone extinct in North America, otherwise known as the Carolina parakeet. The bird used to be seen from Mississippi to New York, but by February of 1918, it was gone forever, just like Martha, the last passenger pigeon (both occupants of the Cincinnati Zoo), or so believed most ornithologists.

Berndt and Gouge de Bar both watched attentively as huge flocks and herds responded to the gunshot, fleeing in all directions, while a half-dozen men sought out their specific target species.

Within minutes, they had destroyed a new section of wall, not with dynamite but lasers, burning clean through with little acoustic disturbance. A man merely stooped to move through the hole. A large mammal would not manage it so easily, certainly not one in a panic.

"Go in, in measured paces. Keep the man in front in sight," Berndt said, reiterating their strategized relay method for removing each quarry from the mountain.

Their vehicles were sequestered in forest not a quarter mile from their striking position. No trail led to this hub of activity, but Lance, Max, and Edouard could hear the commotion from where they stood, uphill some thousand feet from the incoming army of poachers and the flight of wild creatures that moved before them.

Lance motioned silently. He heard what to his ears was the unmistakable gamboling of one of the domain's most venerable, least understood residents. It was not exactly *what* he heard, but the stunning, sudden absence of any sound whatsoever accompanying what had to be the stalking behavior of the seven sabertooth cats whose forebears had lived in these forests for a million years or more.

"There!" he whispered, restraining any temptation in himself, or the two men by his side, to raise their firearms.

"They will not attack unprovoked," he added. This was not the first time he'd seen the giant felines. Although James had rarely traversed these slopes, preferring instead to spend the majority of his time near to the chateau, Lance and occasionally Edward had laid the gridwork and surveillance that were intended to protect the entire estate. Lance had frequently come in contact with beasts of every dimension and nuance, imbibing the sacred code of reciprocity.

Another series of gunshots ricocheted across the maze of valleys, prompting the escapist flight of tens of hundreds of creatures, some of whom were snared and dragged shrieking to their certain doom. Creatures with an uncanny resemblance to such beasts of former glory as the *Archaeopteryx*, saola, auroch, saiga, moa, quagga, leaf deer, Hyacinth and Spix's macaws, a lowland gorilla, an Eskimo curlew (last seen in 1923), a creature without a name . . .

Lance saw the men working their prey, hauling in one after another. He aimed. Max, too, aimed.

"Not yet," Lance said. The men were closing in.

"What are we waiting for?" Max asked, positively astonished by what he was seeing.

"Not yet . . . "

Suddenly a metal arrow ripped through the throat of Edouard, who stood beside them. Before Max could react to the horror unleashed, Lance shot the culprit in the face, but more men were upon them and more animals in their wake.

Down below, along a highway engulfed in rising fog and increasing barometric pressure, the same chaos could be heard by Mans and the two gendarmes from Nevers. They had spotted the SUVs. Now they had to decide whether to go into the forest, or wait for backup.

ᔕ

Father Bruno had been up for hours, pacing, thinking, praying to his God, and rifling through the memoranda book of the Secret Brotherhood attached to his church. They were Benedictines from an ancient order, the original one, with hidden vaults at Le Thoronet, Silvacane, Clairmont, and Fontenay, under the very remains of Cluny itself. And most sacred and vouchsafed of all . . . in a hidden garden of antiquity with four rivers and a low-lying mountain, invisible pillars of alabaster defending its ramparts, defying the world, and within, a tree in whose braided bark and knotted telemetry was all the harbinger one needed here in this life. Now he felt destiny closing in and thought that there was only one way to shed the burden engulfing him.

From his bedroom in the steeple wall of the priory adjoining the church, he uttered the prayer of Prime and placed a phone call to his niece's answering machine, spoke softly, briefly, then hung up.

Forgive me Father, he pleaded.

He stared at the bottle of pills for what seemed an eternity. A plastic bottle of mountain spring water. Three pillows. An escape from all he imagined he had done.

But just as he reached for the easy solution, his mind froze on the fact that there was nothing easy about it. No solution at all, rather, eternal damnation. He could not escape the truth, not in the faith to which he was sworn.

Now real panic swept over him. He had already placed the call to his niece. It was imperative that he call her back, leave a second message, apologize for what he had said.

What did I say? In his confusion, he couldn't exactly remember. Only that he was going to kill himself. That the chateau stood at the entrance to eternal life, held the secret for which so many thousands, tens of thousands of good Christians had martyred themselves. Were those deaths, the Crusades, the mendicants giving up everything any different than his own ultimate sacrifice this night?

He heard the loud gutteral call of a crow just outside his window. *A crow!*

He opened the drapery of his bedroom window, looking out toward the church courtyard below just as a large bird flew off. There on the window's ledge was a slice of bread. He gazed in horror at it and mumbled a prayer to Saint Benedict.

But no rationalization offered him the peace he needed to set things right. He closed the window, went to the side of his bed, picked up the phone, and dialed the number of an old and trusted colleague.

CHAPTER 43

As Martin sped northwest of Geneva, past the outskirts of Bourg, Margaret continued to pore over the three-and-a-half pages of signatures, trying to divine some connection, but it was proving a task beyond even her considerable historic, cultural, and artistic expertise. What were Ulisse Aldrovandi, Engelbert of Nassau, Willem Vrelant, Catherine of Cleves, and the famed naturalist Linnaeus all doing in the same group? She certainly recognized the name of Sir Thomas Browne, but who were Thomas de Cantimpré, Konrad van Megenburg, William Turner, John Ray, Christopher Merret, Francis Willoughby, and someone named Skippon? She had absolutely no idea. Painting was not the common thread, as Catherine was no painter, but a patroness. Ulisee painted fantastic animals, hybrid monsters, some real, some invented. None of them would have made the grade, according to Linnaeus. And Engelbert of Nassau, one of the greatest bibliophiles of the Renaissance. The combined mystery was no more than a monster of possible extrapolations that lay on three meager pieces of paper in her hands.

But the connectivity, or lack thereof, only got worse. She read aloud to her husband: Antonio Vivaldi, Beethoven, Buffon, the great French naturalist, *Le Remède de Fortune*—not exactly a signature, but a description, and she knew of it—the anonymous painter claimed to have discovered "naturalistic landscape" under the reign of Charles V. What's more, there was the Boucicault Master, sometimes associated with one Jacques Coene, whose own renowned *Hours*, with its remarkable requiem mass, would travel from one chateau or political dynasty to another until finally landing in Paris, in the hands of Madame Jacquemart-Andre of the famed museum by the same name.

Boucicault ... Margaret tried to wrap her mind around it, having consulted on a purchase for the Getty of one of the great images of all times by Boucicault, *Adam and Eve in the Garden of Eden,* part of a huge manuscript of heartbreakingly beautiful detail work, unlike before and since. Value: tens of millions of dollars in today's market.

As if that weren't enough, there was Étienne Chevalier, the royal treasurer of Charles VII, another great collector of *Horae,* Egerton, René of Anjou, Master of the Delft Grisailles, and Bezborodko, a Book of Hours designation she had seen with her own eyes at the Amsterdam Bibliotheca Philosophica Hermetica. The Master of Guillebert de Mets, a signature that she remembered from the so-called Gold Scrolls group from the Walters, in Baltimore. She knew Pierre Gourdelle, whose aquarelles of various birds were executed between 1550 and 1560. And there was Isaac Van Oosten, a 17th century Flemish painter of birds.

One Louis Jean Pierre Vieillot she'd never heard of. And others: Johannes Laurentzen, Hippolyte Salviani, Christophorus Gottwald, de Réaumur, Erik Pontoppidan, Dru Drury, Regenfuss, Carl von Meidinger—all names unfamiliar to her.

But suddenly her eyes seized on a no-brainer—leaping right off the page, Robinet d'Estampes, treasurer to the Duc Jean de Berry, a member of the House of Bavaria and Holland, and the greatest patron of manuscript illuminations ever. Followed in no particular order by Konrad von Gesner, the great 16th century Swiss botanist, glaciologist, and, by some estimates, the founder of modern zoology, and next to him, Titian, whose signature she recognized instantly: Vecellio, for Tiziano Vecelli, or Vecellio. Palma Vecchio was there. And Philip II. Velásquez, Giorgione and Sir Thomas More. There were no dates. But she knew her history.

A *Who's Who* of ... of what, she had no idea. Except there was one common denominator that did strike her as interesting—Nature. Every one of the artists she recognized had created a masterpiece after the garden theme. Most of them were Utopians, like More, or the Velvet Brueghel the Elder, during the long aftermath of his trip to Italy in the late 1500s. Paradise scenes like *The Entry of the Animals into Noah's Ark*, which Margaret had seen a year before at the Getty Museum in Los Angeles, and she had read the accompanying commentary by Adrianne Faber Kolb in her book for the exhibition. Kolb analyzed the abundant species present in the various menageries collected by the Burgundian royals in Ghent, Brussels, and Antwerp, beginning with the audacious collecting of Philip the Good sometime after 1446, according to Kolb, which included lion and lynx, wolf and ibex.

Margaret's mind leaped to the most gorgeous illuminations in the history of the art form: the Masters (with a capital "M") of obscure lineage. Those who were called Masters were done so because their true identities remained uncertain. Others had putative ID's, the greatest of all before her: a signature that read *Bening*. The father and/or son, purported painter(s) for the richest woman in history, Mary of Burgundy.

"Mary of Burgundy," Margaret whispered out loud, her finger lightly touching the signature. "Can it be?"

Martin glanced over at his wife. "Yes. James says the Oliviers are her direct descendants. I saw her picture on the wall of the chateau." He was not as overwhelmed as Margaret appeared to be.

Chateau? Her picture? The concept did not register, initially, nor did Margaret react. But then the notion began to rise in her throat. Like a winning lottery number, but one that was no longer valid. Like worthless Confederate money, too many centuries had passed for there to be meaning or substance to vague clamors of a family tie.

"Martin, tell me exactly what is going on. And what is this?" She had come to the messy ball of yarn, so to speak, at the conclusion of the list of signatures. Half words, letters, numbers, symbols printed in a kind of gothic woodblock that had blurred on the edges, like wet ink upon Japanese paper, leaving a linguistic Rubik's cube or four-color problem of unintelligibility. "This I don't understand."

"Clues from the 1780s or '90s," Martin said mysteriously. "Look for the name Gruuthuse. However it's pronounced. See it?"

"Yes. Gruuthuse." It was there, lodged in the middle of a stream of strange linguistic bombardments that had no breaks, one long continuous word but four times the length of that childhood *supercalifragalisticexpealidocious*.

"The house and the museum. I know one of their curators, Luis Adornes, old family from Genoa, in Bruges for centuries. I consulted on some fine painted Renaissance maps for them just two years ago, remember?"

Martin had forgotten, among all the illustrious clients from whom his wife had received wire transfers for just being her brilliant, ebullient self. He was thrilled that others appreciated her as much as he did.

Now he appreciated her even more.

His iPhone vibrated.

"Read it."

Margaret lifted the persistent little nag that had been snapped onto a holder in the BMW.

"It says: *straitbroogunfire*."

Martin wasn't hearing right. "Again?"

Margaret read it slowly.

There was an exit half a mile away. Martin took it, pulled the car over, and examined the small screen for himself. Now he understood. There could be little doubt.

CHAPTER 44

"Here's the deal." Martin began to explain how the primer—the three page book in his wife's hands—was, according to James, a mere appetizer for what, allegedly, awaited them in Bruges, or "broog" as James had indicated hurriedly, with his thick, gardener fingers, on the iPhone. Gunfire. Head straight for Bruges and the Gruuthuse.

Had the poachers gained access to the chateau? Should we go back anyway and try to help? But how? I'm no commando, and neither is Margaret. James seemed so urgent about the book. Perhaps the poachers were, in fact, after it? But that would mean the book was at the chateau, not in Belgium. His mind spun out possibilities as he headed northwest at 160 kilometers toward Bruges. He thought repeatedly to turn around and head straight back to James. But the message on his iPhone was loud and clear, and he kept his foot on the gas.

Margaret took in the bombshell with reserve. If what her husband had described or, more accurately, if what Uncle James had said were true—and by all indications, there was no doubting him—then the history of art was about to change forever. More important still, she had married into a family with ties beyond comprehension, in terms of royalty. And there was *something else,* a dangling modifier that suggested some kind of biblical significance to the chateau which Martin's father, Edward, and his brother James had managed to keep secret until now. Little wonder there were those who coveted the secrets and the wealth. And now, from the looks of it and all that Martin had conveyed, gang warfare had overtaken the splendid estate in the name of some sordid battle over who should possess some rare animals. It was that inane, Martin had said. But he also gave an alternative explanation, which Margaret herself had already figured out: This skirmish and the death of Martin's father were part of an ongoing mêlée, the most important struggle ever waged, whose stakes involved nothing less than ownership of the greatest assemblage of art of all time. And if what James had said was not merely symbolic but literal interpretation, possession of the very wellspring of life itself—the Garden of Eden.

Margaret's heart was pounding. On the practical side, she knew that Martin could fairly decipher a Memlinc (or Memling, as some preferred) if he saw one. And he knew his real estate. If the chateau was all that Martin said it was, there was no question as to its enormous value. There were no estates left in one piece of that size anywhere in France, to her knowledge. How it had escaped the eye of authorities was a puzzle, unless, of course, the "authorities" had within their ranks some higher power to whom they were all obedient. The president of France? The pope? The queen of Holland? It sounded altogether preposterous to her mind, but there was no doubting the power of the Renaissance Orders, and the Golden Fleece exerted a force upon the imagination altogether unique.

The Order's history was the most convoluted of any, and the primary players were none other than those very same patrons of the arts who had jump-started the Renaissance.

Mary, born February 13, 1457, died March 27, 1482. The one child of the Duke of Burgundy, Charles the Bold, and his beloved partner, Isabella of Bourbon, Mary had inherited the largest kingdom between Istanbul and London when her father died in battle, at Nancy. She was nineteen at the time and suddenly at the mercy of Louis XI, king of France, who took over her rightful duchy and strove to marry her off. She rebelled, secretly meeting with her allies in Holland, gaining strength, and taking for her husband the future emperor of Austria, Maximilian. By this gesture she set the stage for 235 years of contention between the French and the Habsburgs, and gave birth to two sons and a daughter who shared between them half of the western world. One of their offspring now appeared to be Martin's ancestor. But which one? And how was any of this going to win them back the book of incomparable value that Martin had described?

∿

James had only just finished preparing his weapon in the downstairs gallery room when the shadow moved across his peripheral vision.

"Put it down," Raoul said.

James stood steadfast, aiming his gun at the intruder.

"I know who you are."

"Then you also know I won't have the slightest hesitation."

"The animals are in the forest. They don't much frequent the indoors. I think you know that."

"Give me the manuscript."

James feigned to look around. They were in the library.

"I have no idea what you're talking about."

Raoul gazed upon his victim with the smile of a berserker, frustrated and amphetamized. But also confident.

"Where is it? You have one minute."

"You're mistaken. I have all the time in the world," as his finger pressed against the trigger.

∿

Jean-Baptiste Simon was less than a kilometer from the chateau when he noticed the fresh tracks of a vehicle that had departed from the long muddy road into the forest, along a narrow lane that was probably used for the removal of deadwood. He got out of his vehicle, took hold of his firearm, and followed the trail. Within minutes, he found the hidden vehicle, a postal truck. He approached with caution, prepared for a hidden sniper, kneeling, moving with stealth.

He reached the truck and, having lifted a rock, smashed the window of the passenger side. He thrust his weapon through the open hole, but no one was there to confront.

He swirled round, prepared for an assailant to fire from the rear, perhaps lunging out of the back. But only the distant cry of agitated birds, and a strange booming roar, met his precautionary antics, punctuated by the distant, unmistakable sound of gunfire, miles away, slanted and confused by the wind and the rain, and the maze of hills and valleys all around.

He searched the vehicle. In the glove compartment—a stun gun, lifesavers, and a notebook that he confiscated. No time to study it. In the rear of the vehicle—cages.

Then he saw the deep footprints leading through mud into the oak forest. Locking his own vehicle, he followed the trail, which went to a wall, from which he could see the sterling white edifice, knowing it at once to be a combining of architectural eras, the 12th century pigeon tower, obvious at a glance, and later additions, the last of them, it appeared from his orientation, to be 18th century.

Simon climbed the barrier, using antiquated gouges in the plaster for finger and toe holds, as well as bits and pieces of exposed iron filigree work. At the top, he used a tree limb to test the wire. It was, as he had suspected, dead. Not even the faintest hum.

From the top of what must have been nine or ten feet, he re-cosseted his weapon, then dangled, and leapt into the mud on the inside.

Simon now stood up in a clearing, raised his gun, and peered toward two subsequent gates, neither of which gave off any buzz, either. He continued following the footprints, surmounted two more gates, and found himself directly beneath the domicile when his cell phone vibrated.

"Yes?" he spoke in a near whisper.

"It's Le Bon," the voice could be heard, though entangled in a very bad connection, "Father Bruno has had a massive heart attack. He's in ER. Julia is with him."

"I'm sorry."

"Whether he will live, I don't know. But there's more to it."

"Wait a minute."

Simon was stunned, eyeing the mansion before him with scrupulous care. But the information hit him with not near the same level of astonishment as the huge bird that walked before him, with eyes that seemed to suggest he might make an attractive mate.

And then the line was engulfed in static.

CHAPTER 45

Bruno's left hand clung to the oval Medal of Saint Benedict around his neck. He lay in the emergency room at Antwerp's Saint Elisabeth Hospital unconscious. The heart attack had been near fatal, triggering subsequent mini-strokes. Bruno's deliberations at the end had left him paralyzed with guilt and fear.

Julia stood outside in the corridor of the intensive care unit speaking with Paul Le Bon and Fabritius Cadiz. There was nothing she could do for her uncle at this point. That would be in the hands of surgeons.

But she had no difficulty deconstructing her uncle's telephone calls up to the time of his near suicide and subsequent heart attack. Bruno had called Julia twelve minutes before eight A.M., leaving a message to warn her of a strange combination of events: the death of the oceans, the death of the forests, the end of the world. He told her to pray for his soul and for the souls of all Creation.

Minutes later he had called back, rambling on about *Paradise Lost*, and apologized for startling her. His faith had been challenged, he declared, and he had nearly lost his footing.

She did not know her uncle well enough to have registered this level of apocalyptic gloom, ever, in his demeanor, his sermons, or his writings. Indeed, he had never revealed so grim a side before.

Not two minutes after his second phone call to Julia, Father Bruno had telephoned a number that was traceable to nearby the monastery of Cluny, as could be easily determined from his cell phone in the sleeve of his cassock, found neatly hanging in a closet near to the floor where he had been found by a springer spaniel from next door. The dog's unrelenting barking had led the neighbors to his crumpled body.

Le Bon had dispatched the nearest police unit to that address, between rues d'Avril and du Merle. Nearby, the remains of the Arts et Métiers from the 1700s and an inscription to the famed painter Pierre Paul Prud'hon, commending the greatest concentration of chapels and architectural features on earth. There were nearly ten acres of cupolas, shining lamps, squares, refectories, libraries, one church after another to serve the four hundred monks that once had made Cluny the centre of learning for all of Christendom.

After the Revolution, much of the town had been sold off for its invaluable white stone. A road was built directly through the nave of the great church.

Eggs Benedict were still warm on a plate bearing the logo of a three-hundred-year-old ceramics factory nearby. A log still burned in the fireplace. But nothing indicated the occupant's evacuation of his quarters. No trace that led in or out of the house. No neighbor had seen or heard anything. And a Volvo remained parked in the garage, which belonged to the retiree, feted by witnesses in the village as a hero, a freedom fighter during World War II who had managed to lead the Nazis astray, thus saving the entire community, and one who had been a solemn, inward man in the intervening half century.

But where was he? And why had Bruno called the elderly former monk right after delivering his doomsday scenario to his niece, which Julia had played back for Le Bon? Both Deblock and the inspector realized that Bruno was on to something. But what?

"He had high blood pressure. Maybe he intuited the end and wanted to say good-bye," Deblock opined. She knew that her uncle had been a student at Cluny. Their age differences suggested tutelage. Perhaps Bruno had studied under Father Bladelin.

"Studied what?" Le Bon asked, not that it would shed any light on the goings-on necessarily. "Anyway, I don't buy that. He called him after his second call to you. He was not intending to bid farewell."

"Look!" One of the officers found what appeared to be a trap door in the floor at the back of the kitchen. They managed to pry it open with a crowbar from the trunk of the Volvo and discovered stairs leading down into the darkness and a tunnel with a dirt floor heading away with no sign as to its destination, depth, or length. Jews, many Catholics, and resistance fighters had used it, according to the neighbor.

And so had Bladelin, for there were his footprints indicating agile movement for a ninety-eight-year-old, beneath the great clocher and past the deep caves under the Abbey Church of Jean de Bourbon, chapels of Saint Martial and Etienne. Cluny led in all directions in the world. But Father Bladelin obviously knew of one route in particular, which is exactly where he was headed.

Three officers armed themselves appropriately, shone their flashlights, and started off after him. There was no mobile phone anywhere to be found in the home. He must have taken it with him.

∿

Simon stared at the creature. The creature stared back at him, and something in its stance, the way it cocked its head at him and shook itself, made Simon think it was almost flirting with him. It was, he was quite sure, an albino or white dodo, *Raphus cucullatus*, weighing easily sixty or more pounds, fussing about in a grove of tambalacoque trees, *Calvaria major*. Both the trees and the allegedly seafaring bird were supposed to have gone extinct before 1700, though there had been some speculation in the early 1800s that both species had been captured by a count and sequestered in the Bialowieza Forest between Poland and Belarus, the largest remaining northern temperate stand in all of Europe. It made sense. Ornithologists had long speculated that the dodo, if it had managed to survive, would have gone on to populate city parks throughout the world with the same frequency as mallards or mourning doves.

Simon's thoughts froze upon the exquisite revelation before him, and then the bird was gone, walking with clumsy but forceful determination into an obscured part of the copse.

Simon continued to the edge of the chateau, moving in a slumped position, kneeling low, beneath the sightline of the large array of leaded windows in a side study. He slowly gazed in. Nobody was there.

He ducked down and shuffled to another part of the chateau, slowly raised his head, and caught a glimpse of himself in a gigantic mirror directly opposite on the wall of a library. He dropped back down, controlling his breath. He'd also seen something else.

Now Simon aimed his firearm and stood up. There before him were two bodies sprawled across a stone floor.

Simon knelt against the limestone dihedral where two walls joined at a thirty-degree angle and reared skyward with all the decorative detail of the Burgundian Renaissance. He went for his cell phone, then thought better of saying a word, even a whisper that might distract from his predicament. He was solo. Simon searched the perimeters, looking for a way in that would not disturb the silence of a clearing storm. The sky admitted fantastic sunlight that radiated atop a thin layer of glistening frost. Clouds swirled away, revealing for the first time in days the magnificent Morvan. He inched his way toward an entrance.

The door was ajar.

Simon moved with nervous stealth down a hallway. It suddenly dawned on him that he had not done this alone, ever. He was not particularly good at it either, feeling more and more like a puppet in an old B-movie, having to brace for the unexpected assailant leaping out from untold doorways and passages.

He heard creaks and shutters everywhere. The house was alive as wind poured through open crannies.

He came upon the library. There the two corpses stared at one another, weapons in their respective hands. They had fired simultaneously. From the looks of it, the older man bore all the markings of the occupant. The other suggested an intruder, dressed in the characteristic fatigues of a poacher.

Both guns were warm. It had happened not thirty minutes before. Within minutes he found an iPhone in the smoking jacket of the older man. With gloved hands, Simon recalled the last numbers that had been dialed. The first was not a number but a text message, which read "straitbroogunfire." The second and last was a local number. He took note of both on a piece of paper.

Simon tried calling Le Bon, but there was no service. He had seen the tower and sought out a stairwell, figuring correctly that the elevation would gain him a few bars of service.

There was the painting of Mary of Burgundy. He could not fail to recognize the legendary political Madonna. Every native son knew her likeness. And there, through the large window, an estate laid out in all directions to the wild horizons. Forest. Forest canopy unlike any he had seen. The insuperable height of the trees and aspects of their character he would have expected in Borneo or the Amazon, not his native Burgundy. And parrots in flight and elephants—*not* elephants, mastodons! All of them moving away from source of agitation out beyond the labyrinth of forested unknowns. But moving where?

Simon staggered, unsure what to do. He tried again to place a call. This time, successfully. "Paul, I'm at the monastery. My phone can be located. Call IW. Get the coordinates. Find out where in the hell this place is and who owns it. And listen carefully. I need two traces. Fast."

And then, on hanging up, he did the logical thing. He dialed the number that Le Bon was now tracing. His phone did not yield up any ID.

An old voice, out of breath and very frail, answered tentatively, "Oui?"

Simon paused, saying nothing.

"James, is that you?" the voice trailed.

CHAPTER 46

I t took Martin and Margaret five hours to reach Bruges. It was early afternoon. They checked into a hotel on one of the main canals. Martin
showered, then lay down on the king-sized bed.

He closed his eyes and within all of a few peaceful moments suddenly
arose from his pillows, panicked.

"What?" Margaret said. She had been standing at the window peering
across the medieval cityscape from their third-story window toward the
lonely spire of Our Lady's Church, behind which sat the Gruuthuse and
museum.

"Sweetheart, a dodo! I've seen a friggin' dodo." And then, following the
trail of the most beautiful creature he had ever witnessed, he declared, "We
should have gone back. James is in trouble."

"I don't know what to say. If it's the right key, the right museum, and your
ancestors have not totally duped their heirs apparent, we should be back
there with book in hand by sometime tomorrow. Can he hold out? Are you

willing to risk it? Because if we locate this book, then there will be everything to gain," she ventured.

He didn't respond. It was clear he was torn and ready to return to the chateau at any moment. He had no confidence in a sweet outcome and could not bear the delay which ensued when Margaret picked up a phone and rang the museum. Her contact was out at a meeting and might not be back today.

Margaret put back down the phone and said, "A slight delay. Are you alright?"

"I guess so."

She walked back to the window adjoining their balcony. She needed a moment to think and looked out across the rooftops of Bruges to the museum they hoped to get into before dark. The original owners had commandeered the trade in barley beer five hundred years before. Around 1900, the palace of Lodewijk van Gruuthuse (who had been born with the title Earl of Winchester and was, as well, a councilor to Charles the Rash) had been turned into the official museum housing Gruuthuse's extraordinary art collection. It was with one of its curators that Margaret had worked.

The historic personage of Gruuthuse had also been a close family friend of Mary of Burgundy, her protector, in a sense, as well as a mentor to her son Philip. He had died sometime in November of 1492 and lay buried in the palace.

Margaret knew Bruges well and had helped clients navigate a history that produced more treasures than any other city in the world with the exception of Venice. The city's portfolio of extraordinary art humbled most would-be purchasers. It took more than a few million euros, more like ten, twenty, or fifty million, in addition to ruthless timing, trusted contacts, and laborious authentications to enter the remaining ranks of those who would possess the great Flemish and Burgundian Masters.

To her right was the Markt Square and high belfry at Cloth Hall. Further on was the Basilica of the Holy Blood and the remarkable Groeninge Museum with its two Jan van Eycks. Still further, the Gruuthuse itself and Onze Lieve Vrouekerk, or Church of Our Lady, four hundred feet high, made of brick and said to be the second-tallest brick structure in the world, just a few feet shorter than Antwerp's cathedral. Yet this one towered in a way that no other building in the world did, something about the context which gave many who beheld it a sense of vertigo, not because of the height as much as the history.

"OK. Phone book, in the desk, over there."

Martin handed it to her, and she flipped through private residences.

"Got it."

She dialed the number and heard the voice of a child. She asked if her daddy was home.

The phone dropped, hitting a table, and a distant voice, "Papa!"

Then, after a shuffle, an out-of-breath "Yes?"

"Luis? Luis Adornes?"

"Yes?"

"It's Margaret Olivier, from London. I'm sorry to call you at home. Your office said you were out at a meeting. I thought it was worth trying."

"Ms. Olivier, of course. How are you?"

They spoke briefly, and he agreed, without exactly understanding why, to meet her at a rendezvous point. From Adornes' perspective, Margaret Olivier could only be in Bruges for some major discovery or query with financial prospects.

Martin and Margaret walked along a canal towards Mariastraat, passing the Begijnhof Convent, still active, the hip Wijngaardplein with its scores of coffee shops and merchandising of history, the 15th century Genoese Lodge, finally reaching the hauntingly beautiful Church of our Lady.

They went inside where Luis was to meet them in front of the lion and the dog, which stood before the tombs of the city's most famous father and daughter: Mary of Burgundy, in her painted coffin that held a box which allegedly contained the heart of her son, and her father, Charles the Bold, Duke of Burgundy.

It was 6:15 P.M. Summer tourists were still taking photographs inside.

∿

Simon had left the two corpses where they lay and headed out past the gates and barricades to a country road. From there, it was less than twenty minutes to the scene of rapidly unfolding chaos. He had heard the gunblasts and had assumed that French police had engaged the poachers. Now he was unsure what to make of the prospect before him: nine old men, bearing an odd assortment of ancient-looking armaments, standing in the forest and holding at bay his partner, Mans, as well as the two gendarmes who had rescued him earlier that morning from the side of the road.

Seated handcuffed in the police car was a bearded male, probably early forties. And nearby several SUVs, all empty of occupants.

Simon aimed his gun at the ensemble.

The oldest of the combatants spoke a French whose accent was undeniable. Simon knew it from childhood as an ancient dialect of rural Bourgogne.

"What do you want?" he commanded. He noticed that two of the men wore armor from another age. One old man had a spear and wore a sword, another bore a hatchet. Who were these people? Weekend warriors dressed in the medieval vogue, illegally hunting wild boar in the old manner, caught unawares by the police but emboldened by their numbers? Poachers in France tended to be arrogant, taking every opportunity to trespass without the slightest compunction, considering it their right. Most Frenchmen would not argue the fact. Hunters, be they poachers or otherwise, had as much patrimony in the country as farmers. There was no room for disagreement.

"Put down your gun!" the old man shouted, fifty paces away.

Simon might get one shot, possibly two, but he could see that his partner and the two cops had already been disarmed. Against nine men, the odds were not looking favorable. People would die.

"Who are you?" Simon asked patiently. He could see no animal corpse. Perhaps they had been surprised on their way into the forest. Simon had tried calling Mans immediately after dispatching his message to Le Bon, but the cell coverage in this part of the Morvan was annoying, sporadic, nil.

Simon then saw a bright instant of reflection off a metal oval on a thin golden chain round the old man's throat—a medal of Saint Benedict.

"You are Benedictines?" Simon asked.

"Yes," the old man replied, lowering his aim through a rifle's line of sight that had been holding its prey until that moment.

"We're not the bad guys," Simon assured him, with a gesture signaling that he would lower his firearm if the monks—for he took them now to be monks, not poachers—would stand down.

"OK. Let's start over," Simon began.

"There are others up the hill," Mans now added, casting his voice into the strange fray, a checkmate with no obvious villains, other than one, who sat without a hint of remorse or identity within the cop car.

Simon tried to read his partner.

Up on high could be heard a sudden discharge of firepower that had been prompted by a classic role reversal, once documented in southeastern Alaska. There, a grizzly bear had, with a single swipe of its paw, beheaded the man who had been trailing him for days, a big game hunter. How had the grizzly managed to sneak up on this attuned marksman? Nobody would ever know.

The old monk, Father Bladelin, left the showdown to his companions and raced away, towards the valley from where the conflict had issued, quickly disappearing. Simon marveled at the sprightly departure and was unsure of his next move.

He spoke in his native Burgundian to the other monks, and they conveyed enough information to suggest that they were appointed, in a sense, to keep out illegal hunting from the region. No more than that. Simon knew he had to get up that hill, and this added bulwark of resistance from a handful of old geezers made his job particularly perplexing. First the old gardener, impaled, then Serko's body, as well as two others in the chateau, and now, these strange altruists. But he had seen with his own eyes what it was they were seeking to protect. They were on the level.

∿

Father Bladelin paced himself like a runner, without surcease, breath, or fear. He kept on in a determined march beyond the wall into the heart of his beloved sanctuary. He stopped to smell the morning air in the cloud-scudding Morvan, then continued into the large inner grove of podocarp and broadleaf forest. The red and black pine-dominated canopy that existed nowhere else in Europe was filled with a profusion of near-tropical understory—butterflies, worms, epiphytes, liana, a constellation of ferns and birds of near infinite variety.

In and of itself, the deadwood meant more beetles and rare white-back woodpeckers than anywhere else on the continent. Scores of creatures, most not seen in millennia, were not at all happy to encounter human intruders. Three-toed woodpeckers amid sixty-meter plus Norway spruce chirped, hooted. A lynx sprinted away from the kill site. Wolves howled, agitated by an entry they had not asked for, feeling terrible fear, not hope. Giant wisents charged through the thick palette of deadwood.

As Bladelin climbed higher into the upper portions of the mist-enveloped valley, thousands of other birds could be discerned racing in and out of the clouds, between the trees. Terns, an Andean condor, goldfinches and trogons, parrotlets and guans.

A small group of slow-moving *Proteles cristatus*, the aardwolf, in addition to caracals, mingled with a giant ground sloth, Burchell's zebra, black rhinos and greater kudu. There were kori bustards, warthogs, and easily two hundred species of "extinct" avians, arriving at length from all directions.

Up ahead, he could feel the weight of agitation throughout the waterlogged sward encircling the scene where death had occurred. As he approached, he witnessed dozens of vipers swinging from branches, slithering in an orgy of the unimaginable.

There, human destiny had performed yet again its moribund exercise of self-destruction and rejuvenation.

Then he caught the unmistakable sense of a large predator, two or three times larger than wolves.

Only one showed itself, while a half-dozen of the big cats, deemed extinct for at least twelve thousand years, had circled the invaders, men who had already violated the forest breaking the pact which had held the delicate balance in thrall since nearly forever. The alpha was the first to see Father Bladelin, as he stood looking up towards the sunlight refracting swirling mists just topping a ridge. The huge graceful animal growled, but Bladelin did not move. He knew the cats were there, prowling, doing their job. The others in its pride waited behind it, out of sight. But this one great cat was a sure study in evolutionary perfection, as fearsome as fossil hunters had made them out to be in countless later displays, since their earliest skeletal finds in Germany. Their upper canines could slash through any herbivore's leathery skin.

By the late Pleistocene, this *Machairodontinae* family of felines had given birth to an even more perplexing killing machine, a unique offshoot of the genus, known as *Smilodon*, the most famous of the sabertooth cats. It possessed larger claws than the African lion, a short tail, and by far the sturdiest endurance, musculature, and speed of any creature in the last 60 million years. It stood the size of a lion but with a heavier, more compact body and could outrun all the first pollinators, including tarantula wasps.

The big cats had hunted the human intruders with a behavior that had long been suppressed. Circling in tandem, striking with a force that had a pulse speed of two hundred miles per hour. Dragging the bodies into the pits. A learned behavior. They weighed, on average, four to five hundred pounds. Their canines were seven inches long. The first poacher's gun hand was severed in a microsecond, before he could pull the trigger; his skull was crushed and his abdomen eviscerated. One by one, the poachers fell beneath the onrushing ferocity of those canines and claws. This was not a meal but a revenge that had soaked the earth in the bad blood of human designs.

Father Bladelin recognized the human blood as he ventured across the same ground not long after the massacre. He knew that the cats had prevailed, as they had periodically in times past, or so the stories of Henry Olivier, the great-grandfather of James and Edward, had relayed: tales of wonder that had accompanied Bladelin's initiation as a Knight of the Order of the

Golden Fleece, along with the other monks down below.

And now the truth of the tigers' collaborative victory was doubly confirmed, as the lone figure of Lance darted from behind a redwood tree. He nodded to the Father, who gave him the sign of the Order, and vanished in the mists.

Twenty minutes later, all eyes were on the approaching old man. Bladelin neared the police vehicle, his weapon by his side. He knew he must ensure that no one get into the domain. If the police were to venture there, or see anything unusual . . . he didn't want to even think through the consequences. Morality, inside the wall, was impossible to debate. Life and death took on different weight than they did outside the wall. He must convey a sobriety that was consistent with a Grand Master's bearing, dignity, and persuasiveness.

"Put down your arms," he called out. "It's over."

CHAPTER 47

Bladelin approached Simon, his Bohemian broadsword of the 15th century in its old leather scabbard at his side. He held his rifle in an unthreatening manner.

"You don't remember me, do you?" the old knight said.

"No. Should I?" Simon asked.

He smiled paternally at the cop whose badge revealed his Interpol wildlife role and name.

"Your accent, inspector, betrays its Burgundian ties. Simon, is it?"

"Yes?"

"Your grandfather studied at our monastery. I was one of his teachers."

"Oh?" *How could he know that?*

"I'm trying to recall. He was a teenager, unsure what to do with his life. A very serious young man, but not entirely proficient at Latin."

He's bluffing. Definitely stalling for time . . .

"I remember. He wanted to be a painter. His name was Henri."

Simon was somewhat impressed.

"And by the time he was thirty-five, he *was* a painter, though not entirely successful, if I recall. He moved to Paris."

"What did he paint?" Simon asked, testing him further. Bladelin might have heard about all this, who knows how. A small community.

"Cows. He painted cows. Marvelous cows. I actually have one of them."

"You're kidding."

"I'm happy to give it to you. A lovely little canvas. How is he?"

"He passed away some years ago, I'm sorry to say. Leukemia."

"Je suis si désolé."

Mans was waiting. "What do you want to do, Jean?"

Simon had already made his decision.

"Let them go."

Father Bladelin knew he had won some Brownie points, but were they sufficient to gain the Inspector's complete loyalty? To a secret, no less, that could not be told? To a strategy that was altogether counter to the law? Nor could the Father decipher whether this native son, whose own grandfather Bladelin remembered teaching the *Lausiac History* by Palladius, 5th century tales of the ascetics, knew anything more than that poachers had trespassed. Benedict had been the name taken by fifteen popes, including the current one. His Rules had ordained the behavior of loving Christians for fifteen hundred years. But there were several dead men up on the mountain and no way to be sure that Inspector Simon could possibly understand what was involved here.

Mans looked at his partner with raised eyebrows.

Simon addressed Bladelin. "What is a group of monks doing behaving like militants?"

"It is a small gesture. We, in turn, would hope for the same from our neighbors if the monastery were ever threatened."

"Which monastery?"

"There are many in this region, as you no doubt are aware. All tied ultimately to Cluny."

"These are international crooks, Father, not small-time offenders going after wild boar or the biggest stag."

"We know that." Bladelin gazed at Simon with unrelenting baby-blue eyes and the poignant power of one of Rembrandt's saints in the half-light.

"Is it some kind of private zoological collection? A wealthy donor to the Church, perhaps?"

"God knows what He is doing." Bladelin gestured to the forest.

Suddenly there was the howl of a wolf, coming from not far up the valley.

Simon looked at Mans, whose mouth had dropped even more. Iberian wolves had not come as far as Burgundy, not that either knew of.

"You see."

Both men paused.

"See what?" Simon asked.

"God speaks through every creature."

"What is He saying? God, I mean. Or the wolf, if you prefer?"

"He's saying, 'Leave well enough alone. Live and let live.'"

Simon was not about to cross this surprisingly effective team of geriatric gladiator/monks, who had managed to turn over one of the culprits. Moreover, they apparently had been able to protect their charges. The cages were empty. He was beginning to feel a certain admiration for them as well as a protectiveness of his own for this place.

"What about the others?" Simon asked.

Father Bladelin gazed at the policeman, trying to divine the underlying man. Was he remotely like his grandfather? Committed to salvation in the form of a forest and all it had come to mean for thousands of years? Bladelin might not think of it as a Pleistocene island, but he knew it was separate, had survived the Great Flood and had provided hospice for all those animals who had nowhere else to go, not into a frozen European continent. They had remained, innocent, without warfare or competition. The authors of the Bible, among them the prophets Matthew and Isaiah, had heard legends of this principality of wild, unspoiled origins and had drawn upon the reports of the earliest travelers.

Even then, three thousand years ago, everyone who thought about it relocated the place on the map, mostly to the Far East, somewhere in the Himalayas or Ceylon or south in Abbysinia. Marco Polo insisted upon the Karakoram. Shelley, who had visited with Mary Shelley and Claire Clairmont for two days during his tumultuous exile in France, placed it in the Vale of Kashmir, not about to give up its secret.

"They're gone," the Father declared.

"Gone or dead?"

"Gone. Forever."

"You're sure about that?"

"Yes."

"We've got no cell coverage here," Mans said. "We need to get this guy processed."

"Right." Then Simon looked at Bladelin. "I may have some other questions for you later on."

"I am at Cluny. Father Bladelin's the name."

"Where are your vehicles?"

"We came by foot."

As the two regional gendarmes, followed by Simon and Mans, drove off in the two police cars, Simon watched the old men disappear into the forest.

"What to make of them?" Mans inquired.

"Daffy old monks," Simon proffered.

But his mind was somewhere else, putting a perspective on all the mundane administrative obligations of his profession: the international treaties and alliances that were meant to protect wildlife, the early directives on birds and habitat and those few anomalies within the greater global system, such as the former Soviet *zapovedniks*, wildlife sanctuaries that were left on their own, left to deep lineages and evolutionary isolation without human interference. No cutting down of trees after twenty or thirty years, as in most of Europe, no concerns about deadwood, areas of protection off-limits to the public and rarely visited by representatives of the scientific community.

There was nothing to say that this property surrounding that chateau might not be left to its own devices and the protective good graces of Benedictine monks, one of whom, evidently, had been his very own grandfather.

Somehow, however, he would have to deal with those two dead bodies. Who were they? What had happened? If police visited the scene—and it was a certainty they would after Simon had asked for the traces—then what?

He had no doubt that there was something very special about this forest, what with the full force of fifteen hundred years of Benedictine tradition protecting it.

A dodo. A unicorn. Wolves . . .

∿

"Luis? C'est moi," Margaret spoke quietly.

"Ahh, Madame Olivier." He shook her hand.

"My husband, Martin."

"A pleasure."

Margaret led the two men to chairs somewhere near the back of the church. They sat down. Martin then withdrew the old key and handed it to his wife.

"Recognize it?" she asked Adornes.

Luis took the key in his hand and studied it, then shrugged. "No. It's old, maybe 17th century. What is it?"

"We were hoping you could tell us," she sighed.

Luis Adornes smiled. He hadn't a clue.

"Any locked bookcases in the museum that might have a keyhole to fit it?" Martin chimed in.

"Now there's an interesting point. Yes, certainly. The museum is closed for the day unless, of course, it is urgent?"

"It is, rather," Margaret confided.

∿

Noon in Antwerp. Le Bon had videoconferenced a half-dozen agents from IW and engaged the reconnoitering of Deblock, his assistant Cadiz, and others in an effort to find out what in hell was going on in Burgundy. The answers came back with increasing disparity. How, Le Bon asked, amid some 3,400 kilometers of marked trails, had nature lovers, local French tax authorities, national park biologists, and the French government failed to take note of this vast forested blank on the map—let alone a missing person by the name of Edward Olivier, Professor Edward Olivier, whose family apparently had title to this largest of domains in all of France, going back many long centuries?

Then there was the brother and the son. Traces with the highest level of security clearances at Interpol had located James' last iPhone messages and, in turn, those going to and from not only Martin Olivier's iPhone but his wife, Margaret's.

What was slightly more difficult now came across in an electronic dossier from unknown authorship, somewhere in the bowels of Interpol in Brussels or Paris. Le Bon was not privy to exactly where the satellite reconnaissance work was done, but there, presently downloading onto the plasma screen in his office, was the work of but an hour or two. As Le Bon looked at the screen, his office phone rang.

"Yes? Ah, oui, it is coming now." It was the senior officer in charge, who had transmitted the pictures in JPEG Raw. A pleasant young woman's voice. Le Bon, a bachelor for too many years, imagined her to be quite beautiful.

"What's your name?" He put her on speakerphone.

"Maggie."

"Irish?"

"Obviously. Cork. Have the images resolved?"

"Just about. I've got our whole group here."

Le Bon, Cadiz, and Deblock hovered around his new computer, which Le Bon had only recently figured out how to use.

"What do we do?"

"Open each image, twenty megabytes, from top left."

Le Bon did so. "But, it's all cloud cover."

"Yes. Keep going."

Le Bon clicked successive images and got the same. One near hurricane of snow, as seen from above, after another, each picture tagged with an ID and a date and technology. USGS-Eros, Landsat 7, Aster, Iconos, Maryland Cover, Landsat 6, Landsat 5, Landsat 4 . . . all the same. And dates going back to 1987.

"I don't understand."

But Maggie did. Each image, taken ninety-nine minutes apart over a period of years, had yielded what must rate as the worst weather region in the country. Either that or consistently bad luck. "You click the last one?"

"Just now . . . ahh! Tout alors."

A single SPOT (Système probatoire d'observation terrestre), shot at 9:45 A.M., twenty years earlier, in infrared. The single thirty seconds of lovely weather out of 116,800 images.

"Freeze-frame it, or whatever you geeks do."

They all stood around the large computer screen and looked at the first sunny morning in two decades, a window that revealed a most extensive forest.

"What are we seeing?" Cadiz asked.

"Pretty healthy woodlands, I'd have to say. A national park, I presume?"

"No. Private property."

"Well, that's impressive. Here, take a look."

Maggie was escorting them on a zoom-in with her cursor that revealed, according to her, huge copses of alder and chestnut, traces of ancient pasture, possibly viticulture, Roman and Medieval archaeological strata, a monastery, Cistercian by association with nearby Cluny. These "categories" revealed themselves without the needed interpretive skills of the computer operator. Two valleys to the east had the designation of "Little Ice Age Margin," although climate change had left the estate cut off ecologically as early as twenty thousand years before the so-called Common Era.

Atop the remains of the monastery was an enormous chateau, as impressive a structure as one would find in Paris or Versailles. One-meter resolution. Oriented on the eastern portion of a slope, far from any A or N road.

But there was a dirt path, where once a Roman road seemed to lie, wide enough for vehicular egress. And, clearly marked, a wall running in a full loop, north/south, calculated to be less than twenty miles in length, seventeen, to be precise.

Rock formations and much taller groves of forest stood out on the highest peak of the property.

"What are those?" Le Bon asked.

"Limestone caves," Maggie ventured.

"No, to the left of that?" Le Bon took his finger and touched the screen where dark shadows streaked at an angle.

"Shadows," Cadiz volunteered.

"Yes, shadows," Maggie reiterated. "Easy to measure, hold on a minute . . . " She rippled a few gradients and did the math. "What's the tallest known tree in France?"

"No idea," Le Bon replied.

"This one is 378 feet tall, and if I'm not mistaken, that would make it the largest tree in the world."

"*Eucalyptus regnans*," Deblock, who hovered near, stated.

"Found in Tasmania. Not France."

"What about sequoias?" Le Bon enquired.

"None in France," rejoined Cadiz. "Oh, wait, there is one next to the Crillon, at Place de la Concorde in front of the American Embassy. Gifted to the people of Paris. And a few others here and there, if my memory serves me."

Le Bon's associates all shrugged.

"I am no dendrologist. I can't tell you what sort of tree it is. There are over one hundred thousand known species of trees, and we certainly don't presume to know most of them. We have a pretty comprehensive bioassay program adopted from IGBP."

"What's that?" Cadiz asked.

"International Geosphere-Biosphere Program. They have a mapping system based on monthly composites from some twenty thousand sites around the world that read in various wavelengths, red, infrared, et cetera. Using their data, we model, scale, look for various types of reflections, luminance, variations in the percentage of closed versus open forests, and so on. There are all kinds of ecological algorithms that result in a fairly comprehensive overview of global habitat. So what you are seeing is a consolidated readout in the infrared, and it has translation parameters across a fairly impressive spectrum of flora and fauna. Birds in flight, not so good. Animals, insects, fish, well, only when we are lucky enough to get a three-dimensional lock on them. Rare when they are moving."

"What about all those little shining points on the tips of the branches, what are those?" Le Bon asked.

"Flowers, I would imagine," Maggie said.

"Then that would argue for the blue gum theory," Deblock pointed out. "Sequoias, to my knowledge, don't have flowers."

"Never seen a sequoia. Couldn't tell you," Maggie confided.

And just as Maggie signed off, Cadiz pointed out something else, a strange, slow-moving shadow. On closer inspection, two separate bodies, side by side high up on a branch of the highest tree. "What is that?" He traced his index finger against the video screen.

"I have no idea," Deblock said.

Cadiz blew up the image in real time. "They appear to be ... appendages?"

"Anteater?"

"No. That's a giant sloth. Two of them. I saw something like that on the Discovery Channel. But that was a recreation?" Cadiz shot a helpless look at his colleagues.

CHAPTER 48

Luis Adornes, Margaret, and Martin passed beneath Michelangelo's *Madonna and Child*, sculpted in 1504 and sequestered to Bruges from Italy, the only work to be purchased by a foreign power during the artist's lifetime. They continued walking outside, past the Basilica of the Holy Blood into the busy Rozenhoedkaai, overlooking the canals. They crossed Dijver Road, past the Groeninge Museum, where Margaret had many times studied the portrait of her namesake, Margaretta, Jan van Eyck's wife, and *The Madonna with Canon van der Paele*, one of the most famous paintings in the world. She bore some resemblance to the artist's spouse.

And then they wandered into the Gruuthuse, walked past an historic guillotine, and finally into a library that was reserved for staff and researchers.

"May I?"

Martin handed the key to Luis, who inserted it into a leaded-glass façade that held the early 18th century wire-meshed bookcases. "Bingo!"

The glass door swung free.

"It can't be that easy!" Martin exclaimed.

It wasn't. They all three stared at the several thousand books before them.

"What are we looking for?" Luis asked. He knew some, by no means all, of the books stacked tightly against one another, dating back many hundreds of years.

"One book," Margaret declared. "Surely you have an index of books, a card catalogue . . ."

"It's all on computer."

"Can you show us? It will be far more efficient."

"Of course."

He led them down a corridor into an elevator, using a striped magnetic card, up two floors.

His office was neatly layered with work, the usual stacks of recent catalogues from exhibitions all over the world, file cards, documents. His computer swiveled out of a sleek recess in the wall.

Luis typed in a password, scrolled down the museum lists, and finally called up a screen that listed each of 127,000 manuscripts, of which perhaps fewer than 1,500 lived in the case he had opened.

"What, in particular, are you looking for?"

Margaret thought for a moment. "Anything from the scriptorium in Ghent?" she wondered aloud. "Or the Bruges counterpart?"

"Ah ha, you're looking for Simon, or Alexander Bening."

"The Master of Mary of Burgundy," she conceded.

"Yes, we have a page. But it is not housed in the library. I thought you said a certain book?"

"Give me a moment."

Margaret, taking a seat, began to scroll through the library index. She knew exactly what she was not looking for—127,000 exclusions to whatever it was she might hope to discover. Rippling through the vast list. Psalters. Breviaries. Miniatures. Leafs. *Les Principaux Manuscrits a Peintures des Princes Czartoryski*. Fragments of a border. Drawings by Popham. *Le Livre d'Heures de Philippe de Cleves*, a set of initials. Now she was closing in possibly, YY, Master of the Dresden Book of Hours, workshops, court painters, marginal borders—a miscellany of enticing pieces to a puzzle. Unfortunately, each and every item was accounted for and spelled out, leaving nothing to chance.

Except for one. ID1292a. *Boxed book. Multiple authorships. ITRE.*

Margaret stared at the single line, her cursor flashing. "ITRE?"

Luis looked at the line, puzzled. "I have no idea."

He typed in the keyword.

ITRE?

Item Relocated. October 17, 1793.

"Interesting. I've never seen that designation. And I've been here over ten years."

"The height of the French Revolution."

"Indeed. That date rings a bell." He googled it. "You see, the week of Marie Antoinette's beheading."

"What day exactly?" Martin asked, taking a sudden interest.

Luis checked it again. "Ah, that was October sixteenth."

"In those days, how long would it have taken for news from France to have reached Antwerp?" Martin pressed.

"Hours," Margaret said. "Men on horseback, village to village, like a telegram."

"You think there was a connection between Antoinette and Mary of Burgundy? Different centuries."

"I don't know," Martin sighed. "I have no idea."

"Relocated to where?" Margaret asked.

"Provenance, Item 1292a?"

The computer froze. A little icon appeared on screen, spinning. And it kept spinning. One, two minutes.

"It's frozen us out."

"Force quit. Try it again," she pressed.

He did, with the same results.

"There must be something in its place. A box, I would imagine," Luis contested.

They walked back to the rows of books. Luis unlocked the case, drew his finger towards the spot, and there found the coral-red silken box and withdrew the volume. A golden crescent was engraved on the outside. But there was nothing inside. Light as air. Empty.

"The box alone is quite valuable," Luis surmised, studying it.

"That's the seal for the Order of the Golden Fleece," he added, taking hold of a black light with an eyepiece from his desk.

"That's odd," he went on. "See that?"

Margaret took the magnifier and scanned the embroidered gold thread. "There! What is that?"

"A number and some letters.

"Nine-seven-three-one-one-two-q-zRvh."

"I know that system; an old card catalogue. Another library. Prague. No, *vh*, of course, Vienna?"

In precise unison, she and Luis both then uttered, "H. *Hofburg*."

The palace. Another long stretch without sleep, Martin was already figuring that this might not be so easy after all.

Margaret thanked Luis, who still had no idea what these two English eccentrics were really cooking up, then she and her husband walked back to their hotel, called their son to inform him there would be several days' delay in their getting back to England, checked out, paying with Margaret's Visa— Martin was still sufficiently spooked by his uncle's original paranoia about such things, as he described to his wife—drove to the train station leaving the BMW in long-term parking, and boarded a first-class cabin on a train for Vienna, to arrive early the next morning.

That night, on the narrow bed of their private berth, Margaret and Martin made passionate love. They felt somewhat like beginners, after however many months and years, which increased the pleasure of it.

When they left the station in Vienna at 6:58 next morning, there could be little doubt that global warming was seriously infiltrating parts of Europe. The temperature was already thirty-three degrees celsius. Wildfires were raging in Germany and Greece.

They checked into the Sacher. Getting to the palace would take all of a ten-minute walk.

"This all makes perfect sense," Martin said as they headed to their room. "At least according to James, who mentioned Vienna repeatedly. On the other hand, I think we've lost it."

Once in their room, Margaret turned on her computer and began to search on-line for any possible clues to the whereabouts of the most important manuscript since the Old and New Testaments.

"OK ... Not difficult," she mumbled aloud to Martin, accessing the basic platform for the public's entranceway to an electronic card catalogue of the Habsburg Imperial Library. Margaret's rather special gifts were all fiery and emergent, an intelligence of quick, broad, multidisciplinary realms, immense knowledge worthy of probably a half-dozen Ph.D.s. Martin gazed in admiration at her frighteningly deft manner with the computer. She plied numerous keystrokes and one particular eleven-digit code.

Her Apple rippled through its encyclopedias of data, a conduit of tens of thousands of books, beginning with highlights of the most treasured manuscripts of the 15th and 16th centuries, Gutenberg Bibles and the richly illustrated *Theuerdank*, the Emperor Maximilian's marriage saga to young Mary in the Burgundy of the 1470s. Standard highlights for browsers.

"But what about that number?" Martin asked impatiently.

"Nothing," she replied, addled. Then a sinking thought came to her. "What if the book has already been sold privately or stolen?"

"How do you find out?"

"Well, since we're not certain the book even exists, I'm on ridiculously thin ice here." Margaret typed in her passwords for each of the key auction houses across Europe, both obvious and not. "Little likelihood. I'm not sure how to even define what it is we're looking for. Bening? Breughel? I just don't know."

"Savery? James mentioned Savery."

"Roelandt. Yes."

She typed the 17th century painter's name. Instantly, two books, one an exhibition catalogue from a June 1954 exhibition at the museum in Ghent, Belgium, another, by K. J. Mullenmeister, the definitive master work on the artist, published by Luca Verlag Freren, 1988.

A quick scan of the on-line highlights led them instantly to what was possibly the artist's greatest work, "Landschaft mit Vögeln," known as the "Wiener Dodo," or, *Le paradis terrestre.* Kunsthistorisches Museum, Inv.-Nr. GG 1082, in Vienna, painted in 1628.

"Oh, my God!" Martin said, peering at the black-and-white reproduction. "That's it."

"What?"

"I mean, I'm not positive. It's from an angle I didn't ever see, and in weather less formidable than what I experienced . . . but that seems to be it. There's the tower!"

"You're telling me *that's* the Olivier chateau?"

"See that bird? That's a dodo!"

Within minutes they were in the lobby of the hotel and then out front hailing a taxi to the museum.

Ten minutes later they walked up through the famous interior entry, a stone stairwell built over the course of two decades, beginning in 1872, for what was once the greatest empire in the world, after designs by Semper and von Hasenauer. Ten minutes after that, they stood in front of the painting, amid numerous other masterpieces.

Martin stared at it.

"Well? Is it?" Margaret asked.

"It must be, but I'm not sure. It seems a tad generic and not nearly as large a house as exists. And those two additional towers, I don't remember seeing them. Maybe it's not. But the dodo. How could he have gotten it so right?"

"Maybe they hadn't gone extinct yet? Maybe he saw one in a zoo. I don't know."

"Now what? What are you doing!"

Margaret peered behind the painting. She felt the back of the canvas. A security alarm sounded. Margaret backed quickly away.

Martin shook his head at her risky indiscretion that had yielded absolutely nothing. "What did you expect?"

Ordinarily, Margaret would have lingered in a museum she knew well but never ceased to marvel at, one of the greatest collections of fine paintings in the world. Vermeer, Velásquez, Titian ... but this time, the alarm hastened their exit.

They returned to their hotel room. Only the arrival of room service interrupted, briefly, their increasingly frustrated search on the computer.

"Try *paradise, chateau*, no. What about *Utopia?*" Martin suddenly exhorted.

She did. Only to find rare-book sales of the last hundred years that went to J. P. Morgan, Mellon, Frick, and a half-dozen other contenders with titles that bore no connection to their quest; though quite a few individual Books of Hours by specific artists or anonymous Masters. Not what they were looking for.

"Go back to the library. Same word search."

This time she uncovered a list of hundreds, beginning with:

"Anonimo di Utopia pseud. Landi, Ortensio, Utopia Didaci Bemardini ...
Alt Mag ...

Brockhaus, Heinrich, Die Utopia-Schrift des Thomas Morus, Erklart von,
Keipzig, 1929, 738-B. 37 Neu Per

Doni, Antonio Francesco, Mondi celesti, terrestri, et infernali ... Venezia,
Moretti 1583, 224456-A ...."

And so on.

"This isn't working," Martin moaned, seriously sleep-deprived. He shuffled into the bathroom and stood over the ornate sink. He stared at his fatigued face and felt ready to throw up.

Four stories beneath their suite, Jean-Baptise Simon flashed his Interpol card for the benefit of the manager. Le Bon's trace had pinpointed the Oliviers' location, and rather than send someone else, Simon had decided to investigate the couple on his own. He was feeling a very personal involvement in the case.

"Four-forty. One of our nicest suites," Thomas Rischka said, instantly acquiring the information on a computer in his office. "They only checked in about an hour and a half ago. Here are their passport numbers."

Simon looked at him, his expression unreadable. "We have that information."

"This is a five-star hotel," the manager punctuated.

"Uh-huh."

"We trust you will endeavor to avoid any disturbance to our other guests?"

Upstairs in their room, which was equidistant between the emergency stairwell and the elevator, Margaret had detected the strangest of all clues, if one were prepared to call it that. "I'll be damned," she uttered.

"What is it?" Martin asked, removing to the bedroom where Margaret sat at a Biedermeier-style desk.

She had opened the infamous "guest registry" just to be sure. And there it was. She had seen it earlier, but it hadn't registered—among so many other outrageously famous names. The signature of Ludwig van Beethoven.

CHAPTER 49

The coincidence was too great. There was the precise code, absent *vh*, which made total sense. The Hofburg librarians would not have needed to reference manuscripts in their own diverse collections. But particularly telling was the absence of a normal category. All the other manuscripts, memorabilia, priceless treasures were accounted for either in the imperial apartments, among collections of Holy Roman Empire crown jewels, the artifacts of Duke Herzog Albert of Saxe-Teschen, Egyptian papyri, and so forth.

In her computer ramblings Margaret had come upon a strange listing at the Hofburg for an even stranger object, one not defined. It might be a manuscript or, for that matter, a diamond from Zanzibar. There was no way to know. Only the dates struck her as remarkably coincidental: "973112qzr" described as acquired 1827, 29, 3. "De-accessed. 1939, 9." Eighteen twenty-seven? *Nine . . . September?*

She typed frantically now. "There! Beethoven. He died March 26th, 1827, was buried in the Alsergasse church on the afternoon of Thursday, March 29th."

"And the deaccession date?" Martin mused aloud. "What is that?"

"The Nazis invaded Poland when?"

"Sometime around then."

"Wait a minute." She typed in the appropriate query. "Right. September 1st, 1939. Nine equals September. Umm . . . no, what about the ninth district here in Vienna? Beethoven lived in the ninth."

"I dare say you're starting to sound like Uncle James, sweetheart. Why make it so easy?" Finding a single book in the Ninth District, more than a needle in a haystack, a preposterous dead-end.

She gazed at an electronic map of the city pondering their next move and thinking, like an addicted gambler, how nice it would be to avoid the Hofburg, if possible. Of course, did *de-access* mean it was gone from the chambers or simply in storage? Gone, her instincts told her. Hitler was on the move, and somebody on the inside feared an all-out war across Europe. They weren't wrong; and *their* instincts told them to remove something belonging to Germany's son—the man whose music was played at Hitler's birthday parties—before the Führer himself came looking for it. This notion, born of nothing more than a colossal wish, made Margaret's task conveniently easier, and she was the first to admit it—a complex (the Hofburg) that took in a vast geography of churches, vaults, thousands of rooms, security guards, and hiding places. Without an insider, it would be impossible to find something that was not advertised. But then, the ninth district comprised probably five square miles of big city life.

In truth, her cockeyed revelation was without merit, and she knew it. They were screwed.

The room phone rang.

"Yes?" Martin said quietly.

"You have a visitor, sir. He's coming up the elevator just now." And the voice, which gave every reassurance of guest privacy, hung up.

"Stairs," Martin said panicked.

"What?"

"A tip from the front desk. Someone's onto us, I guess, and they're coming up."

Margaret unplugged her computer, threw it in her bag along with the precious guest registry, gathered their respective few other articles, stared into the hall through the Claude eyepiece of the door, then scooted out, hurrying down the stairs two, three at a time.

Within a minute they had exited the hotel out the front.

"Merde!" Simon cursed, realizing he had missed them.

He raced downstairs, breathing hard, his hand skimming the railing, only to reach the entrance in time to glimpse a hotel Mercedes taxi with two occupants that matched the profiles of Martin and Margaret Olivier, a half-block away, moving fast. He had intended, with any luck, to quietly unravel the mystery enshrouding these two people. He had no idea what they could be up to, whether they had had some hand in the murders or were themselves fleeing from the murderers.

Simon called his team back in Antwerp on his cell phone. "Anything?"

"Jean, Hubert tells me you secured the crime scene?"

"Yes. Pending a thorough interrogation of the one suspect."

"Well, now there are three of them. We've managed to hack the Oliviers' computer. Pretty impressive technology to do so, I must say. What was happening in Vienna in 1939, and what does *nine* mean to you?"

"Nine? Let's see. ... That would be September. September 1939. The month Hitler invaded Poland."

∿

The driver looked at them politely, without saying a word.

"A minute, please," Martin sighed, turning to his wife for help.

"There's a bunker, some kind of museum in the ninth commemorating Austria's freedom after the war. That wouldn't do. Liechtenstein Museum, no, it's contemporary. Freud's house . . . " She scanned the little *Lonely Planet* guide she'd grabbed. "The birthplace of Schubert. But he's not in the guest registry, nor did he live in the ninth."

"But I thought you said the ninth?" Martin was perplexed. "Maybe it means the month of September?"

"No. How could I have missed *that*? It's the Ninth Symphony."

"Fuck!"

"What?"

"James said the same thing. Beethoven visited the chateau, then went home and wrote his Ninth Symphony."

"How does James know that?"

"He doesn't," Martin admitted.

But it was enough to catapult Margaret into an even greater frenzy. The problem was, from Martin's perspective, they were truly grasping.

"'Ode to Joy.' The poetry of Schiller. I know it." She began to recite, "Joy, thou lovely spark of the gods, daughter of Elysium." And concluded, "thy holy realm, O heavenly one! *Deine Zauber binden wieder* . . . Thy magic joins again . . . *was die Mode streng geteilt*; that which custom has torn apart . . . torn apart and, there is a missing sentence, I don't remember, oh . . . it ends with . . . "wherever thy gentle wings are spread." She thought to humm, her zeal then actually uttering the upward rising "Da-da-da-da. . . ." then ceased with embarrassement, aware of the taxi driver grinning at the two idiots behind him, while the meter rolled on.

"Margaret, what does all this buy us?"

She typed in more queries on her computer, which was tied to her own iPhone. "Oh, shit."

"What?"

"He lived in some seventy-two separate houses over the course of thirty-four years in Vienna. Something to do with chronic stomach problems."

"Yes, but where is the Ninth Symphony?"

"What do you mean?"

"Did he write it in Vienna?"

"Of course he did!" And she scanned the available information. "Yes! 323 Landstrasse."

Their driver looked into his rearview mirror, amused. "There is no 323 Landstrasse."

"But there must be," Margaret replied pleadingly.

The driver, who had been patiently waiting for a destination up until this point, his meter ticking away, checked his own book of maps. "Ah. Now that is Ungergasse five, at Beatrixgasse," and he pulled out into traffic at last.

Landstrasse angled at a slightly parallel direction before merging with Ungergasse.

They were there in little time. A pizza parlor occupied part of the street level of a large, several storied building that seemed to stretch for blocks in all directions, a maze of dense housing.

"I don't think so," Martin weighed in. "It's a relatively new building."

"Wait a minute," Margaret replied. "I'm not sure it's all that new. In one of those apartments, the composer dashed off the symphony. He was there in 1823 and 1824."

They hopped out and paid the driver who sped away.

The Oliviers walked in to the pizzeria. "We've got to order something," Martin concluded.

"They have espresso. Orange juice."

"Two."

As they sat down, Jean-Baptiste Simon entered the front door, a rolled newspaper in his tanned hands. The restaurant was nearly empty, save for the British couple. He grabbed a booth thirty feet away. The young waitress, tattooed, a prominent earring in her nose, placed a menu before him, then continued with drinks on a tray to the Oliviers' table.

"Danke. Wir hörten dass Beethoven hier einmal lebte. Wissen Sie wo und in welchem Stockwerk? Gibt es eine Gedenktafel?" Margaret's German was rudimentary but had become a necessity in her profession.

The waitress had heard that Beethoven once lived somewhere upstairs. She begged a moment and went to ask her boss, who sent her back with information known to millions of the artist's fans. Erster Stock, first floor, directly above the corner portion of the restaurant, where the oven was set.

"Vielen Dank."

They took the stairs and found the private apartment within a minute. No name on the outside.

"Just do it," Margaret said.

Martin knocked. A child answered, unafraid, gazing with mute and earnest obsession. The mother arrived presently.

"Yes, may I help you?"

"You're American?" Margaret enlivened.

"That's right. And you're obviously British. What's the problem?"

"No problem. This is rather awkward. We're musicologists and . . . "

"Beethoven. Right. You're not the first. Come in."

"We're awfully sorry . . . "

"That's alright. There's a plaque around the front of the building. Most of the tourists head to the 19th, where he wrote his Pastoral Symphony. "

By the time Martin and Margaret were safely inside, Simon had staked out a position that guaranteed a quiet confrontation when the Oliviers reappeared, but for the one architectural feature that defied logic and which Simon could not have anticipated. An unusual back entranceway served the building structurally when centrally forced air had been installed, compliments of the Marshall Plan.

Supposedly, Beethoven's apartment had included an additional room with a toilet along that rear hallway, now used only by maintenance people. Unknown to all but the autistic child, there was, indeed, something there.

"You're welcome to explore it," the woman said, escorting them to a small, irregular door, which was unlocked. "At least a dozen people have searched there for anything connected to Beethoven, and that's just in the two years my daughter and I have been living here. By the way, the door in back allows you to exit but not get back in."

CHAPTER 50

Martin led the way, convinced that they should never have left the chateau. Margaret's contention was that just maybe someone in power at the Hofburg had, under terrible circumstances, made a split-second decision, predicated upon no other intuitive gambit than that Beethoven had been part of the chateau's history. This person must have known that, must have been in on the secret. There was a hiding place, one that nobody would have ever expected, and this person decided to protect the book from the Nazis by hiding it there. Hitler was preparing to ransack all of Europe, but of course could not hurt Austria, or not exactly. He was Austrian himself, after all.

An alternative theory, which Martin now voiced—a few billionaires and their once loyal knights had sequestered the damned book in a cave, up a tree, in some vault in Zurich, or perhaps in the library of the chateau itself. That was far more likely.

As he and Margaret crept crazily along the dimly lit passageway, a third person drew toward them. It was the little girl, strangely taken by this odd

British couple. The girl knew something not even her own mother had grasped. Something about Margaret, an aura that only a child of her nature could recognize.

The girl held up four fingers.

"Four?" Margaret responded. "What do you mean?"

"Four is four," Martin said impatiently. "What do you mean, four?" he said stupidly to the girl. Margaret looked at him hopelessly. The little girl held out her hand, Margaret took it, and the girl led them forward.

They followed a circuitous route beneath cylindrical polyurethane heating ducts and badly botched wiring that piggybacked on the exoskeleton of plumbing pipes encrusted and dripping.

A small crawl space, unlit, allowed for only one.

"Martin, your lighter?"

He withdrew the Tiffany gadget, inscribed with his name, and handed it to Margaret. Margaret leaned down and peered into the dark.

Inside the cubbyhole, she ignited the flame. A shelf in the corner gave way to another dark confine.

"Do I dare?" she mused.

"Go for it. Be careful."

The little girl, who could not have exceeded eight years, a petite eight, nodded affirmatively.

Margaret proceeded. The lighter went out. She fumbled with it, again and again. Then it happened. The flame shone and directly before her was a wall of stone. She had no more room to maneuver. End of the line.

"It's weird. I can't breathe back here!" she cried.

"Get out!" Martin exclaimed. "There's steam rising!"

∿

Outside, in the building's first-story hallway, Simon, counting the minutes, had grown suspicious. He knocked on the door. The American woman answered, expecting her daughter and the odd couple.

"Yes?" she said with a start, having opened the door without hesitation, only to try to close it as soon as she saw the unfamiliar face.

"I am looking for my friends," Simon said in fluent English.

The American caught the vibes and discerned a hidden gun, which Simon always carried. He knew she spotted the bulge. He'd been careless.

"They left five minutes ago."

"Out your window?" he tried to smile.

A crack in the ducts? Half-dozen people taking their morning hot showers? Whatever was causing it, Margaret had to get out. The steam was rising like hot water in a kettle.

Martin took more of an initiative now. He crawled in after her to pull her out by her feet.

"Wait, I see something," she managed, reached forward with the light, ever so slowly, to a crumbly ledge of plaster. And there, vaguely discernible, a number, carved above the ledge. The number 4 and nothing else. Had it been there from the beginning? Margaret was no dummy when it came to sculptures. She could read plaster better than most people. This was an old number 4, not a modern one. The number was upside down. What did that mean? Had someone in later years replaced the plaster with inadvertent sloppiness? Or was this a deliberate ruse? Her brain went momentarily slack.

All this for that? Her mind could not grasp the simplicity of their dead-end. *A four* . . .

Feeling dizzy and not a little claustrophobic, she began to force her way backward, squirming from the most awful, dark abyss she'd ever landed in, Martin pulling her with all his force.

By the time she'd been hauled out, her smart, summery business attire was covered in dust and plaster of Paris.

"Where's the girl?"

"Vanished."

Through the pipes, they then heard Simon questioning the mother. "What else did they say?" He sounded menacing.

"That backdoor the woman mentioned. Go!" Martin whispered urgently.

They moved like widgets in a furious contraption until reaching the door and pouring forth into a courtyard. Finally, they found themselves on a brick pathway leading to the back of the building.

From there, they ran, both fortunately wearing appropriate shoes for the occasion, as it turned out. In fact, Martin had not changed his shoes since arriving on the Continent. They still bore dried mud from his journey onto the slopes where the falcon had landed on his arm.

They could not find a taxi and feared to head out around the massive block back towards Ungergasse. So they walked, fifteen minutes, lost.

Margaret hailed an elderly woman who carried a basket of groceries.

"Gnädige Frau, können Sie uns den grossen Park, in der Nähe von dem Hilton zeigen?"

She pointed the way, silently.

On a bench adjoining the large pond with its fast-arriving hopeful bevy of garrulous ducks—mandarin, white-headed, wood, and ferruginous—in the calm shade of a venerable grove of Fehme Eichen (justice oaks), Tanzlinden ("dancing limes" or linden trees as they are called in North America), and the odd common beech, Margaret sat stunned and disappointed.

"So are you going to tell me or what?" Martin exhaled.

"Four. The number four was carved into the stone. Nothing else."

"Four?"

"Yeah."

"We're being played for fools."

"Maybe not," and she withdrew the guest register.

"What?"

As Margaret scanned the signatures again, her eyes lit on one in particular. "Vivaldi?" she conjectured aloud. "What about him?"

"Beethoven's Ninth."

"From nine."

"Then that's it," she declared. "*The Four Seasons.*"

"Wonderful. Venice in the summer. That should be easy."

Margaret accessed her server and then searched for Vivaldi thumbnails. "He's here."

"Who's here?" Martin said wearily.

"Vivaldi's buried at Karlsplatz."

"Margaret, don't do this. Everybody is buried in Vienna."

But no one, not even Martin, ever prevailed upon Margaret Olivier when she got on to one of these malarial-type fevers. And now it was a map of Vienna that she pulled out of no hat, examining the mundane particulars, only to sit back with an exhausted lament. "Karlsplatz is huge. It's the goddamned epicenter of the entire city."

"Naturally. And I suppose the book is buried with him, since Beethoven didn't quite pan out, at least in that respect?"

"We don't know that."

"We know squat."

"Martin, there are no dates on the primer, only the names of visitors to our chateau."

"Now it's *our* chateau?"

"Well?"

"Alright, go on."

And she led him through her circuitous ratiocinations, involving four centuries of chicanery, desperate hide-outs, and fair-game littering the major funeraries of Europe, all based on her own incredible fabrications, fueled by the innocuous three pages of signatures in her hand, and coming to a head at the most logical of all obscure sites, the secret resting place of the greatest nature composer of all time—a man who had been lost to posterity until just before Hitler invaded Poland.

Vivaldi was a prodigious maverick, once the toast of Venice. Women adored him. He was the concertmaster for a house for wayward girls, a nunnery, half-dozen opera houses. Kings and queens lavished praise upon his works, but then, oddly, his career was over, and he hastened to Vienna on a commission that never materialized. There, he died in exile at a lowly saddler's house. His corpse was moved in the night to an anonymous grave.

The kicker, in her opinion, was not what Martin would have expected: Hitler was not likely to bother with Vivaldi's tomb, Margaret inferred. He had Poland to conquer. No, the book they were after was buried before Hitler, before the fanfare of Vivaldi's rediscovery. Incredibly, the vast majority of his works, more than seven hundred of them, were unknown prior to the unearthing of a large bundle of his handwritten manuscripts at a monastery near Turin in the early 1900s. The man was a stranger to his rightful posterity. Except that, obviously, a few people knew of him. People of great influence, members of the Order of the Golden Fleece, who had preferred that Vivaldi never be rediscovered.

Her mind was working it through, because she could *see* it.

"We're not going to find it there," she finally admitted.

"I could have told you that."

"But we might find out where it went *from* there!"

"More clues."

She showed Martin the information on her computer. "Look, Italian composer/conductor Alfredo Casella hosted a weeklong Vivaldi revival in 1939 called "The Four Seasons" here in Vienna. You really think whoever had possession of the book was going to risk an opening of the lost tomb, assuming of course there was the slightest chance the book had been stored there?"

"Why would it have been? I mean for God sakes, Margaret—why a tomb, versus, I don't know, anywhere less . . . "

"Less what?" she pressed. "Sacred, priceless objects are buried in tombs, Martin. King Tut was buried in a tomb. Grave robbers tried but failed to get him. It's not just the Golden Fleece. Knights of Pythias, the American Legion, Shriners, Masons, and the Knights Templar, to name but a few, have all had their secret hiding places. Imagine what lies hidden in the graves at Cimitero Monumentale, in Milan, Highgate Cemetery back home, not to mention Père Lachaise in Paris. Martin, tombs have always been repositories for many of the world's greatest treasures. Everybody knows that."

Martin just shook his head.

It all made sense, at least to an historian like Margaret, who had no emotional connection, particularly, to her now deceased father-in-law. She had never felt much for him and so did not quite share her husband's controlled sorrow, which was softly on the rise throughout this ordeal.

"You OK?" she said.

"No, not entirely," he asserted wearily.

∿

Simon was already on them. The game had become remarkably simple. Every time they used their respective iPhones, incorporating Margaret's Wi-Fi connection, Interpol had them down to two feet. The satellite technology was frighteningly accurate. Simon was in no hurry to apprehend them now. He knew they were on a mission, their eccentric itinerary and speed suggested as much. His instincts wrestled with two opposite theories. If indeed they were involved in murder and an international poaching ring, then their exodus to Vienna must be tied to accomplices, perhaps some connection to the Emirates. An embassy or a bank. Ungergasse 5 made little sense, however.

On the other hand, if they had fled the killers or killer of Martin's uncle, Simon had only to come forward and openly exonerate them.

But he sensed there might be more to it, as he walked a block behind them along the Ringstrasse towards the Resselpark, Central U-Bahn, and sprawling campus of the Technische Universität.

"There!" Margaret said.

Le Bon's team had pinpointed their coordinates: 48/11/57/16/22/12/. "It appears to be a car dealership," Cadiz said, checking against a commercial template.

Le Bon called Simon. One ring, then a recording.

"What the hell's he doing?" Le Bon asked Mans on another line.

"What are you talking about?" Mans, at that moment, was supervising the final taping of a police line around the entrance to the chateau.

The Oliviers entered the Daimler-Benz dealership. Simon watched from a kiosk nearby.

"Alright, dear, now what?" Martin plied with strained effort.

"I'm thinking. Study the cars like you're interested."

A salesperson engaged them. "Kann ich etwas für Sie tun?"

"Bathroom? Gibt es eine Toilette?" Margaret asked.

Once inside, she sat on the toilet with her computer in her lap. The signal was weak. The wheel spun. She waited. Two marks. Three marks. Back to two. *Fuck this!* Then suddenly, four.

Ancient burials, Karlsplatz . . .

A network of tunnels leading from the new subway to the Technical University. In 1818, some building or group of them had evidently been destroyed at this approximate spot. An earthquake? War? Or simply the march of progress? There was a burial ground. Poor people. Vivaldi among them. He had died in exile from a heart attack, anonymous, without any fanfare. Only recently had a plaque been erected at the university to commemorate his demise.

She flushed the toilet, packed up the computer, stepped back into the showroom, and asked to speak with the manager. Martin had no idea what she intended.

"Yes?"

And Margaret proceeded to explain how she and her "colleague" were with the Ministry of Culture and needed access to their trap door.

"Trap door? I'm sorry? You are English?"

"UNESCO. British Embassy."

Martin admired her bullshit. Very smooth.

"A tunnel or stairs, an old hidden place, something locked up, down below. The coming exhibition."

"Madame . . . "

She leaned in, persuasively, producing a document, any document, from her computer bag.

"We are archaeologists for UNESCO, and we have a plane to catch." She smiled at him.

And before he bothered to examine her credentials, he suddenly remembered one detail from years before, when he was newly hired, plumbing.

"Plumbing?"

"Yes. The plumbers had been instructed to avoid a room."

"What room?"

He led them into a basement cluttered with the remains of centuries. At the rear of this rat-infested array of decaying walls, crawl-spaces, and wet asbestos, they found the signs of a 17th century original hole in the wall.

"There. You'll excuse me if I don't join you," the manager said.

"Has anyone else been snooping around down here that you know of?"

"There was a music professor. I don't what he was looking for."

"When?"

"Last year."

"Did he find anything?"

"I have no idea."

"We'll be a few minutes," Margaret said with a slightly perturbed air, the tone easily readable. The manager gave them space.

"Take your time."

"Dig, Martin."

"What do you mean, dig?"

"You heard me."

They scratched away for five minutes.

Then they both heard it. A hollow-sounding something.

A strangely eroded dirt shaft that suggested previous occupation.

"What are you doing, Margaret?"

As she clawed at the thin veil of dirt, she gave him a look that silenced further discussion.

And then it was done. A tunnel faintly lit from the light source of the basement room the manager had left them in.

"Margaret, wait here."

"No way."

They went together. Looking for the number 4, anything to justify what was beginning to look like a wild-goose chase. They imagined what they must look like to the manager, a crazy English couple, no longer resembling a preeminent and incredibly successful real estate agent and an internationally renowned art historian.

Nothing. They searched for twenty minutes. Scratching at the faint outlines on outlines. Nothing.

When suddenly: "Oh, Lord!"

A metal box. The same golden seal. No way to open it.

"Just take it," Margaret urged, knowing they had found—not a book, for the box was no larger than a pillbox—but *something*. . . .

"I can't. It's somehow encrusted in."

They found a rock and started to bash it. Ordinarily, Margaret would never have employed so destructive a technique. But she was like a madwoman now.

The lock sprung open. Martin slowly pulled apart two eighth-inch layers of metal. They peered inside.

There was a tiny, tightly knit scroll. Margaret unrolled it and gazed upon the two handwritten English words: "There's more."

"Dig!" she barked.

"There *is no more!*" Martin shouted. "Just some sadistic game of clues leading nowhere. Vivaldi isn't here. His bones aren't even here."

"But why would they say *more?*" Margaret pondered, as if she hadn't heard anything her husband had just uttered.

"I don't know. To prove that greed is gullible? To sport with idiots?"

And then it struck her: the list of signatures, the word searches for the National Library.

Paradise . . . Utopia . . . "Utopia!" she cried.

Martin just looked at her, with a dim view as to this compulsive behavior that had so overtaken his normally much reserved spouse. He'd never discerned the trait in his wife—an obsession suggestive of slot machines and cocaine. She was losing it.

"Utopian dreams, illusions. That pretty well sums it up, or at least in reverse," Martin added.

"Wait a minute, who was it who said utopia in reverse?"

"I don't follow."

"That's *Erewhon; Nowhere* spelled backwards. The title of Samuel Butler's novel. An Englishman writing in a venerable English tradition."

"You lost me."

"Martin, didn't you once tell me that one of your predecessors had been buried in Canterbury?"

"Nothing my family has ever said or done would surprise me at this point."

"Canterbury, right?"

"Oh, yeah. But that was long ago."

"All of this is long ago!"

"Right, my great-great-grandfather, or maybe four times removed. My father never said much about it. Only that there was a family plot at one time."

"At the Church of Saint Dunstan's?"

"How did you know that?"

"I know everything."

"I've never even bothered to go there. What would be the point?"

Margaret rolled her eyes. "The point, dear, is English Utopian tradition. Who wrote *Utopia?*"

"*Erewhon* or *Utopia*?"

"*Utopia.*"

"Sir Thomas More, of course."

"Precisely. More. The word *more*. It's on the register. Sir Thomas More signed the register."

"Margaret, we're covered in dirt, and this is getting tiresome. Anything can be a clue if you imagine it to be so. Leonardo is on that list. Leonardo invented submarines. Does that mean we search every submarine whose moniker starts with *L* or *V*?"

"Sir Thomas More was embalmed at St. Dunstan's."

"No. As a matter of fact, his *head* was embalmed there, *maybe*. In his sister's coffin, along with what's come to be called the Roper aisle. An archaeological foray some years ago came up with nothing. No head."

Margaret was impressed. "How do you know that?"

"An institutional client of ours wanted to lease the church but waited to see if there was indeed a famous head involved. More was beheaded, recall."

"Yes, I know."

"Well, there was no head. And nobody said anything about an illustrated manuscript."

Margaret was stumped, pondering under pressure. "Of course they didn't. They stole it."

"There were two dozen members on the expedition. The press was standing by as scientists and scholars opened the tomb. It was empty, Margaret."

Margaret sat down in the dirt, greatly perplexed.

"If it's any consolation, More's oldest daughter was named Margaret. She wrote a book entitled *Four Last Things*, received letters from Erasmus, and history knows her to have been brilliant, endowed with 'transcendental talents,' as one biographer wrote."

"But it makes perfect sense. The tomb, a utopian tomb, would have been the likely repository," she ruminated aloud. "And what if that were the last thing?"

"We can't reach forever. There's no time. I'm sorry, dear. I suggest, and with utmost haste, that we return to France. It's time you met my eccentric uncle and saw for yourself the rather extraordinary inheritance we're going to have to deal with. It's obvious these clues were planted for the benefit of the Nazis or anyone else who might be looking for the book to throw them off course. I don't know how we'll ever find it now. I'll break the news to Uncle James."

Margaret hadn't given up. Not that easily. She carefully removed the guest register from her computer bag and studied the signatures and their accompanying clues, looking for anything that might tie the Hofburg, Hitler, the invasion of Poland, Savery, Beethoven's Ninth Symphony, the last days of Antonio Vivaldi, in exile from Venice, and the hugely tormented Sir Thomas More together. Any particular spacing, regularities, irregular . . .

"Martin!"

It had been there all along. A system.

"Look. No dates, right?"

"Uh-huh."

"No chronological order whatsoever. Don't you find that odd? Saint Francis in the middle, Giotto next to Gesner, the Queen Mother beside Fra Angelico?"

"James admitted as much. Why, you think the book is fake?"

Margaret had all of seven percent power left on her computer. She remembered a certain file. A study of the Van Eyck brothers from the 1930s she had been utilizing. The artists' signatures were there. She brought up the file and compared the signatures with those in the book.

"Magnify it," Martin exhorted.

She did, five hundred percent. They were precise matches.

"It's no fake. The artists were in on it."

"In on what?"

"A deception spanning hundreds of years."

"Deception of whom?"

"The future."

"Margaret, please. You're starting to sound like my uncle." Then he stopped in his tracks, so to speak. "Actually . . . "

"Well, go on, what?"

"Come to think of it, James did mention that it was something of a mighty secret from the very beginning. And only from the time of the French Revolution did they actually go to the trouble of *hiding* the book. For that matter, it was all supposition. Maybe Saint Francis took it to Assisi. Or perhaps it was purchased by someone like Morgan or Carnegie or Frick, from the Hermitage, and is squirreled away in New York?"

"Martin, look at this and tell me what you see."

He examined the page, where Margaret's finger was nearly touching. "What?"

"An indentation or pressed seal. Much like reverse printing."

"I can't see it."

"Look more closely."

"There is a minute impression."

"After the bona fide signature of Charles II."

"Which one was he?" he asked. His wife necessarily maintained a phenomenal grasp of European history. Martin did not.

"He was the last emperor of the Spanish Habsburgs. He died in 1700."

"Right. What does that get us?"

"He was the last direct heir of the Order of the Golden Fleece, which your ancestor, Duke Philip III, created in the year 1430."

"Seventeen hundred. OK? But if you're wrong, another dark alley which your insatiable intellect delights in illuminating, absent the slight hint of actual proof?"

Margaret scanned the three pages with her magnifying glass. "Impressions after ten names, and only ten: More, Vivaldi, Fra Angelico, Charles II, Savery, Beethoven, Saint Francis, Gandhi, the Queen Mother and . . . what's that? Do you see that? What is a lonely little letter *e* doing among these other giants of history?"

Martin examined the *e*. Something clicked in his mind, but he could not yet grasp it.

"I have no idea," he replied.

He gazed upon his wife with a sudden sensation he had not felt since the first year of their marriage, a love as breathless as Margaret's own tenacious antics as she frantically pursued her hunches and detective work. The air had become oppressive.

"We need to get a fresh lemon or anything like it," she gasped.

"Right."

They made their way back to the surface of the earth. Martin stopped to compare a few of the new models of Mercedes with his own BMW.

"Martin!"

They headed outside and found a small grocer. Margaret plucked two lemons and headed for the first bench they could see.

Margaret applied the juice to the primer.

"I hope you know what you're doing—those three pages have to be priceless. Don't ruin them!"

Margaret gave him an annoyed look, lightly spreading the juice across the page.

"There, see it?" She held the pages up to the light. "A check, as if those ten names had been checked off, or on to, the list. Except this one." She pointed to the last name in the primer.

"*e*?"

"Nearly so. At least among nine of the signatures."

"The Queen Mother is dead. That means her daughter has it. I know her. Remember? We simply go to the palace and appeal to her decency. We are the rightful owners, after all."

"Uh-huh. That'll work for sure," Martin said, noticing that the *e* before him in the guest registry had been written in the manner of a child's scribble—or the studied gesture of a formidable someone who preferred a shorthand guaranteeing anonymity.

And that was precisely what he now remembered with all the familiarity of home, sweet home.

"Margaret, when I was a kid, my dad gave me a copy of *Alice's Adventures in Wonderland*, a first edition. I must have been seven or eight."

"Right?"

"If I'm not mistaken, he signed it simply, *e*, for Edward."

Margaret's eyes followed those of her husband down to the third finger on his right hand, as Martin slowly twisted the lapis and gold ring, long familiar to his hand, and thus entirely overlooked, until it had presently been gingerly extricated.

"Father gave me this when I got into law school."

He turned the ring around and there was the word, *congratulations*, followed by an *e* for Edward.

They looked at one another with a holy-shit sort of shared relief. The great book they had been searching for, a manuscript that by Margaret's reckoning would be worth an entire museum, a billion pounds or more, was back at the chateau somewhere.

"Good news, except for the fact that the chateau is enormous, chockfull of basements, attics, secret tunnels, hidden holes-in-the-walls and trap-doors, not to mention tens of thousands of treacherous acres surrounding it. Probably caves, rocky alcoves, I mean, it's a wilderness."

"It's got to be there. That is what your father is telling us."

∿

As Simon watched the Oliviers tossing a couple of pieces of fruit into a garbage container on the street near the front of the car dealership, he took a phone call from Le Bon.

"Yes, Paul?"

"You're not going to believe this."

CHAPTER 51

"This is turning out to be one of the more interesting seventy-two hours of my career, I must confess," he began.

Simon listened silently.

"How fast do African antelopes run when they're frightened?" he asked.

"Fast. Especially steenboks and dikdiks. As fast or faster than cheetahs, at least half the time. What's up?"

"And how long can they keep up a high speed?"

"Paul, obviously it depends on the species, some for days, if it's a large one, like the nyala, the defassa, the gemsbok. I mean there are numerous species and races—sable, roan, kudu, klipspringer, now there's a beauty, *Oreotragus*. . . . What are we talking about?"

"In the last four hours, we've gotten five separate sightings of what appears to be the same ungulate. The fifth was called in a few minutes ago by a French traffic cop who saw it race across a freeway, leaping over the concrete barricades, in and out of traffic, and just before the TGV traveling 230 miles per hour nearly clipped it. Before that, a hunter, some school children, a tour bus driver, and a man who said he'd been pruning pear trees in his garden when it leapt past him."

"Any zoos reporting a missing gazelle? It sounds like some species of gazelle."

"Are you sitting down?"

"Actually, no. I'm walking about one hundred meters behind two suspects in heavy traffic, but please continue."

"It had one horn, Simon . . . . I know, I know. But this was no rhino."

"Go on."

"First sighting, four hours ago. Just south of Reims in a forest between the autoroutes N51 and D9. Running like the wind."

"Yes. I know it."

"Approximately ninety minutes later, stopping to drink in the Aube."

"Just north of the D441."

"Exactly. Then, just forty minutes later, it nearly caused a pile-up at the interchange of the D444 and E511."

"South of Troyes."

"Exactement."

Simon could see the itinerary. What was happening was astonishingly clear. He stopped before crossing the busy Ringstrasse. The Oliviers were on the other side, heading toward the park, now out of eyeshot. He'd lost them. And at that moment, it didn't matter any longer. "Paul, that's three sightings. What about the fourth?"

"Just southwest of Montbard, heading toward Semur."

"How long ago?"

"Forty-five minutes."

"And the fifth?"

"It crossed the A6 near Guillon."

Simon's mind was abuzz. The chateau and the docks of Antwerp were virtually in the same precise longitude. The animal was making a beeline to its home. Running madly across Western Europe like a purposeful dog chasing after its human companions on a country road at top speed, through fields of wheat, beet, potato, green bean, on the edge of cities and towns at an astonishing speed. Over perilous railroad tracks and freeways; past smoke-stacks, huge factory outlets, like Ikea; along concrete as hard as the ice of the glaciers from which its ancestors had once fled. It had survived human chaos. Pleistocene hunters who thought nothing of driving thousands of the animals over cliffs to then feast upon the odd tongue.

Simon imagined all of the world's natural history concentrated in this one rogue who had managed remarkably to get out of the fast currents of converging waters at the Antwerp docks—out of Belgium altogether, moving with the agility and the homing determination of migratory fowl, back to the place where, for thousands of generations it had found peace, along with all the other plants and animals. They had grown up there, or migrated under conditions that would have killed them anywhere else. If this unmistakable creature of noble conformation could survive the A6 drivers who typically exceeded 150 kilometers in their Mercedes and Citroens, then nothing could deter it now.

And Simon felt equally empowered. He knew what he must do. Father Bladelin had made it clear enough. The chateau and its domain *were* unique in all the world. It had to be protected. Moreover, a plan was already blossoming in his mind.

"If it is the same animal, it has been averaging forty miles per hour nonstop since it escaped from its container," Le Bon calculated.

"Where is Hubert?"

"On his way into IW with the suspect."

"Who is at the Olivier estate?"

"Local cops. Guarding the crime scene. What are you going to do?"

"I'm going to the chateau. Listen, Paul. Save that animal. All points. Every cop. Tell them to leave it be. No interference. Leave the scene, de-secure it. I want your absolute guarantee on this."

"Certainement."

"As for this animal, nobody approaches it. It knows where it's going. You need to get those local cops the hell out of that crime scene. It's positively critical. They've got to evacuate the area. Get 'em out, Paul, back to wherever they came from. No one, absolutely no one is to venture anywhere near the Olivier estate. Do you understand?"

"It's done." Le Bon wasn't sure he did understand, but he was not about to question the Deputy Director of IW.

"Should we keep the trace on the Oliviers?"

"No. Shut it down. It's over. We're good."

∿

Martin and Margaret hailed a taxi and sped to Vienna's international airport. Martin tried to prepare her for James' eccentricities and his uncle's firm belief that contrary to all reason, this "farm" of strange origins to which they were now headed played host, according to James, to the original

Garden of Eden. Not some metaphor of the French garden aesthetic—no pastoral tradition built by the several centuries of commanding sums, millions upon millions of French francs, euros, exquisite taste in architecture, and every last detail of interior design, but nature's own prolific capacity across a continent—a biological fact that had begun hundreds of millions of years before there was ever a place called *Europe.*

Margaret had her doubts. Paintings of paradise tended to be flamboyant, sometimes drawn from life but more often from the tragic lives of caged animals caught in the wild, shipped from places like Brazil and Indonesia to ports such as Le Havre and Rotterdam, then displayed and paraded by bored sycophants and royals. After the French Revolution, the demographics of French life shifted severely to Paris, Nice, Montpelier, and other urban entrepôts. People wanted excitement, not brown bears and wolves. They craved nightclubs, coffeehouses and, most of all, better plumbing and bananas out of season. Somehow, inconceivably to modern aficionados of country living, the huge chateaux and fountains had become colossal tax burdens and broken-down headaches. The mansions were hospices for rodents and hornets, and the owners could do nothing to curtail the adamant hunting clubs whose members zealously trespassed, shooting bullets, in essence, through those very paintings of Eden.

In France, Brigitte Bardot had tried for years to curtail her countrymen's bloodlust and that of the rest of the world. But she was a lone voice, bolstered by a few hundred thousand young vegetarians at best, or that's how Margaret understood it.

Still, she too found the whole scenario of the Olivier domain, and the artists who had secretly sojourned there, so incredible as to offer at least one alluring alternative to the imagination—namely, that it was all true.

∿

Simon did not board their tight connection to Paris. Not with a flight to Geneva twenty minutes later. He knew the schedule better than they, the time of day, the trouble they'd have getting around Paris en route down to Burgundy.

In fact, Martin would have preferred the Geneva flight, since he now knew how to drive the ninety minutes or so to the chateau. He had stupidly gone for Paris, better seating.

By 5:30 that afternoon, Simon was sitting in the library of the chateau. The two corpses still lay in the tandem puddles of blood on the floor nearby.

His call to Le Bon had evidently succeeded in removing the site of the chateau from any further scrutiny by authorities, at least for the time being.
There was no tape demarcating a crime zone, no policemen hanging around
their cars. No sign whatsoever of surveillance. The historic property with its
surrounding gardens and impenetrable forests, white turrets, majestic architectural medley, and imposing facades rested like a giant bird hunkered
down on its nest—privileged, wild, and undisturbed, or so it seemed.

The rains had come again. Simon thought he heard distant thunder.

But there was something in addition to the distant rumbles of an angry
sky: a deep, undulating half-cry, half-roar. And then Simon looked through
the mottled light of the stained glass to the face, the very mouth that uttered
those unbelievable sounds out near the wall.

An elephant, or more precisely, if Simon wasn't mistaken, a woolly mammoth, poised ever so gently in the rose garden. Unlike the mastodon, the
mammoth's tusks were curved gracefully, or this one's were.

It wants to play . . . Jean-Baptiste stared at the most fantastic creature he
had ever seen. The beast was gazing towards the chateau in the rain. This
colossal, amazingly gentle introvert had somehow remarkably been spared
the wave of extinctions across Europe and the world. The implications were
breathtaking, but he was not sure how such knowledge was likely to play out
once unloosed. The genie out of a bottle syndrome? Science was notorious
for screwing up enormous chances, opportunities, virtue, because scientists
were capable of rationalizing self-interest and exercising no restraint. If the
truth were to be known, Jean-Baptiste, like his grandfather, was uncomfort-
able even walking through the forest, stepping on living things and, more
than likely, inadvertently killing them: moss, lichens, toadstools, invisible
things that humans rarely appreciate.

At that moment he heard the opening of the electric gate and then a car
pulling up. Simon readied himself in hiding, checking his weapon. He had
had time on the flight to Geneva to figure out where he must take this inevi-
table confrontation. But he did not presume to have any answers.

Martin was the first to enter the main hallway, calling to his uncle. Margaret was right behind him, expressing no small amazement at the size and
scope of the domicile.

"It's magnificent," she said. "Where's that Memlinc? It will tell us a lot."

"James?" Martin called out. They entered the library.

"Oh, no!" Margaret heard her husband moan. And then she, too, beheld
the horror.

Martin knelt down over his uncle. James' left hand still clung to the small oval, the Medal of Saint Benedict, whose succor had benefited James in his final seconds, though this balm was not expressed in a gesture of any discernible bliss. Only the hollow gaze of a man who had entered the other side. On the floor beside his right hand was a weapon, the one he had presumably used to kill his assailant, though not in time to save his own life.

Margaret stood frozen with fear, looking around the room, noticing the knight in armor in a corner and all the various medieval paraphernalia. And then she focused on the other corpse.

"Martin, who is that?"

"I have no idea, but I would have to imagine he is the murderer. There were poachers. James knew they were coming for him."

"What are we going to do?" she said with none of her characteristic brio.

"Call the police."

"That would be me, Mr. Olivier," Simon said, moving from a corridor into the library.

CHAPTER 52

"I followed you both to Vienna. I have no idea what you were doing there, and I will never ask you," Simon began. "I know that all this is yours. But you may rest assured, I am here to use my position . . . " and he trailed off. "That is to say, I have no intention of ever divulging what has really happened here. Nobody would believe it, in any case."

As Simon spoke, his attention veered from the floor, with its two dead occupants, to the mirror, in which was emerging a veritable concord of creatures descending from out of the forests towards the wall, or over it, and onto the grassy clearings and "English-like parkland," as the French always thought of such manicured gardens.

Now Simon turned and faced the carnival of animals directly.

Pachyderms, strange mammals, giant reptiles, and colorful birds to delight the ages. Since childhood he had dreamt of such a moment. He was, despite his own grandfather's early retirement from the monastery, a deeply religious Christian who yearned to truly *believe*. Here before him was the Creation, and it was his time to act accordingly. He would not fail to be of service. He would never feel alone again on Earth.

Simon now fully understood that the poachers had become the prey. The residents here had protected their own, as perhaps they had always done. Simon saw through all the lurking chaos and understood one thing: what was needed of him now was the actual truth of himself, not just what he had been trained to do as a wildlife enforcer, not just what he loved. But who he was from his earliest upbringing.

"My uncle informed me that there was trouble next door," Martin began, having risen unsteadily to his feet, Margaret in tow. "Some enormous real estate deal that would jeopardize the peripheries. He called it 'edge effects,' the same thing that's happening along the sides of the highways throughout the Amazon. 'Incremental deterioration of the ecosystem stability.' I am, of course, no scientist, but this is a pretty obvious crisis we face, no matter how large the domain."

Margaret looked at her husband with astonishment. This was not her mercenary house agent of a husband speaking.

Simon paused for a moment then, drawing on his years of experience, replied, "The way I see it, we have several distinct solutions. First, the satellite data. Pretty remarkable, I must say. And what it shows is a constellation of important historic and archaeological remains on your property. World Heritage status. But I suspect that would not be in the best interest of this estate. This is a crime scene of interminable unresolve. It is my case. And that's a good thing, I think. Because it makes it my choice to keep its clues, accessibility, and resolution delayed forever."

Words Martin was grateful for. A search party would never do, as far as he was now concerned. The mountain and its tapestry of valleys should remain forever free of humans.

"That does raise, I'm afraid, a very sad problem. My driver, Max Hardiman. My uncle's scientific assistant, a wonderful young man named Lance Sèvre, a local ecologist of high standing, I would assume. And a rather famous museum director, Edouard something-or-other."

"Revere?"

"That's it."

"Mon Dieu."

"I know him. What was *he* doing here?" Margaret chimed in.

"I'm not sure. But all three went up the mountain to fight the poachers. It was medieval. Bizarre. Terrifying. And I fear the worst. There will be people asking questions."

"Did your driver have a family?"

"Not that I am aware of," Martin replied. "But that fellow Lance . . . I really have no idea."

"There's no need to worry," a voice declared, as Lance, having heard all the preceding discussion from one of the many hidden trap doors in the chateau, made his modest entry, unarmed.

"Lance!" Martin cried out.

Simon whipped around with his gun raised. Lance put his hands up but it was only the sudden entry that had ignited this reaction on Simon's part. He was not the sort of person who liked such surprises.

"It's OK. That's Lance. He's on our side," Martin exclaimed. "And that bird, I know that bird!"

It was Eyos, the falcon, who rode now upon Lance's shoulder.

Simon put his gun down. "Are you alright?" he asked.

"It's over," Lance replied somberly. He knelt down beside his old friend, James, and touched the old man's forehead with a kiss.

Then he looked outside and saw Alice, the huge mammoth, repeatedly digging her foot into the grass.

"She is again in mourning, this time for the death of her dear human friend, James Olivier," Lance said quietly.

"What happens now?" Martin asked, having absolutely no idea.

"I believe I have the solution to the problem of the adjoining land," Simon began. "That deal is tied up with an Arab potentate who was backing the poachers to add to his extensive illegal collection of endangered animals. Moreover, we already know that a local official has been nabbing stags and wild boar out of season. He will not gain much credibility with the constituencies he has been courting when he is arrested. And by constituencies, I refer to those business groups that have lobbied for the acceptance of this very destructive proposition, by none other than that very same filthy rich prince. He had negotiated to buy all the adjoining land. My agent in the United Arab Emirates informed me just before I got here that the potentate in question lost his diplomatic immunity a few hours ago. He is in custody in the Persian Gulf somewhere, charged with financing the poaching ring, whose ringleader is *that* man."

He gazed at the corpse before him on the bloodied stone floor.

"And I believe that I could gain the cooperation of a certain important individual," Simon continued. "A local gentleman I know, a retired farmer who actually held the lease on thousands of acres surrounding the Olivier estate. He did not own the land, but his tenancy was sacrosanct in rural France."

"Oui, I know him," Lance said. "He stays very much to himself."

"Yes. That is true," Simon replied. "But what is important is that as long as he grazed the odd sheep, he was untouchable. Acreage given to simple vegetables and a nicely cured cheese. That is an enterprise, however modest, whose authority has always been revered by the French government. Wouldn't you agree?"

Lance showed a hint of a grin.

"This much can be said with unambiguous affection about the French way of life, its subsidies and love of farming," Simon added.

"He is the father of somebody I know well. And he will never concede his portion of land. Moreover, the local politician I referred to will lose all his support, particularly when the investor is exposed for the corrupt sonofabitch he really is. And that socialism for which France is made fun of abroad—train strikes, protests, the inability to ever form a consensus, an onerous tax system—will, in fact, prove to be very useful, in this instance. The slightest pressure put on the Ministries of Agriculture and the Interior by these investors will end up in court for two centuries. Viva la France!"

"You're really a cop?" Margaret asked.

"I ask but one favor of you, madame et monsieur." Simon concluded.

Martin nodded. "What did you have in mind?"

Jean-Baptiste Simon looked out into the area where the wild grasses merged with the deep forest. All eyes followed his. Right there, at that instant, a remarkable creature had just stopped and turned to gaze across the few hundred meters towards the chateau. To all who beheld it—or imagined that they had—the animal was unmistakable.

"I should like, sometime, to bring my daughter and my granddaughter to this place. They have never witnessed a unicorn."

CHAPTER 53

I t was two more days before the Oliviers returned to London and the at-
tentions of their son, Anthony. Martin had been gone just less than a
week. In that time, his world had changed. But the book, which had taken
them to Bruges and Vienna, was nowhere to be found. They had spent an
entire day and most of one night searching throughout the chateau for it. In
every drawer, closet, and partition, in the cellar, the attic, outbuildings, barns,
the chateau d'eau, and, of course, in the several libraries.

There was no book that they could find. Could it have been an invention?
A wonderful decoy intended to distract treasure hunters from the overwhelming temptation of a Pleistocene island outback—the aggregate of all
those species that would otherwise have gone extinct?

One thing appeared clear to Martin, the book, wherever it might lie, was
no longer the essential anodyne, as James had thought of it. Jean-Baptise
Simon had calculated enough impediments to ensure that the sale to developers of the adjacent acreage would collapse in the scandal of allegations and
revelations.

Martin had decided that the cost of keeping up the chateau need not pose an insurmountable burden. Forty thousand square feet of habitable interior could easily be over-dusted and vacuumed (ask any man), and Lance had ably proved himself the finest caretaker in all the land. Moreover, he was not alone.

In sum, with its religious exemption from taxes and an absolute policy of zero forest management, very little money would be needed to maintain one of the largest private estates in all of Europe. The frugal, practical ecologist who was Saint Benedict would not have wanted it any other way.

Margaret had gone to bed. Anthony was in his dimly lit room googling bibliographies and assorted arcana his mother had fed him. She was not giving up. Martin sat at his writing desk in the library thinking through the previous days. Sometime after midnight, third glass of sherry in hand, he opened his vault to review documents, his and Margaret's wills, powers of attorney, medical guardianships. He was looking for something. But was unsure what. And then it struck him, calling from nearly forty years before.

He turned and stared at the elaborate book-lined walls, suddenly overcome . . . trembling.

CHAPTER 54

There was the first edition of *Alice's Adventures in Wonderland* and the companion *Through the Looking-Glass*, which Martin had remembered in Vienna.

He removed the boxed set from the library, returned to his comfy chair and browsed through the mint-condition works. As he had remembered it: the *e* on the title page. Two things, however, that he had utterly forgotten or missed. This was a presentation copy from none other than one "CL Dodgson" to Martin's great-grandfather, with a sketch, looking very John Tenniel-like, of Daniel Olivier sitting on the grass of the chateau with two huge dodos. Publication date, 1865. Bound in a distinctive gold and red triple-gilded fillet-of-border, with azure endpapers coated for eternity. Or so it seemed, until Martin felt the slight razor-sharp cut to the back inside cover, wherein a single sheet of Bible-thin paper has been hidden.

Martin removed it. There were the words he had never seen: "Do Not Open Until I Am Long Gone."

Martin stared at the ever-so-fine sheet of narrow, faded paper with its incredibly tiny and flawlessly handwritten missive:

My dear Martin,

Someday you will be reading this and I shall be in another place and time. By now you will have been to the chateau and pondered its meaning. And you'll have also learned of the Book, and tried to envisage it, based upon a remarkable little guest registry. Do not agonize over its hiding place, as your Uncle James has. I never worried about it. If our ancestors were as clever as I believe them to have been, then they surely hid the little Book somewhere in the forest, near where I am probably buried myself, high up in a dry cave of primordial limestone, near to a flowering gum tree, the tallest one in the entire estate, and probably the largest tree in all of Europe. That would be my guess, but it's only a guess. Should you be tempted to search it out, however, be sure to walk gently up there, and enter the cave with a dim light that will not disturb the insects, bats, and countless species found nowhere else. Tread carefully. Disturb nothing.

As for the Olivier domain, as long as you emanate unconditional love in your heart, the animals will not even notice you. Or, if you are lucky, as I have been, they will befriend you. They know nothing but love.

Leave the Book in place, however. Some future chronicler of humanity's foibles, and the rise and fall of civilizations, may have need of it someday. Hopefully, you will not.

Never tamper with the estate, Martin. Please. It is not a game of chance, or power. Nor is it an option to sell it off in bits and pieces. From what your uncle and I have ascertained, this plot of precious, anomalous turf has proved to be the only sanctuary worth mentioning in twenty-five thousand years, a safe harborage for tens of thousands of species, millions of individuals otherwise doomed by forces well beyond their control.

I was never a religious man. But, as you will have discovered by this time, our family history is oddly linked to an Order of Knights, many of whom happened to be Benedictines, wonderfully practical monks. They have been loyal friends of the Oliviers for centuries. I would urge you to maintain that trusting association with them. You never know when there will be need of their assistance, wisdom, and understanding. They also happen to be quite deft in the medieval arts of defence. One monk in particular, a Father Bladelin who lives near Cluny. He was my friend.

May you live a long and happy life. And I hope you will find a partner who can give you as much joy as your mother gave to me. Then you will understand those immortal words of Mark Twain, or something approximating them, "Wheresoever was Eve, There was Eden." This has been my experience, as well. Your Mother, bless her soul, was my salvation.

Good luck, always, your loving Father, Edward.

A
TREATISE
OF
PARADISE,
AND THE PRINCIPALL
. contents thereof:

Efpecially
Of the greatneffe, fituation, beautie__,
and other properties of that place : of

CHAPTER 55

Martin put down the book, which he had grown up with, and wiped unexpected tears away. The fantasy, enriched by Tenniel's drawings, had entered his bloodstream just as it had been imbibed by so many millions of other children and adults around the world. He took a deep breath, contemplating the days ahead and the vague clamor in his head of unknown machinations that would have to be worked out by a certain inspector for Interpol, a man who had, like Martin himself, gotten the religion of paradise.

It was all too much to think about at two A.M. He had not slept in nearly a week. He would do so tonight, however. Better than he had slept in many, many years.

ACKNOWLEDGEMENTS

I wish to thank my editor, Laura Wood, for her scientific and artistic acumen and passion; Kathryn Atwood for her editorial suggestions; Carl Brune for his wonderful design sensibilities; Paulette Millichap and Sally Dennison, publishers, Rebecca Loftiss and Jennifer Beard of Council Oak Books. And finally, my greatest thanks, esteem and admiration for Jane, for whom this novel was conceived, and for everything she is, and for all that she does to sustain the great ideal that is the legacy of the French countryside.